VOICES OF THE SOUTH

DEBBY

Other Books by Max Steele

The Cat and the Coffee Drinkers

Where She Brushed Her Hair

The Hat of My Mother

DEBBY

by
MAX STEELE

LOUISIANA STATE UNIVERSITY PRESS
Baton Rouge and London

Originally published by Harper & Brothers
LSU Press edition published 1997 by arrangement with the author

Manufactured in the United States of America
06 05 04 03 02 01 00 99 98 97 5 4 3 2 1

Library of Congress Cataloging-in-Publication Data
Steele, Max, 1922–
Debby / by Max Steele.
p. cm.
ISBN 0-8071-2160-6 (p : alk. paper)
I. Title.
PS35537. T27825D43 1997
813' .54–dc21 96-45594
CIP

The paper in this book meets the guidelines for permanence and durability of the Committee on Production Guidelines for Book Longevity of the Council on Library Resources. ∞

For M.R.S.

DEBBY

Chapter 1

IF YOU squinted your eyes, or if you were as nearsighted as Deborah Hall, the flowers on the rug would grin back at you like faces: red, blue, odd-shaped faces, with green leaves protruding as impish ears. When she first came to Stonebrook the figures on the rug had been company to her, more real than the matron and the women who walked close to the wall without looking up. She had found names for the rug-pictures: "Thomas" after her husband; "Allan," a different one, after her oldest son; and "Grover," a little small one named after her baby. When she found time to be alone in the room she talked to them; and when she was out of the room, scrubbing floors in the back hall and kitchen, she planned what she was going to say.

In the center of the rug, at the entrance of the aisle between the two iron beds, another face, larger than the others, stared out into the room in such a way that no matter where she stood, the eyes were watching her. This was Nurse Janet. Deborah stood on this large, worn flower while dressing and undressing and at any other time, such as now, when she could be alone in the room.

"Mrs Hall. Deborah Hall!" The matron stood at the

foot of the stairs. "Mrs Hall! Mr Merrill is waiting for you."

"I'm going away." Deborah spoke to the people in the rug. She stepped backward off the face of Nurse Janet. "You too." Nurse Janet's face was so worn now that her cheeks were splotched with patches of burlap which showed through the tender nap. At least Deborah had destroyed that much, and by herself.

She could not remember exactly what the real Nurse Janet looked like. But she remembered the first day, seven years ago, that she had seen her. The night before, Deborah and the children had not gone home. Night had come suddenly. They were playing in a pasture stream, she and Allan. They were building a dam. The water kept breaking through and they had gone, without noticing the time, farther up and down stream to find rocks and mud. Then suddenly it was night. They slipped up to a barn to sleep in the new hay. Moonlight slanted through the half-open door and a silly chicken thinking Christmas had come, sang them to sleep.

The next morning the dam was gone. The rocks were still there but the water ran smoothly over them as though they belonged there and had never been anywhere else. Deborah and the children crossed the road and started across another field, where blackberries grew near the edge of the stream. Blackberries made a good breakfast. Allan was running on ahead of her, and she was carrying Grover on her hip when the horse and buggy rumbled over the wooden bridge.

"Deborah Hall." A strange woman's voice called after her. The horse had stopped. Deborah glanced around. A woman was climbing down out of the buggy. Deborah gathered her skirts up to her knees and ran across the field, hurrying Allan before her. Where blackberry vines covered a new growth of water oaks, they turned suddenly toward the branch. It was their Secret Path and no one could follow them here. They ran quietly, their bare feet making no noise on the smooth rocks. Deborah stooped where vines twisted overhead. When she raised her head again, they were in the Secret Room. No one could find them here. The vines screened them from the road and crossed the stream to make a little room with four walls of green, and a blue top. The floor of the room was sand and the furniture was all rock. Deborah stepped up on the flat rock table to reach a basket of bread which was hanging on a branch above the dew. She had just lifted the cloth to see if ants had come there during the night when she saw the strange woman standing on the path looking at her.

"You're Deborah Hall, aren't you?" The nurse spoke in a soft tone, as though she were talking to pet kittens.

Deborah did not hear: she was intent on studying the clothes the woman wore. She looked at the white straw hat, the dusty blue dress that came to the top of the high-topped, button shoes, and at the handkerchief which showed from the starched cuff. The woman moved uncomfortably before her open gaze. Deborah glanced down at her own clothes. Her brown checkered dress, which once had reached her feet, was now torn off midway between her ankles and knees. She was barefooted and her feet were muddy. Thomas had said when he went off to the World War that he would bring her back some shoes, and some dresses, some clothes for Allan, and some . . . what else was it he had said? That had been such a long time ago. Maybe this woman knew. Deborah looked up; and a smile, almost not one, twisted the corners of her mouth.

"You don't know me, do you, Deborah?"

Deborah's smile relaxed into the soft curve of her open lips.

"I'm Nurse Janet, the county nurse. Several people have told me you've had a hard time since the death of your husband and so I want to help you."

"Thomas, you mean?"

"Was that his name? Your husband's?"

"Tom was his name, but *I* called him Thomas. He's gone to War."

"Mrs Hall," the nurse spoke firmly, "the War is over. This is 1920."

"I know it."

"Well, then, you must know that Mr Hall is dead."

Deborah sat down on the flat rock table. "That's what Mitchell said." And now this strange lady was saying the same thing. But when a person is dead, the neighbors bring in food, and you have a sitting-up, and a funeral, a coffin, a grave and a headstone. Thomas had not had any of these things. If he were dead then he would have a gravestone that she could go to a thousand times each day, instead of to the upper field where she kept expecting to find him plowing.

"Who is Mitchell?"

"Mitchell. That's Thomas' brother who came up here last year. He's the one who sold all our furniture. Except the bed. And the stove. He didn't sell the stove. He said it wasn't worth selling."

"Did he give you the money?"

"No. He didn't say anything about any money."

"And the neighbors let him do that?"

Deborah dropped the basket which she had been holding between her knees. She shifted the baby from her hip and pressed him tightly to her.

"I know," Nurse Janet said, "the neighbors haven't been

kind to you. But they're sorry now. They want me to help you."

Deborah looked at the baby.

"And the children too. That's a big job for a woman to bring up two children by herself."

Allan had quit playing in the stream and now was sitting on the bank, listening carefully.

The nurse held out her arms for the baby. "What's his name?"

"He's a Hall!" She could not smother the alarm in her voice. Everyone always preached to her about this last baby. All of the neighbors had said, "It's disgraceful, having a baby when your husband's been gone so long." Even Mitchell, who had been so kind to her, was angry, and left before the child was born. Yet he was the best baby in the world.

Deborah was astonished that the nurse knew how to hold a baby. She was so tall and gaunt she didn't look like she'd know how to handle anything as small as a baby. But then the child began to cry.

"Shhh. Shhh. What's his name, Deborah? His first name?"

"Grover."

"Shh, Grover. We're going to be buddies. You and me. We're going to be buddies."

"Grover Cleveland!" Deborah recalled the middle name with surprise. "Grover Cleveland. Thomas used to talk about a man by that name, so I called this one that."

"Shhh, Grover. With a fine name like that you don't want to be carrying on so." The baby wailed louder. "Is he sick?"

"He's hungry." Deborah held out both arms for the baby, and the nurse gladly handed him over. "He's a hungry little baby. Yes he is." Deborah unpinned the top of her dress which opened to the belt. She held the baby to her left breast and then looked up at the nurse. "I've got plenty of milk."

"Show her, Mama," Allan hollered.

Deborah laughed and shook her head.

"Show 'er. Show her what you can do."

Deborah leaned back and laughed. When she stopped for a moment to breathe, tears were standing in her eyes. She was thirty-five, but she looked like a delighted child. She was scarcely taller than an eleven-year-old girl; perhaps five feet, surely not an inch more. Her honey-colored hair was plaited into two braids which she had twisted into a diadem about her head. In the back some of the strands had pulled loose and now floated as fine as cobwebs in the gentle breeze. The childish aspect came, not so much from her smallness as from a certain graveness about her face. Her eyes, perhaps, were responsible, for they were shadowed in deep hollows. They did not, however, sink back into the deep sockets, for the lids showed plainly, giving a sculptured quality to that part of her face. But the mouth was soft, and the lips parted naturally in a gentle curve. She wiped the tears from her eyes with the back of her hand.

"Show 'er, Mama. Show her."

"Show me what, Deborah?"

Deborah hesitated for a moment. "Nothing. He just acts like a dunce sometimes."

"Just one little old stream right here." The boy drew a circle on the ground. "Just one little drop then." He held his hand, palm up.

The nurse frowned and half-turned away.

"It's just a game we sometimes play when I got more milk than the baby needs."

Deborah noticed the distant look on the face of the woman

who had come to help her. She wondered what the nurse would do for her. Would she help with the farm as Thomas had done? Cut wood and plan the meals? Farm and help with the cooking? Could a woman do these things that Thomas had done?

"Can you plow?"

The distant look vanished: the nurse returned. "What?" she asked.

"Can you plow?"

"No."

"How then are you going to help us?"

For a long time the nurse chewed her bottom lip. "I'll think of something." She watched Deborah who was moving the spread, clawing hand of Grover from her full breast. Deborah slipped her forefinger and the middle finger between the child's lips and her nipple, then gently laid him in her lap. During the nursing a circle had been washed white and clean on the child's dirty face, and another white circle had been cleaned around the nipple of the firm breast. "I'll have to think of something," the nurse said.

"Maybe we can plant cotton again. When the time comes."

"Maybe," the nurse said. They stood up, the nurse helping Deborah.

"And if we make a lot of money on it—Thomas said we would, one day—maybe I can have another dress. A red one."

"Maybe." The nurse led the way up the curving path under the twisting vines.

"And when the cotton's laid by and in the shed we can play in it. All of us. Thomas sometimes used to play when he wasn't too tired. Once in November when the weather was warm we took off all our clothes . . ."

"And we'll have a lot to eat!" Allan ran on ahead of the nurse and turned to look at her face while she answered.

"Yes." They entered the field and walked slowly toward the road where Nurse Janet's horse tugged at the high grass along the ditch.

Oh, we're gonna be rich
And fall in a ditch
Hinky, dinky, parlay voo!

Allan sang as he ran across the field, circling back when he had run too far ahead.

"You've had a good time with the children, haven't you, Deborah?"

"We have a good time!" Excitement made her voice high in pitch.

"And you'll have a good time again." The nurse helped Deborah into the buggy and watched while Allan climbed into the back seat. She got in, picked up the reins, said, "Giddayup" once and the horse started off in a trot.

Standing before the open trunk in Stonebrook, Deborah Hall remembered that day as though it were the only day of her life. She remembered how the horse swished his tail, how the wind blew at her face, and how Allan didn't say a word, and Grover slept through it all. In her memory she had come directly that day to Stonebrook, but in reality it had taken Nurse Janet almost a month to place the children in an orphanage and to secure papers for Deborah's entrance into the Home for Delinquent Women.

During the seven years at Stonebrook she had hated Nurse Janet so much she could not even remember what the woman looked like. If she found, in a book or in an old magazine, a picture of a hideous man or woman, or of a sneaking animal, or an imaginary beast, she would sit and look at it for hours, thinking how that must be Nurse Janet. Her revenge, the only one she could think of, was in taking the picture around to the other women and saying, "Who does that remind you of?" "Who does that put you in mind of?" or "Who does that favor?" And, if the women were happy and wanted to please her they would say, even though they had never seen the nurse, "Miss Janet." Deborah would smile and take the picture to the next group of women. But as often as not, the women were unhappy and when asked what person the picture looked like, they would say: "You!" Once they had snatched a picture of an ape from her and written on it: "Mrs Hall."

She wondered if the women would miss her. Sometimes after other women left she felt an emptiness about the home which no amount of talk could fill. Sometimes one of them would say, "Honey, I'm gonna come back here one of these days and get you away. Would you like to come live with me when I get back on my feet and start making good money again?"

She liked the way the women were dressed when they arrived and when they left. Always they came in, beautifully colored, smelling sweet of lavender soaps, verbena sachets, and pink face powders. But within a few weeks they shed their bright colors and were left pale, straight-haired and smelling of bucket soap. Deborah always watched with sadness this fading of the beautiful ladies; and when she saw the matron taking the beads and rings from them to place in a brown envelope with writing on it, she muttered to herself all morning, or until she was told to shut up. But then, and they were the days she liked, suddenly one of these pale women would appear again, painted and glittering, smelling sweet, and with jewelry enough for a family reunion. The lady would say, "I'll be back for you, honey," perhaps leave a keepsake, and then be gone forever.

It was these keepsakes Deborah was now packing into the trunk: a broken string of amber beads; a photograph which was too small for her to see; empty, but lovely, odd-shaped boxes, pink, blue, and rainbow colored; a sliver of lavender soap, and another soap, almost new and shaped like a rose; and—she handled it as though it were an egg—a frosted pink glass bowl that contained a little gray powder puff and was half full of powder. She placed this bowl in the corner of the trunk.

"Mrs Hall! Mrs Hall!" The matron's voice was impatient. "Mrs Hall, Mr Merrill is waiting for you."

Moving slowly as though the shrill voice had not echoed up the stair well, she folded her two petticoats into the trunk which was the only possession, besides her clothing, she had brought with her to the home. She pressed the petticoats against the pink glass bowl and then, pausing to look about the room, she closed the trunk.

There would have been for her a finality about the act if, only six months before, she had not in the same way as this morning been called from her scrubbing to pack her clothes for departure. When she remembered the incident and the days that followed, in which she had tried vainly to cook for a mill village family, she had to sit down on the trunk and shut her eyes. The matron, though, had promised her that this time she would not be mistreated. She did not really believe the matron; yet since that was her only hope for kindness she repeated the matron's words, over and over: "You'll be happy again, with children about."

"Mrs Hall!"

Deborah pushed the trunk to the top of the stairs. Then, in front of it, she began pulling it down the steps. It made a hollow noise that echoed through the house and delighted her. Bump, bump, bump. She reached the landing, dragged the trunk across and started down the steep stairs. Boomp, boomp, boomp.

"Woman!" The matron appeared at the foot of the steps. Her face was red, but instantly she began smiling. "Mr Merrill will help you with the trunk if it's too heavy for you."

While the man came forward and up the stairs, the trunk, which had been uncertainly balanced between steps, slipped once more. Boomp, Deborah said to herself. The man lifted the trunk easily to his shoulder. He must be a giant, Deborah thought. He was a tall man, large of frame, and heavy now with middle age. His hair was so brown that in certain lights, such as that of the late afternoon sun streaming through the landing window, it looked red, and in places gold. The back of his neck, too, was red; and Deborah wondered about this giant who had come to take her away. His huge hand, which balanced the trunk, could, if it hit her, send her sprawling across a room. She stood midway on the stairs and tried to think of some reason to go back to her room; just for a minute, just until she could become accustomed to the idea of going away with this man, until she could tell the three good faces on the rug Good-by and stand for a last time on Nurse Janet's face. But the matron was watching her and she could not find reason to turn back.

Perhaps, she thought as she reached the foot of the stairs and started toward the front door, perhaps on their trip they would pass her house where she had lived with Thomas; or even the stream where she had met Nurse Janet—she would know the place. And if they did she would somehow get the man to stop, and then she would run away. This time no one would catch her.

"Good-by, Mrs Hall. Work hard and be good."

The man paused for Deborah to reply, but the little woman walked on down the steps and down the curving drive without answering.

The children would be there waiting. Grover, in her

imagination still a baby, would be asleep in the crib beside the big bed where she slept with Allan. "You'll be happy again, with children about." That's what the matron had said! Is that what she had meant? Deborah turned around suddenly and waved joyfully to the woman standing watching from the steps. She climbed into the big touring car and waved good-by to the woman and to Stonebrook.

Chapter 2

SEPTEMBER; and a lake of goldenrod flashed into view and whirled out of sight down the road. Hills sank beneath them, and the valleys flattened out. The touring car rushed on through the late afternoon and the tall trees and poles near the road rushed past in the opposite direction. Beyond the trees, though, across the fields, the low foothills were speeding in the same direction as the car. The world was going so fast in so many directions, why didn't it fly all to pieces? Deborah opened her mouth again. She had discovered that the wind rushing past the car breathed for her. All she had to do was open her mouth. She was glad she didn't have to stand up in a wind like this. But people working in the field didn't seem to be noticing it.

"Looks like a tornado's coming!" she shouted above the roar of air. Mr Merrill pressed down and the car screeched almost to a stop. "Where?"

"The wind. The way it was blowing back there."

"Oh," the man laughed and the car speeded on again. "This the first time you've been in a car?"

"I don't know." She could not remember the truth. Sometimes, on Sunday afternoons, she went down to the big gate at

Stonebrook and watched the cars chase down the road. Sometimes, in her imagination, she went with them. But then the land had stood still and she had been able to study each farmhouse, and each line of willows that cut across the sky.

Darkness was filling up the valleys. It flowed like a river and its streams among the low places flooded the road and finally overflowed the hillsides. Ahead of them, the red of the sky guttered out. Back at the home the women would be washing up now for supper. "Star light . . ." On the horizon, hanging on a needle of a tall pine tree, one star glittered like fire on ice. "Starlight, starbright, first star I see tonight . . ." She shut her eyes to make the old wish: "I want Grover." The wind pressed firmly against her eyelids. This was the way to ride: with eyes pressed shut by the wind and with mouth open so that breathing was effortless.

When she opened her eyes the car had stopped. Mr Merrill was standing on her side of the car with the door open. "Well, here we are."

They were in a driveway at the side of a big, white house. The porch was lighted; and as they went up the steps, Mr Merrill carrying the trunk on his shoulders again, the screen door opened. A tall thin girl stretched out her arm to hold the door. Deborah stopped for a moment. There was something bad wrong with the girl. The girl's waist was too near her knees. The dress had a light blue, sleeveless bodice that fitted tightly down to her belt, then flared out in a dark blue, pleated skirt which came only to her knees. Deborah wondered if the girl could walk. She had heard once of a girl baby being born with just one leg, but this girl had been born without any thighs. Mr Merrill set the trunk down.

"Mrs Hall, this is Rebecca. She's the oldest."

"How d'you do?" The girl smiled and twisted the little black curls that had seemed to be stuck to her cheek.

Deborah looked about her at the wide porch. If they would let her scrub this porch she could make the job last all morning and could watch the cars passing. She was tired of back halls. She would ask the new matron.

The rug in the living room was rolled back so that one end of the room was bare. Surely, she thought, they don't work this late. A boy was stretched out on a long sofa, his hand hanging off the side.

"Get your feet off of there!" Mr Merrill spoke sharply. "That's Britton." Britton stood up slowly. He had, she was happy, both thighs. The girl, however, seemed to have no trouble walking; she kicked the rug and it rolled out flat. "I've been trying to teach Britton to dance," she said. "The charleston."

"This way Mrs Hall." Mr Merrill led the way through another room into a dimly lighted bedroom.

In a maple bed a dark-haired woman was propped up on two pillows. Her hair lay, like ropes, in two braids on her shoulders; and over her gown she wore a navy blue sweater. The dark hair and sweater and the dark hollows under the woman's eyes made Deborah remember a game she had played as a child: "Ain't no boogers out tonight . . ."

"Well, here we are!" Mr Merrill switched on the overhead light and stood at the foot of the bed watching his wife's expression as she inspected the woman he had brought in.

"So you've finally decided to come live with us." Mrs Merrill fumbled among the glasses and bottles on the table for her spectacles. "Have a seat Mrs Hall. Dad, take her coat. We were expecting you several days ago."

Had they been on the road that long? Deborah wondered. She had lost all sense of time. She sat down on a low chair near the foot of the bed without taking off her coat. With the light on, the woman in bed looked much less fearful. Her spectacles reflected the light in such a way that Deborah could not see the piercing gaze. Who did Mrs Merrill remind her of? Was it Nurse Janet? Someone, but she could not quite remember who.

"Did Mr Merrill tell you about your work here?"

"No'm. He just said I was to come here for you to see."

"I told her everything I know about the work." He started out of the room. "I'm going to put the car up."

"I don't want you to get the wrong idea," Mrs Merrill spoke to Deborah. Her voice, in conversation, was low so that what she said seemed like a special secret between herself and the other person. "Usually there isn't as much work to be done as you see tonight. I don't know what the rest of the house looks like but this room's a mess. I'll be up next week, the doctor thinks, and then we can start getting the house back in shape. We've got a cook but she's not much of a hand at housecleaning."

Deborah sat motionless. How did the rest of that game go? "Ain't no boogers out tonight . . . ain't no boogers out tonight cause my daddy killed them all last night."

"Of course I won't have as much time to help with the house as I used to. Not until I wean the baby." She looked at the corner of the room beyond Deborah's chair. Deborah turned and saw the cradle for the first time. It stood up on tall legs and was covered with net. As in a dream, Deborah moved to the cradle. She leaned over and looked at the small baby. She had remembered him as being larger. Her star-wish had come true. "Grover," she whispered, no louder than a cat's purring. "Grover." She was trembling and she wanted so much to throw back the net and lift the baby that her arms became as heavy as two sacks of meal. The baby's hand clutched for a moment at the air. "He's still alive," Deborah said. She held out her hands to remove the net.

"Don't!" The voice was full of alarm. "Don't touch him!"

Deborah, her hand poised, glanced at the strange woman.

"I'm sorry," Mrs Merrill said. "I didn't mean to sound like that, but we have such a hard time keeping him asleep."

Deborah turned back to the cradle.

"You can see him tomorrow."

"It's been a long time."

"You like children?"

Before she could answer, Mr Merrill was standing in the door. Rebecca was with him.

"Rebecca, did you get the young ones to bed?"

"Yes, m'am." Rebecca sighed as though she had told her mother that same thing a dozen times.

"Did you leave supper on the table?"

"Yes'm. All except the meat and it's heating."

"Dad, you and Mrs Hall had better go eat."

"I'm not very hungry. I don't think I'll eat," Mr Merrill said.

"First time you've ever . . ." Mrs Merrill stopped when her husband frowned a signal for her silence.

"I've been smoking a lot this afternoon; and I'm not very hungry."

"Well, Rebecca, show Mrs Hall to the table."

Deborah followed the girl to the kitchen. The floor there was as hard and slick as a bathtub. She wondered now if she should speak for the front porch which would soon grow splintery. She studied the floor as she drank the glass of milk at her place. There were blue and white squares, and black lines and red ones. Given a chance she could make them shine like china.

Rebecca stared at the linoleum beyond the table. "Did you lose something?"

"No."

"Do you see something?"
"No. I was just studying."
Rebecca smiled, then turned quickly away. She was giggling when she spoke again: "Do you study often?"
"Who does the porch belong to?"
Rebecca floundered. "Why, well, why, I mean it's ours. It's part of the house."
"Whose floor is this?"
Rebecca looked as though she was being dragged into a dark room. "I don't know what you're talking about."
"I'm talking about the floor."
"Well, my goodness! It's ours, I guess. The house is ours. And the floors and windows. All of it."
The girl is new here, Deborah thought. Tomorrow she would ask the sick woman if she could have the kitchen floor to scrub. But if the morning sun hit the front porch, she would ask for it.
"Which floor do you scrub?"
"Not any. And I don't intend to."
"Is that because you're . . ." Deborah stopped, suddenly embarrassed.
"What?"
"The way you are?"
"And how am I?"
"Just fine, thank you," Deborah said absently but politely. She was wondering if she should mention the girl's legs. "Do they give you much trouble?"
"Who?"
"Your legs."
The girl held her dress up to the top of her knees. "What's wrong with my legs?"
"I mean the way your waist is so low. Almost down to your knees. I thought . . ."

Rebecca began laughing like a dunce-fool. "That's the style. Haven't you been anywhere?"

Deborah felt cheated that she had pitied the girl. It wasn't fair to go around fooling people like that, making them think you were built one way when you weren't.

"My waist is up here." The girl clasped her hands midway between the belt and the neck. "Excuse me a minute."

When the girl left the room Deborah looked at the table. Back at the home they would have fought over a meal like this, but here there was no one to make her wait for the bell to ring. Yet she was not hungry. She put the half-empty glass down and waited for Rebecca to return. She heard loud laughter in the bedroom; and she hoped the baby would wake so that she could pick him up. She yawned, and listened to the clock, and waited.

When Rebecca returned she said, "I'll show you to your room. It's right over the dining room."

It was two hours past Deborah's bedtime and she was so sleepy she had to hold onto the rail of the staircase and half-pull herself along. Rebecca left her at the door of a small room which had slanted ceilings and a huge fireplace with a chimney that stuck out into the room. Deborah noticed as she undressed that the floor was covered with a rag rug with no faces. Her trunk was near the closet door but she was too tired to open it. She unlaced the high topped shoes, pulled them off by the heel. She knelt on her left knee with her right foot flat on the floor. The knee made a rest for her forehead. Mrs Merrill had said, "In the morning you can see the baby." She pressed her forehead against her knee. "Help tomorrow to come. Help tomorrow to come. Help tomorrow. . . ." She said it over and over until she believed she had said a long enough prayer. The bed was soft and she sank deeper and deeper. Beyond the window a half-dead oak was clawing at the moon.

The next morning Deborah could not believe that she had been asleep all night, that a bed could be so soft. She was going to like it here. She might even stay. She thought of the baby in the cradle. Certainly she would stay; she would like to see anyone make her leave. The matron had said, "You'll be happy with children about." But then there was Mrs Merrill who said, "Don't touch him!" And what were children for, pray God, if they weren't to pick up, and hold, and love? She hugged the pillow to her chest to warm the spot. But she had discovered during the years at Stonebrook that only a baby knew how to warm a body. Even a hot water bottle wouldn't warm through and through. Sometimes, especially in the night, she could hardly believe that Nurse Janet had taken her baby away, the other child too, but a baby who couldn't even eat. She did not worry much about the other child, but often she gave a sick sigh and shook her head wondering how the baby, who couldn't even feed himself, could live without her. But he had lived. There was a baby downstairs this very minute, and whether it was her baby or another one just like it, it was a baby. And best of all, the lady had said, "Tomorrow you can hold him." And tomorrow was today.

She dressed quickly, wearing her large coat over the dress which was really too old to be worn without a coat. At the door to the sick room she knocked softly three times. No one answered. She cracked open the door and peeped into the room. Mr Merrill was handing the baby to the woman in bed. The woman quickly covered herself and said: "You'll have to wait until later to come in."

She went down the hall to the kitchen. A Negro woman

who said people called her "Bertha" was frying two eggs and two strips of bacon. Bertha stared; Bertha stared and giggled. "You the new woman they been talking about?" Then she laughed again. Deborah felt uneasy, but to hide her feelings and her knees which felt as though they might tremble, she sat down at the table. "You're going to have to wait for your breakfast," Bertha said. "Mr Merrill, he's funny that way. If his wife isn't at the table, he won't eat with anybody else, not even the children. Claims it makes him feel like he's the father of an orphaned brood. He won't even stay in this here house two minutes if Mrs Merrill isn't in it. Off he goes. You going to have to wait." Bertha pointed toward the front of the house.

Deborah didn't like being driven from room to room. If they hadn't really wanted her, didn't want her now, why had they come and got her? Back there she knew everybody and ate with anybody.

One happy thought remained: the two little girls she had heard about last night. They would like her; children always liked her. The baby would like her if she could find a way to see him. She could endure Mrs Merrill's saying "No," Bertha's motioning her out like a dog, and even Mr Merrill's gruff-ruff voice, if she could only play with the children and hold the baby. But already there was a big doubt if Mrs Merrill would let her near the cradle ever. She sat on the edge of the long sofa and waited for the children to appear.

But it was Britt who came in. He mumbled mumble not plain enough to be understood and then hid behind a newspaper. Deborah watched him silently for almost an hour, it seemed, and decided he wasn't much of a talker. Rebecca came in and she talked more. She said, "Good morning" and picked up part of the paper Britt had finished.

"Isn't there some more of you?" Deborah finally asked.

They stared at her.

"I say: Isn't there some more of you?"

Rebecca said, "You mean my legs. I told you about them last night."

"Some more children. Aren't there two little girls here?"

"One little girl and one little devil," Britt answered.

"They're mean?"

"Betty is. She can be if she takes a notion," Rebecca said.

"And she usually does." Britt was behind the newspaper again.

"Usually," Rebecca agreed. "But Julia, Julia never gives anyone any trouble. You won't even know she's around."

Deborah felt a creepy impulse to glance behind the sofa. "Lord God!" she said.

Britt began giggling as though choking and then Rebecca. They would stop for a moment, begin again. Finally Britt left the room in his long strides. Rebecca followed. Outside on the porch they laughed and whispered. Let them whisper, she thought, they can't say I haven't got any manners and that's more than can be said for some people I know.

After breakfast, which she ate alone, she returned to her room and touched everything in it: the cobblestoned hearth, the chimney which stuck out into the room, the little rocking chair, the rag rug, the hearth broom of purple straw, the soft bed and soft pillow. She had never seen a room she liked more. "The cradle," she said, "will fit fine in that corner over there."

At thought of the baby she tiptoed back down the steps and into the dining room where she was stopped by loud noises in the kitchen. A child laughed and the sounds, which had seemed to be meaningless, became clear. Bertha was telling the children funny stories. Now would be the time to meet them.

"She looks just like this," Bertha said and the children screamed with laughter.

Deborah could not wait to see who looked like what. She opened the door. Bertha was down on her knees with her eyes rolled back until only the white showed. Her palms were pressed flat together in front of her. The children were still laughing and Bertha was trying hard to look sad. Deborah smiled, but then she saw Bertha's expression become suddenly guilty and foolish.

Bertha was talking about her! She stood motionless with her hands held tightly against her sides. Stand still, she thought, and she will go away. It was a rule her father had taught her when strange dogs pawed and sniffed and frightened her. She had found that the rule usually worked as well with people. As long as they were only talking about her, she could stand as still as her father had said. He had not told her what to do if they should ever strike, as they had at the place where she worked before.

Bertha stood up slowly, turned her back, and walked over to the sink. The children stared at her with open mouths. Betty, the mean-looking, small one, had a square haircut, straight bangs, hair straight down at the side of her face, and cut straight around her head. She dropped the spoon in her plate. Julia was the one with the long blonde pigtails and sure enough, even when you stared at her, you couldn't be sure she was there. That was because she looked through you and all around you as though she herself were seeing nothing.

Deborah had not wanted to meet them like this. Everything was ruined. They would laugh at her now, in that special laugh she sometimes heard when strangers were whispering across a room. Since breakfast she had been waiting to see them. Now she would have to wait for a better time. She stepped backward, turned, and left the room. The jumbled noises of laughter and talk followed her through the dining room. She went into the living room, but she could still hear them, then onto the porch.

Nine o'clock; and the September sunlight had not yet reached the porch. Perhaps it wouldn't. If the porch remained in shade all day she would speak for the kitchen. A porch without sunlight would be miserable work in winter. But then Bertha was in the kitchen. She sat down on the top step and watched the light edge gently up the walk and up the first step. It was moving in the right direction. Perhaps, after all, there was a chance that she would neither freeze to death nor have to stay in a room with Bertha. Perhaps she could, as she had planned, stay here on the porch each morning and watch the cars. She pulled the coat with its huge, capelike collar closer about her neck. She folded her dress about her legs to the top of her shoes. Then she hugged her knees and watched the sun slide up the steps.

Cars droned past and the dew dried away. She was in the sun now. She patted her foot in time to a tune that kept playing in her head. "Oh, my grandmother lives on yonder little green . . ." she sang in a low voice to herself. There was giggling behind her and she turned around in time to see a curtain fall. Betty screamed and ran. "Dunce," she said. "That's what she is. A little dunce."

Once again during the morning she heard whispering behind her, but she did not turn her head again until Bertha opened the door and let it slam.

"Lunch's ready, Mrs Hall. You want to eat now or wait and eat with some of the rest?"

"Whenever it suits you best."

"It doesn't make any difference to me. I stay here till five anyhow."

"I don't want to wait that late."

"I don't mean that. I mean we don't have any certain mealtime now that Mrs Merrill's sick. Everybody just eats when the notion strikes."

During lunch Rebecca and Britt came into the kitchen, spoke to her, told Bertha, who was eating at the cook table that they were not hungry, that they would be back later, and left. Mr Merrill stopped in the kitchen door to announce that he would eat later. The two little girls would not enter the kitchen. They stood in the dining room and called Bertha. She went out to them, and without closing the door, whispered until they giggled and went away.

Without knowing why Deborah was compelled to push back her overloaded plate and go up to her room. She lay crosswise on the bed with her head hanging off the side. If she wanted to be sick she had only to lift her head or to swallow hard. She breathed in shallow breaths and watched the cracks wiggle the length of the floor.

She had done nothing to these strange people. Why had they come and got her? Why were they torturing her? Only the woman in bed had been nice to her. She would feel better if they would let her in to see the sick woman—and the baby.

She had not let herself think about the baby since she had been turned away from the door that morning. She had planned that after lunch she would think about it and nothing else for a long time. She had been waiting on the top step until this afternoon when the time would come in which she would allow herself that pleasure. Then she could think about how he would feel in her arms, how the light fuzz on top of his head would tickle her chin and how he would listen when she whispered to him. Now that the time had come to think about him, she didn't feel like it. Something was wrong in this house and it concerned her.

During the afternoon she tried again, and again without luck, to know Betty and Julia. Julia was a little lady, and for a while Deborah thought they would be friends, but Julia was only acting polite and grown up. She did not really want to be friends. She sat in a chair with her legs crossed just so and her dress pulled down over her knees. She was a grave child when she was in the house, as though she were only visiting for a while and would shortly leave. Everyone seemed to treat her as though she were company, using her name in every sentence they spoke to her. They didn't seem to consider that she was a seven-year-old child and not a grown lady. She said, "Yes, m'am," and "No, m'am" when Deborah spoke to her and she stared without smiling, but she would not stay in a room with Deborah. "Come on, Betty, we're supposed to play outdoors." Betty would follow her. Anything anybody wanted to do was all right with Betty, provided it was mean. Betty would leave, brushing back her bangs and turning, at the last minute, to stick out her fat tongue. So what was the use of trying to get along with people who could not be got along with? Only one person could help her now.

Everything, she felt, would be all right once she saw Mrs Merrill again. There had been a secret in that room which she had not understood, but which she would find out now. On her Grandmother's farm all the paths—those from the barnyard, from the fields, from the house, those in the plum thicket—all led eventually to the spring. Here in this house, no matter which rooms or halls you wandered through, you reached eventually the door of Mrs Merrill's room.

When she pushed open the door the room was dark. Mrs Merrill was asleep; the baby was asleep; and only the clock was awake. Deborah sat in the chair she had sat in before and studied Mrs Merrill's face. She felt rather impolite about coming in and not saying anything. She wanted to ask: "Are you asleep?" but then if Mrs Merrill wasn't inclined to talk in her sleep, it would be a shame to ask her. She watched the sleeping face. She was near enough to reach out and touch it gently—or to slap it and say, "Wake up! Wake up!" Yet she was content to sit with her hands on the chair arms watching the secret face. When the eyes trembled under the purple eyelids Deborah almost laughed out loud. She had come down to be near the awake woman she had seen; this was an almost entirely different person. Who are you when you're asleep? And will you wake up and be the same person you were before you went to sleep? Certainly you never feel the same, but other people always know who you are. But someday when you're asleep they'll grab you up and bury you before you can say Jack Robinson, and won't you feel foolish then? That was something to think about.

Cars droned past; far off somewhere a dog barked; a screen door crashed shut, and a boy's voice, high and sharp, cut through the air: "Kings," meaning time-out.

"What is it?" Mrs Merrill fussed at the pillow without opening her eyes. Then she sat up suddenly, her eyes wide with fear: "What is it?"

"He said 'Kings,'" Deborah answered.

"Who?" Mrs Merrill looked suspiciously from Deborah to the cradle.

"A little boy."

"Was he in here?" Mrs Merrill stared skeptically at the cradle.

"No. He just hollered 'Kings.'"

Mrs Merrill, wide awake now, lay back and shut her eyes. She rubbed them a moment with the fingertips of one hand; then slowly opened them toward Deborah. "How long have you been in here?"

"A long time."

"Isn't there something else you could be doing?"

"No'm."

"Have you unpacked your things?"

"No'm."

"Didn't Rebecca show you the closet? And all the drawers in that chest are empty except for some linen in the bottom one."

"She didn't say anything about it to me."

"Well, there's no hurry. But sometime today you can get your clothes unpacked and straightened out."

"I'm not going to unpack my trunk." She had packed it with such care at the home. She was suddenly filled with doubts.

"Your clothes will stay wrinkled if you leave them in."

"I'm not going to stay here!"

Deborah Hall's voice broke and the words rolled about the room like beads from a string. She had not known that she would say these words, or that all morning she had been thinking them over and over. The words breaking loose surprised her as much as they did Mrs Merrill. But now that she had told herself the news, she was impressed by the truth of it. "I'm going to leave."

Mrs Merrill watched her the way a mother watches a child climb a ladder. "Where're you going?"

"I'm going to clear out. Going to pack up and clear out." She was going to cry too. Already she could feel the sobs trembling in her throat. She beat softly on the chair arm with the side of her closed fist.

"Why, Mrs Hall! Has anybody said anything to you?"

"No'm."

"Then why do you want to leave?"

Deborah shook her head from side to side as though the

subject were too complex ever to explain to this woman who was propped up there without a care in this world.

"Mrs Hall, I think I know how you feel. Everything's strange here. The house, and the family. It's not like the place you're used to, but don't you think in time you could get used to us? We aren't mean people. Maybe if you'll just wait awhile you'll feel better."

Deborah was lost. The whole world she had known for so long had disappeared, and if she did not start now, this minute, to search for it, she would be lost forever. "I've *got* to go."

"But where, Mrs Hall? Where do you think you're going?"

"I'm going back." Her chin was trembling, and the room was floating in tears. She could not say whether "back" meant to her Grandmother's, or to Thomas, or to the home. She only knew she meant some place that was not this one.

"Back to the home, Mrs Hall?"

Deborah nodded that that was where.

"You can't go back there. Not if you ever want to leave again. You see this is the second time you've been away, and if you go back now they'll think you don't ever want to leave again."

"I don't." Her face was wet, but she was making almost no sounds of crying.

"You mean you'd like to stay there the rest of your life?"

"Yes," she nodded.

"Then I suppose," Mrs Merrill had lowered her voice until it was again intimate and full of delightful secrets, "I suppose it was wrong of us to have taken you away."

The scene of her leaving came back to her and Deborah began crying aloud. "I didn't ask to come here."

"Mrs Hall, I know you didn't. And I'm sorry. We

wouldn't have brought you here, though, if we hadn't thought we could give you a good home. And that in return you'd be a big help to me."

There was anger in her grief; she had been trifled with and now everything was lost. "You didn't have any right to."

Mrs Merrill shut her eyes for a long time. When she opened them, she spoke slowly, as though to herself: "That's something that's always puzzled me—what right we have to touch the lives of others."

Words, words, words, and they didn't mean anything. Not a thing at all. They didn't tell Deborah she could go back to the home; they were just a singsong. Nevertheless, she could cry louder than the woman could talk, and that was something to do.

"I'm sorry. I'm just as sorry as I can be. But if you're determined to leave, I'll send you back. Not today though; nor tomorrow. Because I think you're just tired right now."

"I'm not tired!" She was beginning to sob because this fool woman, who didn't understand anything, didn't even know how all your insides can sink down into your stomach and leave you heavy with weakness.

"Mrs Hall, I'll send you back, but I'm not going to put up with any such carryings on. Now if you're going to cry like that, and not be sensible, well then go on back up to your room."

Deborah rose to the surface and swam to the door. In the next room, right in the middle of the room, she realized that the pillow she was going up to was not her small tan one that was back at the home. She didn't even have a pillow to cry on! The full horror of the fact closed in on her and she cried out so loud she was afraid for a second the woman was going to jump out of bed and beat her to death. Then: Deborah wished she would.

Chapter 3

DEBORAH went to her room and for a week, except for meals, she stayed there crying to herself almost continuously. After the first shock of finding herself alone among these people her tears had little to do with the thoughts she was thinking. She cried simply because weeping, after seven lonesome years in which she had not, was as refreshing as a warm bath. After that she cried because she knew that that was a certain way to bring the children to the upstairs hall where they would play within her hearing, often peeping in at the unshut door, but never entering, never saying even so much as "Pea Turkey" to her.

Betty might be a little devil all right, all right, but that didn't mean Julia, with all her long blonde and braided hair, was an angel. Deborah listened carefully to their play. Julia would say in her quiet, calm, ladylike voice, "I wonder would this break if we dropped it down the stair well." There would be a crash, and Bertha or Rebecca or Britt would holler: "Betty!" Betty would scream back, "Julia told me to." But of course no one believed Betty, and Julia would call down truthfully, "I did not." No one seemed ever to think of screaming at Julia, not even Betty. Maybe, Deborah thought, maybe it's because she's the only one with blonde hair. That's why they treat her like a grown visitor, like a somebody. She wished that she and Julia could be friends. She didn't want Betty as an enemy, not after seeing the way she kicked Britt in the shins, but she wasn't sure that she wanted her as a friend. Some people it was safer to be enemies with. So she cried about that until she had hiccups. She could not stand to cry another day.

She went downstairs and, knocking only once, entered Mrs Merrill's room. "You've got to do something about me," she cried.

"Yes," Mrs Merrill whispered. "We have. I was hoping though that maybe after the newness wore off you'd be a little better satisfied."

"I'm not." Deborah sobbed. "I'm not I'm not I'm not I'm not."

"Mrs Hall, won't you stop for a minute? Just until I can find out some things I've got to know." Mrs Merrill, wearing a maroon bathrobe, was sitting between the bed and the cradle.

"I can't stop." Deborah stood in the doorway. She turned as she spoke and pressed her forehead against the door sill, rolling her head from side to side so that the sharp wood cut pleasantly into the flesh, drawing off to there some of the pain.

Mrs Merrill pulled the net up over the cradle again. "Come sit down."

"There's no use." The sob in Deborah's voice rejected the chair and the entire world.

"I'm going to call a doctor." Mrs Merrill had tried every persuasion she could think of.

"I don't need a doctor." Deborah gasped for breath. "I told you all I want is to go back and you won't let me."

"Don't say I won't let you. You heard me phone Stonebrook, Mrs Hall."

Deborah for a moment lifted her head and stifled her sobbing. "What did they say?"

"I've told you a dozen times."

"Did you ask them to take me back?"

"Mrs Hall, you heard me say we wanted to send you back."

"What did they say?"

"They said," Mrs Merrill sighed, "they said you were to stay here till they could find a bed for you."

"What happened to my bed?"

Mrs Merrill was undecided whether to answer or not. "I explained to you. Someone else has your bed now."

"Who could that be? Did they say who?" She thought for a minute, then began crying anew. "I'll bet it's Lizzie Johnson. She was always after me to trade mattresses with her. Lizzie Johnson's got my bed!"

"Hush! You're going to wake the baby again."

"I can't help it! Lizzie Johnson's got my bed."

"Lizzie Johnson hasn't got your bed!"

"She wanted my bed and now she's got it. And it was my bed."

"Lizzie Johnson hasn't got your bed, so be quiet."

"You don't even know Lizzie Johnson!" That, of course, made the tragedy worse, because when your bed gets stolen by someone people don't even know, you haven't much chance of getting it back.

Mrs Merrill took advantage of Deborah's moment of blinding grief to lead her to a chair and make her sit down.

"Now sit here and we'll talk about Lizzie. Who is she? Was she a friend of yours? Tell me about her."

"Lizzie stabbed a man. Poisoned and stabbed him."

Mrs Merrill stepped back, as though from an unexpected corpse.

"And chopped him into little pieces."

Mrs Merrill sat down on the bed, her mouth open.

"And fried him and ate him!"

"Mrs Hall!"

Deborah smiled. "That's what she used to tell me, but I still wouldn't trade mattresses." The smile vanished; the tears came back. "And now she's got it anyway."

"No, she hasn't."

"Well who *has*? Did they tell you who?"

"Yes. You remember I told you yesterday. The three girls who were in that roadhouse fight are being held out there until the next trial."

"Did the matron tell you that?"

"I don't know who it was. Whoever answered the phone."

"It wasn't the matron. I'll bet you didn't talk to the matron."

"Who else could it have been?"

Deborah wailed. "Lizzie Johnson!"

Mrs Merrill lay back on the bed. "Oh my Lord," she whispered. She sat up and stared at Deborah, as though to see through the tears and through the very bones of her skull. "Do you think that's possible? Do you think maybe it was Lizzie?"

"I know it was."

"Why? Did she used to answer the phone?"

"No."

"Well, why do you think it was Lizzie?"

"Cause she doesn't want me to have my bed back."

There was no consoling Deborah now. Lizzie had stolen her bed and then had lied about it. And over the *telephone* at that!

"Come on, we'll go phone again."

While Mrs Merrill went through the intricate process of phoning, Deborah sat on the bottom step, hugging the newel and leaning her head against it. "Is that . . . yes, well I hate to be bothering you again . . . this is Mrs Merrill . . ." She looked over the top of the telephone at Deborah as she talked.

"Ask her has Lizzie got it? Ask her if Lizzie . . ."

Mrs Merrill shook her head. "Shhh." Then: "Well, yes, you told me about those three girls . . . yes, I read about them . . . well, I know and I think you're awfully brave . . . three, I know you must have your hands full . . . I know . . ."

"Excuse me a minute." Mrs Merrill put her hand over the mouthpiece. "Go on out on the porch till I get through talking. I can't hear a thing with you blubbering like that. Go on."

Deborah stood up, then started to sit down again.

"Go on. Do you want me to hang up? You know I don't have to phone."

Deborah left and sat on the side of the porch where the two o'clock sun was shining; for the day was one of those in autumn more kin to winter than to summer. Beyond the shrubbery which grew at the porch edge, the two little girls were playing house. Deborah could see them through the thinning evergreen.

"You forgot to knock on the door. You got to go back out and knock on the door." The big one was talking.

"Not if I'm the Daddy, Julia, I just walk on in."

"Betty, you don't play fair. You *got* to knock on the door."

Deborah couldn't see the door. She could see Betty and Julia though. They both had bundles; Julia's was in a blue baby blanket, and Betty's in a pink.

Mrs Merrill came to the door and called her in. They sat down at opposite ends of the long sofa. Mrs Merrill had put on her glasses and now was fingering the rim piece above the ear. "It'll be a week before you can go back. At least a week, maybe longer."

"Did you talk to the matron?"

"Yes."

"Did she tell you anything to tell me?"

"No. She asked how you were getting along."

"Did you tell her 'just fine'?"

"I certainly did not. Did you want me to?"

There was of course, Deborah thought, no reason to answer a woman who didn't even know that when someone asks you how you're getting along you're supposed to say, "Just fine thank you how're you."

"She said," Mrs Merrill was saying, "that she doesn't know where your folks are—there's no record there—but she believes you have some."

"I've got folks." Deborah Hall's voice was flat, as though she had said the sentence to herself so many times it no longer had shape or meaning.

"Do you know where?"

Deborah thought of her Grandmother's farm. The nurse had taken her straight from there to the home. In her mind Deborah had moved the stream where she had eaten blackberries to the back field of her Grandmother's farm. And in her mind she had paved a road which went straight, without curves or turns, from the farm to the home. "It's on out beyond the home. Ycu just go straight on down that road." She had stood at that gate a thousand Sundays and gone down that road to her Grandmother's. Anybody could find the way.

"Do you think you could find the way?"

"Certainly. I used to live there."

"Well, I tell you what I'm going to do. I'm going to call

Mr Merrill, and if he can get away from the office this afternoon I'm going to have him take you to find it."

She quit crying altogether when she learned that Mr Merrill would be there at three to take her. She went up to her room to put on her big, cape-collared coat—which she had been persuaded, against her own good judgment, not to wear down to breakfast every morning. So now, when she needed it, as she knew she would, she had to go all the way back upstairs for it. It seemed to her all she had been doing for the last week or more was to walk up those steps every few minutes to see if her hat and coat and trunk were still there. By the time she had stood in the middle of the room for a while, and had put on her coat and stood there for a while longer, Mrs Merrill was calling from downstairs. "They're in the car waiting for you."

Mr Merrill and Britt were in the front seat; Betty and Julia were on two little seats that pulled up out of the floor, and Deborah sat alone on the back seat watching the cars go by, the posts, the streets, and the houses which now were growing farther and farther apart. When they reached the country, Britt and his father changed places. The car growled and jumped at something in the road. Then it sat afraid to move.

"Let the clutch out *slowly*!"

"That's what I did."

Betty and Julia stood up to see what was wrong with Britt's feet.

The car moaned and shuddered.

"See," Britt said.

Mr Merrill sat up and looked at the floor. Then he looked at the wheel. "You've got it in gear. Britt, you've got more sense than that!"

"Gruff ruff ruff," Deborah said to herself.

"You did it too." Britton's voice was weak.

"How in the hell did I know you left it in gear? Any fool'd know better."

Boom boom boom! Deborah thought.

"It's not all my fault if I'm a fool."

"Let me have the wheel."

Britton got out of the car.

"I don't blame him. Don't blame him one bit. I'd walk home too."

Mr Merrill slid over and gripped the wheel. But then here came Britton climbing in on the other side like a beat dog.

Betty leaned against the front seat and said in a high voice: "Britt can't drive, can he Daddy?"

"No, Bubber can't drive."

"I can drive though. Can't I Daddy?"

"Not yet."

"When I get big I can drive."

"Maybe."

She turned around and announced to Julia: "I can drive." Her straight hair blew into her face and she brushed it back with the side of her hand. Julia looked out the side of the car.

"Daddy said I can drive."

Julia studied the roadside.

"Julia, Daddy said I can drive." She turned back and held to the front seat.

"Quit breathing on my neck!"

"Britton, don't talk to her like that."

"Well she breathes like a horse."

"Daddy, tell him not to talk to me like that." She waited a moment, then she lifted her chin to the level of the seat back and blew at Britton's neck, lightly, as though it were a dandelion. Britton moved over to the corner of the seat. Betty edged over back of him.

"All right, Dad. She's just trying to aggravate me and she's going to get her little face slapped."

"Betty, leave Bubber alone. He's got delicate nerves, you know. He can't stand being teased. Not even by a child. So sit down like a good girl."

Betty sat down on the edge of the little seat. She looked at Julia for a long time: at her face, her braids, her thin legs, her socks, her feet, and back to her face. "Are you carsick Julia?"

Julia shook her head: no.

"Are you mad at me?"

Julia nodded no.

"Daddy let's go faster."

Julia turned and stuck out her tongue.

"Daddy, Julia wants to go faster."

"I do not."

"I'm driving fast enough."

Humph, Deborah thought. You're not driving at all. You're not even doing a good job of holding it back.

"She said she wants to go faster."

"I did not."

Britton turned around: "Julia, are you carsick?"

"Not yet."

If you had great big donkey ears, Deborah thought, you could hear what Julia was saying without any trouble at all.

"Do you feel like you're going to be?"

"Kinda."

"Did you bring your lemon?"

Julia held up a half of lemon.

The car slowed down. Mr Merrill turned his shoulder but not his head. "You recognize that place, Mrs Hall?"

They were in front of a large, brick building which sat on a hill far off beyond a high, iron fence.

"You talking to me?" Deborah asked. It was not her Grandmother's farm if that was what he wanted to know.

"Yes," he said. "Do you recognize it?"

She looked again. It wasn't her Grandmother's farm and that was a fact. "No, sir."

"That's Stonebrook. That's where you've been living for the last seven years."

She had never seen this view of it—except once before—when she was leaving. When she thought of the home, she thought of her room, how the yard looked from the porch, how the road looked through the gate. This was not the place she saw when she remembered Stonebrook. If she had looked into a mirror and seen someone else's face instead of her own, she could not have felt more foolish.

"I don't know how you expect to find your folks' place. You can't even recognize Stonebrook."

"Well, because," she had to explain everything, "their place doesn't look anything like Stonebrook."

"Oh," Mr Merrill said.

The day hung so evenly between winter and summer that when they were in the hill-shadows they were cold, and when they were on the road between the sunny fields of late afternoon, they were comfortable.

Then suddenly the car turned a curve in the road, and before Deborah had time to think, it turned another. Something was wrong. The road should have been straight. There was no need to go turning curves to get to the farm. Here was a bridge no had told her about; someone had opened up a new river down there. All of this was past strange. She was lost.

"Are you keeping a look-out back there?" Mr Merrill asked.

She jumped everytime he boom-boomed at her. "Yes, sir," she said. But there wasn't any use and she knew it. There was nothing left to do but cry, so she did that.

"Here we go again," Mr Merrill said. "Forty days and forty nights."

At six percent, Deborah thought. That was the way men talked. She cried louder, but tried to watch at the same time; because if the farm did happen to be on this hideous road—and she knew it wasn't—she didn't mean to miss it. She looked at every farmhouse and building, wiping her eyes only when a building was not in sight. Betty had turned around and was watching her. Deborah looked out of the side of the car so that her eyes would not meet the little girl's. Betty moved to the back seat and stared right into her face. Deborah looked out the other side. As if it weren't bad enough to be lost, she had to be cooped up here with a monster-child. Betty stood in front of her and tried to see her eyes. Deborah held a square handkerchief rag to her brows and hid her face. The child stooped down at her feet and peeped up under the rag. It was the funniest sight you ever saw, her crouching there peeping up like a little animal. In the middle of a sob, Deborah laughed out loud.

"Oh, my God!" Mr Merrill said. "Don't tell me she's going to start laughing now."

Even Britton laughed. Betty sat down on the floor and examined Deborah's high-topped shoes. She touched the toe of one with an outstretched finger. Deborah waited to see what she'd do next. The child traced pictures on the shoe, traced the seams and the eyelets and hooks.

"Why do you wear shoes like that?"

"To keep my feet warm. What you think?"

Betty's lips moved. Then she said the words aloud: "What you think?" Evidently she liked the sound of it. "Say that again."

"What you think." Deborah cut the sounds off short as though she were saying the same word three times: "rah rah rah"; as though it were a winning cheer: "Ziz boom bah!"

"What you think!"

"What you think!"

"No," Betty stood up and held to Deborah's knees. "I said it first. You've got to say something else, playlike. What-you-think?"

Deborah didn't know what to think. She looked across a pasture that was rolling by. "Cows," she said.

Betty laughed; then they both laughed. "Now you ask me."

They played until it became hard in the twilight to see anything new in the fields to think about. It was Deborah's time and she was looking for something in the car she would know the name of. "Julia," she said. Julia was holding her head out of the car. She was sick. Deborah pushed Betty aside and moved up to the little seats. She put one hand on Julia's thin shoulder and with the other she held Julia's burning-hot forehead.

She patted the child's shoulder and said: "Go ahead and be sick."

Julia made noises and spit. Deborah pulled her head back into the car, and without turning her around, wiped her mouth with the large square rag. The child tried to move but Deborah held her still. If she sees that it's me, Deborah thought, she'll run away again. She wanted to hold the little girl a little longer; then, if she ran away, it wouldn't make so much difference. She brushed Julia's fine hair back from her forehead and whispered, "Now then." Julia turned and looked at her; and was still. She didn't want to run away; she didn't try to move.

Deborah gazed across the fields, stretching gray in the growing twilight. Betty came and stood on the other side of her and held to her knee. But it wasn't necessary to think of anything now; it wasn't a game; and when you felt like this you didn't have to think. All you had to do was keep from bursting.

The car moved through the evening just as though darkness was not there, all about it. Once Mr Merrill asked her if she had seen the place and she told him no sir she had not. She and the two children moved to the back seat and made a warm spot in the chill night air. Mr Merrill, because he was a man and wanted to break into that warmness, asked if she thought they were near and she told him that night time had come and she could no longer see the way. She didn't tell him she was paying no more heed to the lighted windows than if they were so many squares of yellow paper.

So Mr Merrill drove up to one of the houses and said did they know this woman in the back seat, did they know her folks, and a man stuck his head in the car so that his ugly face almost touched her and said no indeed he did not, that he had never seen her likeness before, or any like it. And Betty would have slapped at him if she had not held Betty's hands.

After that, after they were on the road again, she was so warm and comfortable, inside and out, she could not tell for a truth whether she was awake or asleep. But no one asked her so she did not have to think about that or anything until finally the car just sighed and sat down. They were in the driveway.

"We'll have to get an early start tomorrow," Mr Merrill

said, speaking in one of his riddles, "so that darkness won't catch us."

She wished they could sit there all night, but Betty was already climbing out and Julia was stirring from the warmness.

The house was so bright she had to rub her eyes; and the floor went up and down hill like a road so that she staggered. But she had to get to the back room. All this furniture moving all over the place couldn't stop her. She pushed open the door. "We're back home!" Deborah said.

Mrs Merrill slid her feet into bedroom slippers and stood up to straighten her robe. The words reached her across the room and she smiled.

Deborah held to the doorknob to keep from swaying. Then, seeing Mrs Merrill's face, for the first time happy, she repeated the whole sentence in the way that children do when they are not sure which new word has delighted their parents: "We're back home."

"I see," Mrs Merrill said, "and I'm glad."

Deborah turned and was trotting toward the stairs when Betty went running past into the bedroom. Deborah paused.

"Mama, what-you-think?"

"Well, I don't know what to think."

"No. You're supposed to say 'Cows!'"

Chapter 4

AFTER the car ride and the warm huddle in the back seat, home was the upstairs room in the Merrill house. She belonged in this house. She knew she belonged here, yet she was not certain that the Merrills knew. A week had passed now since that night, maybe longer, but she still did not know Britton and Rebecca. They seemed always to be leaving the room she entered. And she herself did not like to be in the same room with Mr Merrill, whose deep voice made her tremble so that she could scarcely answer him. But she had enjoyed holding Betty and Julia in the back seat and playing games. They had not played since then because the children would not leave their mother's room, and Deborah did not like to play games in front of Mrs Merrill who looked as though she had never been a child, had never played a game, had never even laughed.

So in Mrs Merrill's presence she and the children were shy with each other and Deborah could not figure how she would ever come to know them better if they would not leave their mother's room. Mrs Merrill, herself, answered the problem without being asked. "Monday I'm going to get up and dressed and then we aren't going to come back in this room during the day." She said too that the meals would be on time, and the children on time for the meals, that the entire family would eat together. Deborah was glad of that because mealtimes were sad times with no one to listen to or watch at the table. Maybe when they all ate together, she would know for certain and the Merrills would understand that home was home and this was it.

She wondered though if she would have a chance to see the baby after Mrs Merrill was up. The only reason she visited the bedroom now was to see the baby and to hope that the children would follow her upstairs. She certainly wouldn't visit Mrs Merrill who was mean as a matron about the baby. She would not let anyone pick him up except herself. "He must first of all know who his mother is. After he gets used to one person, then it won't frighten him to be handled by anyone. But first he must know his mother." Deborah did not say a word. Yet after that when she first came into the room each day she would whisper to him, "Here I am," and then as she went out, "I'm going." When Mrs Merrill would pick the baby up, Deborah would leave the room.

Sunday everyone was excited about Monday, and Monday morning they were excited about Monday afternoon which was when Dr Bronston had said Mrs Merrill could dress. There were a thousand things to do before Mrs Merrill got up. For almost an hour Deborah had been trying to finish what she had to find out. She repeated and repeated but as yet it remained a mystery.

She stood in the back hall and breathed deeply with her eyes shut. Then holding her breath she walked across the screened-in back porch, out into the yard. There she let her breath out. Mrs Merrill, with a curious expression, was watching from the back-room window. Deborah had seen her there before but she hadn't had time to speak. Deborah shook her head; she almost had it that time if she could just think of the word. She started up the steps shaking her head. Mrs Merrill was holding the door open for her: "Are you taking exercise?"

"No'm," Deborah said. She wished Mrs Merrill would go away, because that time was almost it. She inhaled a breath so large she had to go up on her tiptoes to finish it. She puffed out her cheeks and stared at Mrs Merrill who had almost gone up on her tiptoes to watch. Mrs Merrill nervously touched her fingers lightly to her throat, as though to see if a string of beads were still there. Deborah ignored her and marched past out into the back yard. She exhaled and looked about to see which way the wind was blowing.

"Is it some kind of game?" Mrs Merrill was noticeably upset.

"No'm," Deborah said as she marched back in.

"Well what are you doing?"

"I'm just trying to find out what this house smells like," Deborah said.

"I hope it doesn't smell like anything."

"It does though," Deborah assured her.

"Even if it does, I don't like to be told," Mrs Merrill said. She watched the little woman inhale. "What does it smell like?"

"That," Deborah let her breath out, "is what I'm trying to find out now."

"I wish you'd hurry. It's not a very nice thing to be told your house smells."

"Everybody's house smells."

"I've lived here fifteen years and I've never noticed."

"That's because you live here. You've got to get the smell when you first come into a place or you can't ever get it."

She started toward the door with her lungs full of house-smell. Mrs Merrill followed cautiously. Then she asked, "Did your house . . . did your house have an odor?"

Deborah exhaled. "Certainly," she called from the yard. She tilted her head and sniffed. Then she looked up at Mrs Merrill who was holding the door open for her: "My house smelled like pine wood and white sand. That's because we scrubbed the floors with white sand." She walked past Mrs Merrill. "And it smelled like Thomas."

"What did Thomas . . ." Mrs Merrill began, fascinated by the subject. "Oh, never mind."

"He smelled good."

"Never mind."

Deborah chose the dining room. "This one's kind of different."

"Maybe it's just the food. Don't most houses smell like whatever's been cooking?"

There were so many things Mrs Merrill didn't know. Deborah couldn't explain to her that she was talking about the odor under the food odor, that mixes in with it, that makes cabbage-cooking smell different in every house. She was talking about the flavor of the air you breathe when you wake up lost in the middle of the night.

"What did Stonebrook smell like?" Mrs Merrill asked and breathed deeply.

"Pee-pee and lye soap."

Mrs Merrill exhaled quickly. "Well I certainly hope this house . . ." She went to the hall and anxiously dilated her nostrils.

"I know what it smells like, only I can't think of what you call it."

"Is it bad? Unpleasant?"

"What do you call those little round things?" Deborah made a circle with her thumb and forefinger.

Mrs Merrill looked at her with a pleading expression.

"Kind of little cakes. Vanilla wafers! It smells sort of like that thin, pretty paper what comes in a box with vanilla wafers."

"Oh," Mrs Merrill said. She looked exhausted as she lowered herself to the edge of a chair.

"And that other thing."

"What other thing?" Mrs Merrill sat up before she had leaned all the way back.

"Empty fruit jars."

"Empty fruit jars don't have an odor."

"If they've been shut up a long time they do."

A silence flowed into the room. Deborah knew it wasn't the kind you wade into and splash. It was the kind in which you stand there gathering courage, shut your eyes, and dive into blindly. She wondered whether she or Mrs Merrill would plunge first. She waited for Mrs Merrill because she knew that she, herself, had not invited the silence.

Mrs Merrill took out her hoot-owl glasses.

"Have you unpacked your trunk yet?"

"Not yet."

"Right now while the children are out would be a good time." She waited. "Let's go up and get your things all straightened out."

"I can do it by myself."

"I know. But I haven't been upstairs in over a month, and I want to see how torn up everything is." She stood up, walked to the stairs, and looked up the long flight of steps. She held to the post and said, "Don't tell anyone I went upstairs today."

Deborah could hardly stay behind her after she said that.

She wanted to take Mrs Merrill by the waist and push her to the top because then they would have a secret together. She had been thinking Mrs Merrill was as mean as the matron—a person to keep secrets from—but here they had one together.

Mrs Merrill with her glasses on again went from room to room shaking her head. Then she went to Deborah's room. The full bedspread had been stretched tightly and tucked, with slanting hospital corners, about the mattress, so that the sidepiece of the bed showed, and the springs. The pillows were propped outside the covers. Mrs Merrill pulled the spread loose and fluffed it out so that it hung almost to the floor. She turned the counterpane back, put the pillows underneath, and smoothed the cover over them.

The sight of the covered pillows sickened Deborah. The soft mounds were like two little baby graves. She would have nightmares if they stayed on her bed like that all day.

"We'll get some new curtains too. The next time I go to town. What I'll do is move the dining room curtains up here and take these for my room where they won't be seen from the street."

Deborah often wondered about people who liked puzzles.

"Mine are about ready for the rag bag anyway."

"You're going to throw away good curtains like these?" Deborah had liked the curtains better than anything in the room.

"No, I say I'll take these for my room."

"Then what'll I do for curtains?"

"I'm going to give you the ones from the dining room."

Mrs Merrill had pulled her into the puzzle; but still it was a shame to throw away perfectly good curtains—and then not have any for the dining room.

"They'll look nice in here," Mrs Merrill said.

"I like these."

"But. Well, it's your room."

"And it's your house," Deborah said.

Mrs Merrill looked as if someone had deliberately hauled off and hit her in the stomach. Deborah wondered what had happened. She couldn't be having another labor pain, not with the baby already here.

"I'm sorry," Mrs Merrill said. "You can arrange it any way you like. I suppose I did just walk in and take over."

"Won't you have a seat?"

Mrs Merrill looked sicker than ever while Deborah glanced about the room for one of the three chairs she had noticed. At Stonebrook there usually wasn't even one chair in her room, and she could never say what she had been taught was proper. She had been waiting so long to say it she wasn't sure the words had come out right: "Won't you have a seat?" But Mrs Merrill apparently understood for she said, "Thank you" and sat down. No, it wouldn't be right to say "How've you been getting along?" She stood and stared at Mrs Merrill, hoping that some words would come to her.

"Have you unpacked any of your things?"

"No. No m'am." Deborah put her hand on the trunk, then slowly lifted the lid. Some of the boxes had slid out of their places; she pushed them back again. She showed each of the boxes to Mrs Merrill and waited for her to say something. At first all Mrs Merrill could say was, "What's in it?"; but then she had understood that they were pretty, *empty* boxes; and she said that they were indeed pretty. Deborah handed her the many-sided one that was colored like the rainbow. Mrs Merrill held it so long, and turned it over and over so many times, Deborah knew exactly what Mrs Merrill was wishing. "You can have that one," Deborah said.

"No. No thank you. You keep it."

"No. I want you to have it."

"I couldn't think of it. Here, put it back with the rest of them."

For a minute Deborah had been afraid the woman would take it; now as she returned the box to its place she wished Mrs Merrill had. She showed her the soaps and the face powder, and Mrs Merrill told her to leave them packed, that there was always good white soap in the bathroom. Nothing was to be taken from the tray of the trunk—except the two petticoats she had used to pack the glass powder jar with.

Mrs Merrill held the petticoats up to the light, running her hands all through them and over them and counting like a schoolchild: "Six, seven, eight . . . this one's got eight places . . . nine . . . places to be mended . . . ten." She looked at everything, unfolded, and counted and counted, and said it was a shame. Finally she sat down and sorted the clothes into two heaps. "Come over here by the window." Deborah went over to the light. "Turn around." Deborah turned around. "Hold up your arms." She did. "Where in the world did you get that dress?"

"It's the best I've got." Deborah said.

"We'll just have to get you some new clothes—from top to bottom."

"I haven't got anything to 'get' with." She hoped Mrs Merrill could think of some way though.

"You can let your arms down now." Mrs Merrill tugged and pulled and gathered and raised and lowered. "We'll get you some. Mr Merrill plans on paying you ten dollars a week, and we'll just take the first few weeks salary and buy some clothes for you."

Deborah didn't know how many clothes that would buy,

but it sounded like a whole closet full the way Mrs Merrill said it.

"Now hold it in here and here, and up, and walk over there."

She held the dress in at the waist. She was so excited by the idea of having new clothes she would have walked on into the closet if Mrs Merrill hadn't said, "All right, now turn around. Lower it just a little. There." Mrs Merrill looked at the entire dress, then right into her face. "You've got a nice little figure when your clothes fit."

When you've been by yourself for a long time, nothing can hurt so much as kindness. Deborah didn't want Mrs Merrill to see what was happening to her face and so she turned quickly toward the closet to hide the tears. She saw the hat and put it on. It was a tall, black velvet one, shaped like a bucket. She pulled it down to her ears. When her face had quit going all to pieces, she turned back around: "How about this?"

"Later. We'll get you a hat after we get the other things. A nice, little hat that suits you."

Mrs Merrill is looking right at me, Deborah thought, but she doesn't even know someone just put a flower on my grave. Because when you said something nice about a person who wasn't even dead, it was the same as putting a flower on their grave.

"Let's go find you some of my clothes to wear, and we'll both be dressed when the children come in." Mrs Merrill led the way downstairs. While Deborah was dressing in the downstairs bathroom, lacing her high-topped shoes, the front door slammed and Betty hollered: "Mama is up! Mama is up!" And sure enough, when Debby came out, Mrs Merrill was standing in the middle of the room in a starched dress. She was unrolling a belt which was so full of starch it might have been linoleum. Deborah sat down quickly before the children could see how funny she looked in a dress that dragged the floor. But they didn't even know she was in the room.

"Wait a minute. Wait a minute." Julia had said to her mother. "You've got your belt all twisted up." She straightened the belt in the back and gave her the end with the snap.

Betty stood in front of Mrs Merrill, watching her in the mirror. "Now then, Mama."

"Now then what?"

"See if you can lift me up."

Julia came over and sat on the couch by Deborah and waited for Mrs Merrill to make another fatal mistake in dressing.

"See if you can lift me up," Betty said again.

"No, I'm afraid you're too big now. Mama's lost her baby girl."

"No you haven't."

"Yes, you're too big for Mama to lift. We've got a new baby now." Mrs Merrill smoothed the stiff dress and turned to see how it fit in the waist.

"Just once." Betty looked at Julia. "Just once, Mama."

"Nonono," Mrs Merrill said. She unpinned the braids of hair from the top of her head and began unplaiting them. "You're too big and heavy to be Mama's baby."

A smile that had nothing to do with humor came on Julia's lips.

"Mama, make Julia stop."

"What's Julia doing?"

"She's looking at me."

"Is that going to hurt you?"

"Make her stop!"

"She's sitting over there like a little lady. That doesn't bother you does it."

Julia's smile turned down at the corners in a mocking curve.

"Mama!"

"Betty, you mustn't be a baby. Julia's not hurting you." Mrs Merrill unplaited the other braid. "Now move. Mama's got to brush her hair."

Betty turned back and raised her arms. "Just once, Mama."

"No, Betty. You can't be a baby now." She looked down at the little girl and brushed the bangs back from her forehead. "We've got a new baby we have to take care of. You want to help Mama tend to it, don't you?"

"Yes."

"Yes, what?"

"Yes, m'am."

"Well, I tell you. You go see if he needs anything."

"Pick him up?"

"No. Don't lift him."

"What do?"

"Just go see if his eyes are open or shut."

Betty stared at Julia a moment before leaving the room.

"Julia," Mrs Merrill said when Betty had gone, "go see that she doesn't bother him."

"She won't pick him up. She won't even touch him. She's scared of him."

"Go watch her though. Mama'll feel better."

In a quick movement Mrs Merrill bent forward and flung the hair over the top of her head so that it hung almost to her knees. She reached out blindly for the brush, and Deborah watched with horror while she brushed until every wave that had been left from the braids had disappeared. She brushed until the hair hung like one black scarf of satin. Then twisting it loosely about her arm, holding the other hand to her scalp, she stood up and coiled the hair on top of her head. She held the coil with one hand and pressed it forward until a pompadour curved up from her forehead. Then she stuck in two combs and some big celluloid hairpins. She touched her nose with a powder puff, put on her gold-rimmed glasses, turned and said to Deborah: "Now let's see about you."

Mrs Merrill pinned the dress to fit Deborah, and threaded a needle to tack the places she had pinned. "When you take this off tonight, you won't have to undo these places."

Julia and Betty came back into the room.

"Was he all right?"

Betty's eyes were wide, and almost black from having been in the dark room. "He had his hands like this." She made a fist.

"And was he awake?"

Betty didn't look at Julia, but she asked, "Was he, Julia?"

"He's sound asleep."

"Aren't you proud of your baby brother?" Mrs Merrill asked as though Betty were the sole owner.

"I think," Betty said; she moved closer to her mother, "I think he's *precious*."

Deborah, who understood faces and tones better than she did words, thought Betty had said the new baby was perfectly horrible and should be thrown in the brier patch.

At that moment the baby cried as though Betty had actually thrown him where he belonged. Mrs Merrill glanced up, then back down at her lap full of basket, needles and thread.

"Did you hurt the baby, Betty?"

"I didn't even touch him."

"She didn't touch him, Mama. I was there watching."

Mrs Merrill began shifting the basket, then stopped. "I'm afraid I have a loose pin or needle on me." Then just as casually as if she were talking about a bag of potatoes she said, "Deborah, would you mind bringing Glenn in here?"

Deborah went alone into the bedroom. She was not trembling as she had thought she would be. Calmly she pushed back the net as though she had done it every day. Leaning near she talked to the baby whose red face was puckered in grief. "Here I am, here I am." Carefully she slid her hands under him and picked him up. She wrapped the blanket closer and rocked him gently, touching her lips to the top of his head. "Shhh, baby." He understood, she believed, for he quit crying, looked at her, then shut his eyes and was asleep.

Julia came to the door and whispered: "Mama says you can keep him in here if you get him back to sleep. She wants to sew in there on the machine." Deborah nodded without taking her eyes from the baby. She sat down in the half-darkened room and rocked gently, listening to the thrashing of the sewing machine in the next room, and presently to the rain on the roof. The baby was warm against her bosom, and she nodded and dreamed as she rocked the baby and herself to sleep.

When she awakened the rain had passed and a brilliant sunset touched all outdoors with a golden glow that was strange and sad. As she placed the baby in the cradle she said, "Mama will . . ." and stopped. The child could never call her "Mama" the way a child should, the way Grover was learning to do when Nurse Janet took him away. Why? Why? Why? She would never be called "Mama" again. She walked to the front door shaking her head. There was too much to be understood in this world.

Where a curtain had not been drawn or a shade pulled,

the sad strange light came into the house. The walls, which in the daytime were neither tan nor rose were at the moment sheets of copper. The long, stiff-looking, and very uncomfortable sofa, which Mr Merrill liked so much, was green now, even though it was ordinarily copper brocade with only a trace of green. The russet-hue draperies had stubbornly kept their own color.

She walked across the living room into the hall and studied the shaft of light coming down the stairs. She stuck her hand out, holding it first this way, then that. She went up three steps and, leaning across the banister, peered into the mirror over the telephone. Her hair, which the matron had forced her to wear in a ball at the back of her neck, was the color it had been when she was a girl.

She looked into the dining room where the large red roses covered the walls in bunches. The glow was not touching them because they were such a deep velvet-red. But about them a thin, fine lace of gold and light blue had suddenly emerged. She stood in the dining room and glanced about her. It was like being in a fancy cage of gold filigree on the outside of which roses had been pinned with little blue satin ribbons. She was delighted by her cage-world.

When she heard the laughter and splashing of the children—Betty and Julia were bathing—she could not tell for a certainty whether she was seeing the noise or hearing it, for even the sounds had been touched by this muted golden calm.

She went into the dark back hall and down to the room where Mrs Merrill was sewing in the window light. She stood in the doorway and waited for Mrs Merrill to look up.

Mrs Merrill took three long, slow stitches, bit the thread, and stuck the needle in the pincushion. "Come in," she said without taking her eyes from her work.

Deborah walked to the center of the room and waited for her to say "Won't you have a seat?" but Mrs Merrill moved over to the machine, stuck the cloth in, and pedaled as though there were only two more minutes left to live.

A flash of gold light caught on the metal rim of Mrs Merrill's new glasses. (The hoot owls were gone with the bathrobe.) Deborah watched the light-bead dance from place to place on the glasses rim, sometimes sliding, sometimes drawing itself out into a fine gold thread, and occasionally disappearing altogether as Mrs Merrill bent her head to the machine and guided the cloth under the needle.

There was a tremendous splashing in the bathroom and Deborah suspected that the children had turned the tub over. "Betty, quit it. Stop!"

"Go knock on the bathroom door for me, will you?" Mrs Merrill asked.

"I don't want in there." She certainly didn't if the place was as flooded as she thought and they were drowning each other.

"Betty!" There was another splash.

"Just knock like this." Mrs Merrill tapped on the machine with her wedding band. "They'll think it's me."

"Clack clack clack." She could make a noise like that. She went into the back hall and stood, hand poised, listening to the splashing.

"Clack clack clack." The noise inside stopped immediately. "Shhh," she heard Julia whisper. Deborah giggled to herself. She rapped three more times. "Mama, we're just playing." She was going to knock again but her hand stayed itself in mid-air. Betty had called her "Mama" and she had thought that she would never again be called that. She stood at the bathroom door until Mrs Merrill called her.

Mrs Merrill was cutting the petticoat loose from the

machine. "Here you are. It'll have to do till we can get uptown." She lifted her glasses and rubbed her eyes. She glanced up at Deborah. "What's wrong?"

"Nothing," Deborah said.

"Something's wrong. Is it the patched petticoat?"

It had nothing to do with petticoats—the uneasy way she felt. She hadn't wanted to go into the back hall to knock on the door and now something had happened to her—she couldn't say what, or how it would last. Maybe it would pass with the fading afterglow. Maybe it would go on forever, or until the right child called her, "Mama."

She looked at Mrs Merrill and said earnestly, "I just wish it'd hurry and be night."

"It is a sad time of day, isn't it?" Mrs Merrill said in that soft voice which hid a special surprise.

Mrs Merrill, then, felt the same way. That was some help. But not much. She looked at Mrs Merrill who was saying that at one time in her life she used to cry at this time everyday. So now they had two secrets together.

A car door slammed in the drive.

"Here he is. Back again." She waited for Mrs Merrill to say something. She heard Mr Merrill's walk on the porch. The front door opened. She didn't know whether to go upstairs or stand still. She waited for Mrs Merrill to tell her. "Here he is," she said again.

"Where's your mother?" he was saying to someone on the porch.

"I don't know." It was Rebecca. "In the back I suppose."

"Mother!"

"He's calling you."

"Shhh," Mrs Merrill stood in front of the mirror brushing the pompadour with the back of her hand and pinching at the hair over her ears. She turned around as Mr Merrill came to the door.

"Well! Well! Up and dressed!"

"It's about time, isn't it?"

Deborah sat down; and for all the attention they were paying her, she could have disappeared.

"Good. Does Doctor Bronston know?"

"He said today or tomorrow. If I felt like it."

"He could have saved his breath."

All her life Deborah had puzzled about that: what you did with your breath when you saved it. Was that the breath you used when you panted after running; or did you use it in your sleep? She rather fancied that some time during the night you went sound to sleep—all over—and quit breathing for a few times and used the breath you had saved during the day. That was why people died in the night. They had forgotten to save any breath during the day. Some days, she knew, some times for weeks she forgot to hold her breath for a little while.

Mr Merrill had said he had a surprise too; for Mrs Merrill to wait there. He went out onto the porch and when he came in he went into the living room. "Wait a minute," he called, and he and Rebecca whispered.

"All ready." He came through the hall to the door of the back living room.

"Haven't we had enough surprises for this time?" Mrs Merrill mocked him.

Deborah followed to the living room. It looked the same to her except that it now was dull again in the electric light. But on the floor was a stack of magazines and books that belonged on the small, square, square-legged table in the corner. There, on the shining walnut top was a tall pitcher: what kind she could not say, for there had not been another like it that she had ever seen.

The sad soft glow which had been over the entire house that afternoon was caught now somewhere in the depths of the pitcher which, Mr Merrill was saying, was made of luster. The gold shone through the wide, dark bands at the top and bottom and on the handle which stretched between. It shone through the deep cream center band where a hunter was sounding a horn to a dog which was leaping at a deer that was disappearing around to the other side. For a handle there was the same dog, not just a picture of him, leaping up the side, the flat triangle of his head turned down to drink from the inside, his ears sticking up in fine curved points, his deep chest and thin hound-loins—a perfect handle. Deborah stared again at the dark brown bands of luster through which were shining that sad light. Would a hollowness always fill her vitals when she saw it, the same hollowness, and pain that had filled her when she knocked on the bathroom door?

They talked about the expensive pitcher in the kitchen while Mrs Merrill, working like a crazy-fool, fried country ham, scrambled eggs, and stirred the bubbling hominy. A delicious blue haze filled the room. Betty and Julia came in to be buttoned up and stayed to watch while their mother opened a jar of dessert peaches. Fullop. The peaches emptied into the glass bowl. If Deborah had been alone, she would have filled the jar again, just to hear it go empty. But Mrs Merrill washed it and returned it to the bottom shelf of the butler's pantry. She sniffed twice and returned to the kitchen, leaving the cabinet door open.

Britton came in and washed his hands just as the toast was being snatched out of the oven, so hot it had to be juggled onto a plate.

And here was the way they were to sit: Mrs Merrill at the head of the table, Mr Merrill sat at her right, because that was where he had ever since they were married, and Rebecca next to him. On the other side of the table another chair was added. Next to Mrs Merrill was Betty, Julia in the middle, then Deborah. Britton sat at the end opposite his mother.

"We're getting to be a big family," Mr Merrill said unfolding his napkin.

"Where . . ." Betty began, but Rebecca interrupted.

"I think we ought to ask the blessing tonight."

That girl, Deborah thought, is full of stylish notions. No one said anything.

"I'll ask it." Rebecca glanced about the table. Deborah watched as they grew quiet and bowed their heads (Mrs Merrill's hand was on top of Betty's head, holding it down). Julia merely shut her eyes and held her hands in her lap. Deborah shut her eyes. For a second there wasn't a sound.

Rebecca began: "As we bow our . . ."

Deborah giggled out loud. Rebecca stopped.

"As we bow our heads . . ."

Deborah laughed again.

". . . in gratitude, Lord we thank thee for this food."

When they opened their eyes, they all stared at Deborah, waiting for an answer. She was still laughing. "As we bow-wow," she finally managed to say, "like a puppy dog."

They all laughed, Rebecca not as loud as the others, Britton louder. They laughed until they were gasping for breath and for sanity to return.

"Now if that wasn't some joke to play on us," Deborah said, but no one was listening. "Getting us to shut our eyes and then barking at God like that."

"What?" Rebecca asked.

"Aren't you ashamed of yourself. Bow-wow heads." Deborah dried her eyes and said to herself, we're having ourselves a good time.

"Mama, what are they laughing at?" No one had noticed that Betty had joined for only a moment.

"We're just laughing."

"Make them stop."

"Why?"

"I don't like for them to laugh at me like that."

"Nobody's laughing at you."

"Julia's laughing."

"She's not laughing at you, though."

"Yes she is."

Mr Merrill looked at Julia. "You're not laughing at Betty are you?"

Julia looked back at him for a long time. She always seemed to Deborah to be making up her mind whether to preach a long sermon or to say nothing at all. Usually she said nothing.

"And she was laughing." Betty pointed at Deborah.

"Not at you."

"See, Julia," Mr Merrill said, "we did a good thing when we put you in the middle. You've got to keep peace on that side of the table."

Julia stared at him again. Mr Merrill held a napkin up before his face and said, "All right, don't hit me."

Julia didn't move her eyes, but a smile came to her face as though it were her natural expression and as though the solemn expression which she usually wore was only make-believe. "I wasn't going to hit you."

Mr Merrill lowered the napkin.

"Mama," Julia said, still looking at her father (for the children lived in a violent world in which it was safer to look at the person you were talking about rather than at the person you were talking to), "Mama, Daddy's a silly man, isn't he?"

"Sometimes he is." Mrs Merrill was spreading strawberry jelly on a piece of toast. She put it on Betty's plate.

"I didn't *want* jelly on it."

"All right, give it to Julia."

Betty looked at Julia. "No."

Britton spoke: "If you don't want it . . ."

"She can't have it!" Betty waited for someone else to start to speak. "Because she's six," she held up six fingers, "and I'm just this many." She held up four.

"What's that got to do with it?"

"Cause she's bigger and I got to eat a lot and be big as her."

"Well, then go ahead and eat it, and let's have a little less noise." Mrs Merrill was drinking coffee but she wasn't eating.

"I don't want it on my plate." Betty pushed the plate away. Mrs Merrill caught the glass of milk as it toppled almost over.

"Ah ah ah," Mr Merrill said.

"Betty, I don't know what in the world is the matter with you today. Are you sick?"

"Don't go putting ideas in her head, Mama," Rebecca said.

Mrs Merrill felt the child's forehead with one hand and her husband's with the other. "You haven't got a fever."

"She's just showing off because you're at the table."

"I am not." She brought her hand down to the table and again the milk glass toppled.

"Betty, now not another word out of you." Mrs Merrill released the glass. "And if you turn that milk over, you're going to get a whipping."

Mr Merrill and Britton were talking about the new pitcher while Mrs Merrill served the peaches. Britton had guessed that it cost sixty-five dollars, but there was no way to tell from Mr Merrill's expression if he was right or a thousand dollars wrong. Mrs Merrill was listening closely.

"Where . . ." Betty started.

"Shhh."

"Guess a little higher."

"Where . . ." Betty said again.

"Not another word," Mrs Merrill said to her.

"Well, Mama, all I was going to ask you is where is the new baby going to sit when he comes to the table?"

"He won't. Not for a long time yet. Shhh."

"It was on a trade so I actually didn't have to give a hundred and ten for it."

"When he comes to the table where will he sit?"

Mrs Merrill glanced quickly away when her husband turned to her. "Over there between Daddy and Rebecca, I suppose."

Betty looked at the space while she finished the peach juice.

"Over there, Mama?" She pointed with the spoon.

Mrs Merrill looked again. "No, I suppose he'll have to sit here by me."

"Where'll I sit?"

"We'll give you Julia's place and let her sit over there. Or you can sit over there if you want to."

Betty looked across the table as though it were a field.

"Way over there where the toast is?"

"Yes, Betty. Now be quiet; I want to listen."

After supper, after the dishes were done, they went in and looked at the pitcher again, and then went to the back sitting room where Britton had built a fire in the grate.

"That's not your coat?" Betty said when they sat down.

"No," Deborah said, "it's your mother's. Her dress too."

"Let me see." Betty had to touch the dress and the jacket.

She had to turn up the collar to see if it had velvet on it, and she had to examine the belt for snaps. "Mama, she's got on your clothes." She waited for an answer. "Why've you got on her clothes?"

"Cause mine is done wore slam out."

"You haven't got *any*?"

"They're all rags."

Betty looked at her, then touched the velvet collar again.

"It's the first time we've all been in here in a long time," Mr Merrill was saying.

Julia was touching her mother's hair brushes and combs without moving them. She glanced up at the mirror. "Daddy, let's build stair steps."

"All right," he said. He pulled Mrs Merrill up beside him and they stood looking into the mirror. "Rebecca," he said.

"Just a minute." Then she stood next to her mother.

"Britton." (Mrs Merrill and Rebecca were almost the same size. They changed places, then changed back.)

"Julia." She was already standing by Britton.

"And Betty."

Betty stood next to Julia without touching her.

"We forgot Mrs Hall!"

"Deborah," Mrs Merrill said. "Come on."

"What do?"

"Just stand. Let's see. Between Britt and Julia."

They parted arms and let her in. She stood for a moment studying the line made by the tops of their heads, and then looking at all their faces in the mirror. She had been thinking about them all so much that for a brief instant she did not recognize which one she was. The top of Mr Merrill's head was cut off by the mirror frame, and only the top of Betty's head showed. Then it disappeared and came up again in front of Mrs Merrill. "See if you can lift me up, Mama." Mrs Merrill reminded Betty again that she was no longer the baby. The stair steps caved in and floated off in different directions. Deborah wanted to go now and think about the way they had looked. There had been a lot of talk and she wanted to be by herself to go over and over it. She had a home now and she wanted to think about it.

"Good night," she said at the door.

"Already?" Mrs Merrill asked.

"Mama," Betty said, looking at Deborah, "let me go upstairs with her."

"No. It's almost your bedtime."

"Just for a minute."

"No."

"Let her go," Mr Merrill said. "So Julia and I can have a little rest."

"Just for a minute. And you'd better come back downstairs the second I call."

Betty tramped up the steps ahead of her. "Now I wonder what she's up to?" Deborah followed slowly, holding to the banister.

"Come on." Betty was waiting on the landing. They went together to Deborah's room and found the light switch. Betty walked to the center of the room and waited. Deborah ignored her, and going to the bed, turned back the cover from over the pillows. Betty shut the door and came back to the center of the room.

"Now what's she after?" Deborah said to herself.

"Come here," Betty whispered.

Deborah looked at the goat-grin on the child's face. Uh-oh, she thought, she's going to try to butt me in the belly. She moved cautiously toward the little girl. Or kick my shins.

"Bend down," the child whispered.

Deborah knelt warily. She didn't want her eye balls scratched out. She searched the goat-grin for meaning.

"Debby," Betty said, reaching out her arms, "see if you can lift me up."

Chapter 5

IN THE back living room the fire shifted in the grate. Deborah who was sitting alone at this late hour leaned forward and knocked her left heel three times against the chair leg. Was it the same fire Britt had started that happy night she lifted Betty? It was burning every morning when she came down, but perhaps Bertha built it. You couldn't look at a fire and tell if it was the same one or not—yet people, who changed as constantly and completely, were always the same.

She had returned to her favorite subject: that of wondering if in the morning after being a sleeping person all night, she would again be Deborah Hall. If she continued wearing Mrs Merrill's clothes would she still be herself? She wished that she could wear Mrs Merrill's clothes always because Betty liked them and because Julia sometimes said "Mama" before she saw who it was. Julia would grin shyly and run away, ever so ladylike on her tiptoes. Mrs Merrill, however, was already busy making new ones that would fit. Deborah insisted though that they be the same cloth and pattern that Mrs Merrill used in her own dresses. And she wanted them long, to the tops of her high-topped shoes. It didn't make any difference what other women wore, she wasn't going to have her legs bare and feeling like they were in a draft. A hand span from the floor was the right length, the only length, now or any time. That was one way of knowing who she was, that she was herself.

She had not always wanted though to be herself every morning. When she was in the sixth grade—she still sat with the third grade because her teacher said she was such a little girl—she had wanted to wake up some morning and be Ellie Mae Wilson who was way yonder smarter than even the teacher.

She hit her right heel against the chair three times. Her feet did not touch the floor; and so hanging there, they often went to sleep. She had to wake them up like this. She leaned down to see if she had hurt the chair. Mrs Merrill had told her to be especially careful of certain pieces of furniture. She could never for the life of her remember which. Except she knew about the long, living-room sofa that had eight round legs and was made of original Sheraton wood. The square-legged tables, there were three of them, were made, Mr Merrill said, of "apple white wood," which was as silly as saying "walnut black wood" when you meant "black walnut." But she was merely to dust these pieces and leave the polishing for Mr Merrill to do on Sundays.

Deborah had worked hard and she had learned a lot this week. She had to if she wanted to stay here—and she could not think now what life would be like anywhere else. Mrs Merrill had said to her one morning, calling her in from the sunny front steps: "Debby, are you about ready now to begin work?"

"Any time you are."

"I've been working all morning. Every day."

Deborah stood there.

"You see, it's that, well, we can't pay you just to stay with us unless you help with the work."

She understood that, but no one had told her what to do.

"I'll probably ask you to do a lot of things the children could do because, when they're in school, I don't want them to have their minds on anything except their schoolwork."

Deborah didn't know what she was supposed to do about Mrs Merrill's children. She couldn't think for them. But Mrs Merrill had a lot more to say.

"Then, as long as you like the work, and as long as you want to stay here, you have a home."

Tonight Deborah sank back in the big armchair and looked at the dying fire. I'll work all night if they'll let me stay here. The clock in the hall had struck ten soon after the Merrills had gone to bed. She was waiting now for Rebecca and Britton, in the living room, to go. Then her day's work would be done. She yawned and stretched. Her shoulders were sore from washing pantry shelves and the glass front door. She could scrub floors forever without being sore; but this reaching up!

She wondered if Mrs Merrill was sore too. That woman, Deborah decided, was a working-fool. She didn't work like an ordinary, white woman. An evil witch had put a curse on Mrs Merrill saying that if one speck of dust stayed in the house overnight she might be turned into a razorback hog and be sent rooting off through the back yard. In a cloud of smoke a dark coal choked out to black.

And I've learned good this week. Every word she had to tell me. Was that true, or had she already forgotten some of the things?

Ellie Mae Wilson could remember—she knew there had been something a moment ago she wanted to think about and now that she found it in her mind again, she breathed deeply and gazed with heavy-lidded eyes at the bright coals—Ellie Mae, what was it about Ellie Mae now? She'd almost thought of it and then it slipped back again. It was something about Ellie Mae though.

She thought about how Ellie Mae looked: tall; corn-colored hair; freckled; ugly as a mud fence; ugly as two mud fences; and waving a thin arm in the air because she knew the answer to the teacher's questions. Mrs Mac Manoway! That was the teacher's name. Mrs Mac Manoway—she looks thisaway. Deborah's eyes pulled toward her nose. At recess Mrs Mac Manoway and Ellie Mae stood under the water oak and talked; or if it was raining, and there was indoor recess, Ellie Mae went up to Mrs Mac Manoway's table and talked.

That was why the other children wouldn't have anything to do with Ellie; that and because she was so tall.

Deborah always liked the girl though. She liked to hear her read: so fast the words didn't mean anything. She liked to hear her answer just anything the teacher wanted to know. Ellie was *smart*. Everybody, even the people who didn't like her said: "Ellie is *smart*."

All you had to do to be smart was talk to Ellie. She could take what you said and say it for you in a different way which sounded fine. Then she'd talk to you sometimes for hours about the things she'd been thinking and saving up to tell. Oh Lord, Deborah thought, what were some of the things that girl used to talk about? She closed her eyes against the heat of the fire. She remembered one afternoon—it was in the late spring—she was going to eat supper at Ellie's.

They were poor people, the Wilsons. They had a bed in the kitchen and that was as poor as white people could get. The kitchen was brown and ceiled. On one side, where the roof slanted low, there was a bed where Ellie Mae's little brother slept. There was a patchwork quilt on the bed and while supper was cooking Ellie showed her every different piece of cloth in the quilt and told her where the scraps had come from.

Then Ellie Mae's father—his name was Mr Wilson—came in, hitching his one suspender strap over his shoulder.

"And this one," Ellie was saying about a beautiful triangle of red corduroy, "was my Aunt Lucy's going-away dress."

Deborah quit listening because she wanted to hear what Mr Wilson's voice sounded like. Deep-frog, deep-frog, she imagined.

"Ain't that Jim Morison's grandchild?" He was talking to his wife in a voice as thin as silk thread; Ellie talked slower, then quit.

Mrs Wilson opened the fire-door and the kitchen flickered in bright light. "Yes," she said throwing a stick of stovewood in.

"Ain't she supposed to be sort of *backward*?"

Mrs Wilson turned quickly and looked at her. Deborah looked at Ellie, and for once Ellie couldn't think of anything to say. Deborah didn't know what was wrong, but something was because Mrs Wilson just stood there with the fire-door open and her hand halfway to her lips. Mr Wilson didn't move. Finally he mumbled, "I thought they were talking. Is supper ready?" and Mrs Wilson clanging the iron door shut, stared at Deborah again; but didn't answer.

"This one, Debby, this one," Ellie Mae was talking fast now and saying everything twice, "is from a pair of old blue pants Grandpa got when he went up to Richmond that time. Up in Richmond."

Maybe they want me to go home, Deborah thought. Maybe they haven't got enough to eat and maybe they don't want me to stay for supper. Well, then, I won't. She stood up. "I got to go home."

Ellie stood up, "You haven't eaten supper yet."

"I know. But I just remembered. I got to go."

Ellie looked at her mother for help.

"Debby, why you haven't been here no time! You can't go rushing off without your supper."

"Yes'm. I've got to go. My grandma doesn't know where I'm at."

"Why, Debby, she knew we were coming to my house."

"No, she didn't. I mean she didn't want me to eat supper over here." She moved to the door. She stood with her back to it and with her hand raised to wave good-by.

"She said you could. Standing on your front porch."

"She didn't mean . . ." Deborah couldn't think of anything else to say. The lump in her throat was growing bigger, so she had to talk fast. "I've got to go home."

She twisted the wet doorknob and started out into the darkness.

"Wait a minute, Debby, I'll go with you."

She would have run on alone except that it was night. Ellie came out and took her hand. Mrs Wilson followed, taking off her apron and rolling it up. As they walked across the pasture they both talked to her, and talked. They were ashamed because they didn't have enough to eat. You could hear it in the sad way they poured their words over her.

When they came up the driveway, Mrs Wilson stopped and waited under the chinaberry because she was bare legged. Ellie walked to the steps with her. Deborah stood on the first step and turned to say good-by. They were the same height now. Ellie didn't notice. Her face was tight lipped, slit eyed, and mean. "I hate him," she said. "I hate him to death!"

Deborah was frightened by the thawing and cracking of ice in Ellie's voice. She turned and ran up the steps and down the long, lamp-lit hall. "Grandma, Grandma. I've come home."

When her grandmother opened the door, Deborah threw herself into the big woman's full skirts.

"Whatsa matter, honey? Did you get homesick for your grandma?"

It was all too awful to think about: there not being enough food at Ellie Mae's. She couldn't tell her grandmother that. Instead she sobbed out words she didn't even remember having heard: "He said I was *backward*."

"Who said that about my darling?" Her grandmother sat down and took her on her lap. "Who said that?"

"Mr Wilson! And Ellie Mae's going to kill him!"

"Well, he needs killing if he said a thing like that." Her grandmother rocked back and forth, back and forth, and sang in a rocking rhythm: "There, there," until there was nothing left to cry about. Then she said, "Now I wonder what he meant by that. Reckon he meant you had eyes in the back of your head? I'll bet that's what he meant."

Her grandmother talked and rocked for a long time. Deborah couldn't remember now what all she had said. But after that she couldn't play with Ellie Mae. And when the other children found out about it, and teased her at recess, her grandmother told her she didn't have to go to school any more. So sometimes, when she had a new dress, or new shoes, she went; but soon there were different children, and she quit going. Her grandmother said. . . . She couldn't remember what now. It was all there to think about whenever she wanted to, but tonight when she tried, it all grew darker and darker, and finally, like the coals, guttered black. Her chin sank to her neck-pocket and she was asleep. The two cane-bottomed chairs creaked with the growing coldness, and somewhere in the house a water pipe was throbbing.

"Mrs Hall!"

The words split her ears and the light split her eyes. For a moment she was both deaf and blind.

"Mrs Hall." It was Mrs Merrill in a flannel nightgown holding a bottle of milk. "What in the world are you doing up?"

"I was just," she said as though that answered everything completely.

"Look. It's after midnight!"

"Have Britton and Rebecca gone to bed?"

"Hours ago. I heard them go up not long after we went to bed."

"I suppose then I'll go."

"You can't stay up as long as they do. And you mustn't try."

"I was just thinking if they needed anything, I'd be here."

"You don't have to wait on them."

"You said you wanted them to think about their books and if I wanted to stay here, I'd have to work."

"I meant," Mrs Merrill said, and from the strange look that came over her, you could tell the cold air had seeped through the gown and was chilling her to the marrow. "I meant, as long as I'm here, you have a home." Her voice was as cold as the air. "Now you go on to bed."

"Good night," Deborah said. She waited for an answer, then switched off the light and let the door click shut behind her. In the darkness, her belt, which had come unsnapped while she dozed, slid silently and wrapped, as she stepped, about her ankle. She rolled the belt about her open hand the way Mrs Merrill did and started up the dark stairs. Without knowing why, she did a thing she had not done in years: she felt through her clothes to see if her navel was still in front.

There was a little poem her grandmother had made up for her when she had bad dreams about a blank face on the backside of her head. She stood on the landing until she remembered the poem:

> If your nose and your navel
> Are on the same side,
> Then you certainly aren't backward
> And you don't have to hide.

That was a beautiful little poem; pretty enough to say in a prayer. Taking her hand from the post, she felt with arms outstretched through the darkness for the door of her room. "I'll bet even God has forgotten that one," she said.

Chapter 6

WINTER came and Deborah worked harder to be sure that she would not have to go back to Stonebrook where a body was never warm enough the whole night through. She wanted to sit up with Mrs Merrill on the nights Rebecca had dates, but Mrs Merrill said it would be foolish for two people to sit up. Rebecca argued that it was silly for one person to, that she didn't need a chaperone and that furthermore Mrs Merrill frightened her dates by coming into the living room and saying, "Rebecca, it's ten-thirty." Mrs Merrill said, "It wouldn't be necessary if you would tell them good night at a decent hour instead of acting so boy-crazy. You act as though if you let them out of sight you'll never see them again." They would begin the arguments in this way, but every time they would end by hollering at each other until Julia, who held to Rebecca, would cry. Julia was not an angel but she did love peace; and surprisingly enough, a tear or two from her would stop most arguments or at least leave them floating in mid-air where later they would be bumped into again.

During Christmas when Julia had a cold in her chest, the plain old croop was what it was, there was not an argument during that time between Mrs Merrill and Rebecca over boys, dates, dancing, or music. Betty though could not calm down enough even to respect sickness. She complained that Julia's coughing and Glenn's crying kept her awake. "Let me move upstairs with Debby?" She had asked every night that autumn following Debby to the stair steps to say good night. Each time her mother had refused to let her, but after Christmas when it seemed that Julia's cough might hang on throughout the winter, Mrs Merrill let Britt move Betty's little spool bed out of the nursery and up the steps. She explained that the move was only for a while, but since no one —certainly not Betty or Debby—had complained, she may have been talking to herself. She must have forgotten though what she had said to herself because now winter was almost over and Deborah and Betty had no intention of being separated. Mrs Merrill didn't try to move Betty back down to the nursery with Julia and Glenn, but she did have to say more and more often: "You sleep in Debby's room. But you're still my child. You're still to do as I say." And Betty did—when there was a switch in sight.

Julia came up every night to sit with them until bedtime which was eight-thirty. Julia was the only one of the three who could tell time and because of that she acted, the other two thought, stuck-up. Julia often stared at Debby in a puzzled way and asked: "Why can't you tell time?" Or, "What is six times six?" When Debby answered "Sixty-six" Julia smiled and hid the smile between cupped hands. Debby liked the way Julia could tell stories she had learned in school but she felt uncomfortable when the little girl asked her school questions. Betty didn't feel uncomfortable, Deborah could tell. Betty just felt plain mad. "You're a baby anyway," Betty would say after Julia had asked Debby a hard, unanswerable question.

Betty said it tonight, for that had become the usual way in which they began the evenings in Debby's room: putting Julia in her place so she wouldn't act too smart. "She's a baby. She sleeps in the nursery."

Julia tried to cough, but she had been over her cold for so long a time she had even forgotten what the noise was supposed to sound like.

"Here, you better put this on." Deborah wrapped her in the black jacket which Mrs Merrill had made for Deborah's Christmas.

"I'm seven now and that's older than you."

I don't guess anything's older than me, Deborah thought, looking at the yellowing wallpaper. Except this house is. She never thought of it until she was in this room, because it was the only room in the house that had not been changed in some way. The wallpaper was almost as old as the house and that was a hundred and ten years. There were new grates and fireplaces in many of the rooms, but her hearth was of smooth round stones, not much larger than biscuits. It was more interesting to scrub than the smooth hearth in the dining room. Her ceiling was better too, because it slanted down on one side so that she could touch it. Sometimes, just at dawn, it reflected the light in such a way you would think you were looking at the sky. It was like waking up outdoors. Now that she had a kitchen chair for Betty, who liked to climb better than she did to sit, and a little rocker for Julia, there were only two more things she wanted for her room.

She wanted the back of the chimney to turn black and hang heavy with soot. Already the soot had started growing like a heavy moss, but near the fire you could still see the large bricks and the patches of new mortar. The other thing she wanted was some night to be able to sit up long enough to have red coals in the fireplace, coals that would lie like poppy petals in the gray bed of ashes.

The brass fire screen and the brass fender were popping now from the growing heat. Sitting with their chairs close together, they watched the flames mount and dance and ebb and bow. They sat quietly and studied the fire: Julia, solemn, and in the black jacket and long nightgown, like a little old woman looking back over all the sad days of her life; Betty, out of the side of her eyes, as though at any minute she would turn and speak a delightful plan: "Let's put water on it!" or "Let's burn the whole house down!"; and Debby, not really seeing the fire, but looking at it because the other two were, and knowing that another evening was passing; passing irrigably.

She formed the word on her lips: "Irrigably." And to her it meant the same thing that "irrevocably" had meant to Rebecca at least three times every day since she had met an odd boy name Bill Fleming, who played with baskets and balls—and him almost grown! The dishwater had been emptied before the dessert dishes were washed and the water had gone down the drain irrigably. The phone stopped ringing just as Rebecca came screaming down the stairs, and whoever had been calling, she whispered as she hung the ear piece back, had gone irrigably. Now this evening was going in the same way. Deborah wished she hadn't laughed with the rest of the family as Rebecca went back up the steps; maybe irrigably for all they knew.

"Debby," Julia said without looking away from the fire, "it's your time to tell us a story."

"I've done told you all the stories I know."

"Tell us about the time," Betty moved over to her. Betty liked to touch the person she was talking to in order to be sure they were listening. She climbed into Deborah's lap. "About the time a man got after you!"

"You don't want to hear that again."

"Yes we do."

"Well, that's all there is to it."

"What?"

"Just that."

"Well, start all over at the beginning."

Deborah leaned back in the rocker, and Betty leaned back against her. Julia moved closer and they waited.

"Well, where I used to work one time, when I left Stonebrook the first time, this man came home late one night and tried to break my door down."

That was the end of the story; the beginning and the end and all of it. They sat looking at the fire, waiting for the room to grow dark and menacing and full of chill. When none of these things happened, Julia said, "Make it a long story."

"And scarey."

"That's all there is to it. Just what I told you."

"Was he a *black* man?"

"He was white. Same as you and me."

"Why wasn't he black?"

"Whut would I be doing living in the same house with a black man?"

"Bertha does. Sammy T. is black."

"That's different. I'm talking about a white man."

"You mean. Did he have white hair, and white eyes, and white lips like a ghost?" A chill had seeped into the room.

"And when you cut his head off, did two grow back?"

"Cut whose head off? I didn't . . ."

"And was he," Betty's lip drew up to her nose and bared her teeth in horror, "was he, oh, just horrible, and ugly and floppety-flop."

"And did he ooze under the door and come floppety, floppety, floppety at you." Julia watched the door as she spoke. She moved closer so that she was touching Debby.

"He just came, like I tell you, and knocked and beat real loud and told me to open that door."

"What'd he want you to open the door for?"

"He wanted in my room and he didn't have any business in there."

"Why'd he want in there?"

"Meanness I reckon."

"What kind of meanness?"

She didn't answer. That was a question they hadn't asked before. They had no business asking that. Children were not supposed to know about mean, half-naked men.

"Was he going to get you?"

"I reckon that was it." Deborah looked away from them and about the room as though she were searching for a pin she might stick in the wall to hold the house together.

"What was he going to do with you?"

"Was he going to peel your eyeballs . . ."

When she turned her eyes from the wallpaper and looked at Julia and Betty again, she saw two little children sitting there; one in her lap and one holding onto her, and they were both asking silly questions. She wanted to stand up suddenly and let Betty fall to the floor. She wanted to tell them to get out of here. This was her room. She wanted to shake her hair loose and tear off her clothes and go running down the steps and out the front door. Naked as a goose egg. She couldn't be bothered with children. She had other things to think about.

"And did he cut your ears off?" Betty's voice was full of awe.

"Move. You're hurting me." She pushed Betty away. "Go sit in your own chair." She pushed Julia's hand away. "And you quit pulling at my skirts. All time pulling at a body's skirts."

"You better quit hitting at my hand."

"I didn't hit your hand."

"You did too. You did just like that."

"If I did, I meant to."

"Yes, and I'm going to tell Mama."

"Tell her."

"And she'll send you away again."

"And that man'll get you again."

"He didn't get me! I'm here to tell you right now he didn't get me!"

They waited. The fight was over. The story was closing in on them again.

"How'd you get away?"

Deborah remembered, but she wasn't going to tell. "That was a long time ago."

They studied the fire again while they tried to think how it could be that something happened a long time ago.

Julia bit her bottom lip with her two new front teeth which looked big and square by the baby teeth. Then she said slowly, "I know a story."

That was the way Julia began all her stories. There was no use asking her to tell it, or to hurry. She had to take her own good time. Betty and Debby waited.

"It's the kind you have to cut out the lights to tell."

She waited for someone to move. Deborah said, "You put them out. Debby's tired."

Julia looked across the room at the light switch, which was next to the door that opened into the dark hall. "Betty, you put out the lights and I'll tell you the story I know."

Betty, holding up her nightgown which was too long, went over, reached up, and pushed the switch. She ran back to the fire and stood, as though cold, before climbing into the kitchen chair. Later all three would go over to turn the lights on.

"Once at ponytime," Julia had only to say those three words and Betty would sit without moving again, "in a dark dark city, there was a dark dark street." She waited while they found such a place in their minds. The firelight in the darkness of the room was almost blinding; and the shadows uncertain in their creepings. "And on this dark dark street was a dark dark house."

"Like this one," Betty whispered on a shallow breath.

"And in this dark dark house was a dark dark hall."

She stopped.

"Go on," Debby said.

Julia watched the door. "And on this dark dark hall was a dark dark staircase. And at the top of this staircase . . ."

"Dark dark staircase," Betty said. It wasn't fair to change a story.

"On this dark dark staircase was a dark dark landing. And on this dark dark landing were some dark dark more steps. And at the top of these steps was a dark dark hall." She sighed. "And on this dark dark hall was a dark dark room . . ."

"Where the Mean Witch lived!"

"Where the mean witch lived. She was so mean she didn't have a mother or a father or any sisters or brothers. She didn't have a dog or a cat . . ."

"Or a pig," Deborah said.

"All she had was just buckets of blood sitting around the room."

"That she got out of babies."

"She'd put the babies in a cradle of nails and rock it back and forth till all its blood came out."

"Little boy babies too?"

"Sometimes," Julia's lips trembled in a smile, "but mainly just little girl babies. She liked to get healthy babies because they had lots of blood." Julia pulled the black jacket close about her chest and coughed.

"She'd go out on a dark dark night, and when she'd hear a baby cry she'd go up to the front door and listen. She'd slip open the door and go to the foot of the stairs and listen again to see where the baby was hiding."

"Upstairs!" Betty gripped Debby's arm.

"She'd take one step on the dark dark stairs, two steps on the dark dark stairs . . ." They listened. Downstairs was a footfall, a real footfall, and another one and another. "Four steps, five steps, six, seven, eight . . ." The steps were louder now and there was no mistake. "Fourteen," Julia said, and then as the steps came toward them across the landing she did not have breath enough to count another one.

The leather heels moved across the dark hall outside. "It's the Mean Witch!" Debby whispered. The doorknob turned slowly. The door opened.

"It's the Mean Witch!" Julia and Betty screamed and ran behind Deborah's chair. "Debby! Debby! Save us! Save us!"

Mrs Merrill stood with the firelight casting black hollows under her eyes and about her lips. She opened her mouth which was hollow with darkness and said, "Bedtime."

She entered and closed the door behind her.

"Debby! Debby!" The children were hanging about her neck so heavily she could not thank Mrs Merrill for the basket of mended clothes she had brought up.

"Come on, Julia, Mama's tired." She grabbed Julia by the arm, then picked her up. "Where're your bedroom slippers?" She sat down in the kitchen chair and reached with her fingertips for Julia's shoes. "Quit that kicking. It won't take much to give me a headache right now." She slipped the shoes on while Betty and Debby watched silently. She stood Julia on the floor, but kept a firm grip on her upper arm. "Next time, Debby, don't wait till you have so much mending to be done. When you find a ripped place, bring it down then. Now come on, Julia." At the door they said good night.

"Let's go save her!" Betty said when the door closed.

"It's too late," Deborah said. "It's already eight-thirty."

"Is it too late to save the baby, too late to save Glenn?"

"When the time comes we'll save him," Deborah said with no plan in mind for it had never occurred to her that she might have to save him from some Nurse Janet or some evil witch. She went to sleep wondering who the witch would likely be and if the time would ever come and if it did would she be able to save the baby, her baby.

Chapter 7

DEBBY, however, could not save the baby from sickness and noise that spring. Every night the living room was wrecked. In the mornings the rug would be rolled up on one side of the room, the chairs pushed back in lines along the walls, sofa pillows and phonograph records on the floor. Rebecca had company one night, Britt the next, and sometimes both of them. When it was Britt's company, Debby could hear Mr Merrill go into the living room, clap his hands together three times and say, "Your mother says 'less noise'." When the friends were Rebecca's, Mrs Merrill, herself, went in to quiet them. Usually they left soon after Mrs Merrill spoke to them, which really didn't make the house a bit quieter, because then Mrs Merrill and Rebecca argued. "I'll be glad when I go off to school," Rebecca would scream. "So will I, and I hope they can teach you some manners and how to behave." "I do nothing wrong. Just you and your suspicious mind." Mrs Merrill moved toward her, her open palm shoulder-high, "Don't you talk to me like that. You're not too old to be whipped." "Well, what have I done wrong? I can't go to dances and now you won't even let us dance in our own living room. What have I done wrong?"

Mrs Merrill lowered her voice suddenly so that it seemed that Rebecca had been screaming as loud as possible. "Nothing," she whispered, "I haven't said a word about right and wrong. I merely explained to your friends that we have a very sick baby in the house. They had enough decency and common sense to leave. I hate to think how you would have acted in their homes under the same conditions." Rebecca began crying as usual. "I would have left too, and I would never have gone back. I'd leave here if I could." The baby cried and Mrs Merrill walked to the door. "You can. Any time you think you're too old to obey me."

Each night during spring holidays the phonograph music was the same, each night the same argument. The house all day was like a fair ground. Glenn's crying was part of the carnival noise; and Mrs Merrill was the dark gypsy walking the length of the house, huddling Glenn in her arms and whispering, "Baby, baby, baby."

The silence which had come into the house this afternoon with Dr Bronston went out through the front door with him. Debby watched the doctor go down the walk. With all this excitement she wouldn't be surprised if they all came down with spring colic or the blue-green leprosy or whatever it was that made Glenn such a miserable baby. Even when he was a well baby Mrs Merrill did not like for anyone to hold him. Now she would not even let anyone see him. Debby tried to find him alone, but Mrs Merrill seemed always to know when anyone was going near the nursery. "Deborah," she would holler from far off in the house. "Don't wake him. Don't go near."

Debby snapped the dustcloth at the small, square wooden column and went back into the living room. This afternoon she had a good job. She was dusting books in the built-in bookcase by the chimney. She took four books off of the bottom shelf; studied the titles which were either too small or too long to be read; dusted and returned them to the left side of a blotter which she moved as she worked to show her which books had been cleaned. If it was her house, she would take all the books out, stack them on the floor, the chairs, the tables —she glanced about the room—the mantel and everywhere. Then she would start dusting and putting them back. That way you could tell how much work you had done; how much more there was to do; and anyone coming in would brag on you for doing such a big job. "Debby," they'd say, "you're just the smartest little lady in the world!" And she would say, just like Mrs Merrill, "You always catch my mess in the house! Have a seat if you can find one." She reached for four mildewed books. And they'd say, "But you've got such a smart little lady here to help you. If she lived with me . . ."

"All of you!" The voice in the kitchen was loud.

"I mean every last one of you!" Somebody was in the kitchen who didn't know the baby was sick. Debby tiptoed through the dining room and into the butler's pantry. She wanted to be there when Mrs Merrill chased the person out.

"You too, Mrs Hall!" It was Mrs Merrill.

She's gone star-craving mad! Debby thought. She turned cold and was aware that she had forgotten after breakfast to go to the bathroom.

"Mama, leave Debby alone. She hasn't done anything."

"No. To hear you tell it none of you have!"

It wasn't Mrs Merrill, of course. The forehead was too white; the hair not smooth; the eyes too bright and the voice too high, too loud, too full of terror. Yet they were calling her "Mama."

Debby leaned against the pantry door and peeped into the kitchen. Mrs Merrill stood by the sink, her arms folded across her thin waist. Mr Merrill stood across the room by the outside door. Rebecca and Britt were at the table. Bertha had disappeared at the wood stove with her back to them all.

"No. No one has done anything. You've all been perfect angels!"

Mr Merrill put his hat on the icebox and left his hand there with it, the fingers tapping the brim. "What's wrong?"

"Oh, Doctor Bronston's been," Rebecca said, "and now then we're to blame for Glenn being sick."

"I didn't say you were to blame." Mrs Merrill wouldn't look at her husband.

"What is it then?" Mr Merrill looked at Britt.

"Don't look at me."

Who sir, then sir, you sir, no sir, not-I-sir! That was what they were playing and Mrs Merrill was mad because she had lost. It was as simple as that. Debby turned to go back to her dusting. She wanted to clean the books on the middle shelf; and perhaps, if no one came into the room, hold the pitcher and look again, as she did frequently, for the color of that autumn afternoon when a child had called her, "Mama."

"Not so fast there!" The words lassoed her.

"Mama, let her go. She doesn't want to hear you rant."

"None of you do. But you're going to. There are going to be some changes around here."

"Before you get started. What's wrong with the baby?"

"He's taking colitis. That's what I've been trying to tell you all for three days now."

"I haven't heard you," Rebecca said.

"Certainly you haven't. Go, go, go. Every ten minutes since the holidays started. If that phone has rung once in the last week it's rung ten million times."

Mr Merrill smiled. "Not long distance I hope. You ought to see the bill for last month."

"That's another thing!" Mrs Merrill certainly could talk loud when she took a notion. And she certainly had taken a notion. Debby tried to remember the quiet, soft voice.

"He was just joking and you know it."

"He may be, but I'm not. Two cars! Maybe you won't be so impudent if you have to start walking to school again."

"I still don't know what's wrong."

"It's this boy-crazy girl, Merrill."

"What's she done?"

"Nothing. It's just that she's so old-fashioned. If she had her way I'd never have a date."

Rebecca stood up and propped her elbows on the window sill. "And the doctor says Glenn's got to get more sleep."

"They'll listen to the doctor. But they won't listen to me. For three whole days now I've pleaded with them not to make so much noise. To go to bed early. I'll bet there wasn't a night this week that living room wasn't full of impudent young fools. Eleven o'clock every night. Playing records! Dancing! Making noise. . . ."

Rebecca turned her back to the room. "You're making more noise than anyone."

"I mean to! There's going to be less noise around here or more. And I'm going to make it."

Debby was completely confused. Something moved under the table. Julia was reaching up for Britton's hand. Betty was under the table too watching Debby. When Mrs Merrill wasn't looking, they waved with their fingertips to each other. Betty cupped both hands over a grin.

"Not once have I asked one of you to turn your hand around here. We've waited on you and cleaned up after you as if you were perfect and absolute invalids. And I don't mind that. All my life—since I was eight years old—I've said my children were going to know what it is to be children.

I don't want you to work—Rebecca, turn around here and look at me when I'm talking to you—"

"I hear you." Rebecca turned from looking out the window. "So does everybody else."

"I don't care. I'm not ashamed of anything I say. You're the ones who should be ashamed. Spoiled. Spoiled rotten. All I ever ask is that you mind me. And Bless Lord you won't even do that!"

"What do you want us to do?"

"What I tell you to. And when I tell you."

Mrs Merrill turned her head only slightly and looked at her husband for an instant. As though that were the signal he had been waiting for, he crossed the room. He put his arm about her shoulder. "They're giving you a bad time, aren't they?"

She threw his arm off and moved to the center of the room. "If you had your way they'd run wild. Do as they please."

"They probably will anyway."

"Not in this house they won't. As long as they live here they're going to do a little as I please."

Mr Merrill took one step; and this time he stood behind her and held her in a bear hug. Debby grinned. It was funny to think of anyone touching Mrs Merrill. It was like trying to think of a cross-eyed Chinaman. Mrs Merrill punched with her elbows. "Let me go." All the fire had gone from her voice. It was weak now and childish. "Let me go." Mr Merrill smiled. Mrs Merrill stopped jabbing long enough to smooth her hair which was slipping out over her forehead.

If she hasn't got sense enough to let anybody be good to her, Debby thought, she may as well not have any sense at all.

Mrs Merrill tried to pry his wrists apart. Tears were standing large in her eyes.

Britton stood up. "Let her go, Dad. You're hurting her."

Mr Merrill leaned over and whispered, "Am I hurting you?" When he did, Mrs Merrill rose suddenly on her tiptoes and bumped him under the chin with the top of her head. He threw back his head and opened his mouth. "You made me bite my tongue," he tried to say with his mouth open. He let her pry his hands apart and stand free.

"From now on . . ." Mrs Merrill began; then stopped to dry her cheeks.

Mr Merrill touched his tonguetip for blood. "What is it you want them to do?"

"All I want is," she stopped again while glistening snail-trails of light, two streams of tears, slid down her face. Her chin was trembling and dimpling, "All I want is for them to show me some respect and not ignore everything I say as if I were a . . ." She stopped.

Everyone looked at nothing. Mrs Merrill hadn't finished the sentence but the words cut through the air like the singing of a saw. "As if I were a black nigger." They would go on filling the room unless someone spoke.

Bertha no longer pretended to be stirring the gravy. She turned slowly and straightened her shoulders. "Mrs Merrill, have I done anything you didn't exactly like?"

Mrs Merrill wiped her eyes with the heels of her hand. "No, Bertha. I don't suppose anybody has. It's just . . ." She began crying again. ". . . that I'm so nervous I can't stand myself." Half-blind she found the door and ran down the hall.

Who sir, then sir? Why it was Mrs Merrill, sir.

"Whew!" Rebecca said, sitting down again.

"She's scared." Britt said. "That's what's wrong."

Mr Merrill wouldn't stay to listen while they talked about her. He picked up his hat again and left the house.

"Wonder what the doctor really said?"

"I don't know." Britt, in the way of those who rarely talk, seemed to choose the words carefully from a thousand he had saved. Debby liked to watch him. His head was finely shaped, his features thin. And now that his hair was no longer trimmed off, it curled when he did not comb it flat with water. "Doctor Bronston," he was saying, "didn't want her to have Glenn." He waited for Rebecca to be surprised; then added: "He told me."

Rebecca's mouth opened; finally she said with awe: "Wonder if Glenn is all right. I don't mean sick. I mean *all right.*"

"His head sure looks big to me," Britt said.

Bertha held the spoon in mid-air. "Why don't y'all politely shut your mouths? You know he's a fine baby. All babies have big heads."

"And he can spit three feet!" Betty said, crawling out from under the table.

Debby wanted to be by herself to think of this sudden change in Mrs Merrill, who was supposed to change only when the mountains did. If it had been Mr Merrill hollering like that—well, that would have been different. That, somehow, was the oddest part to her: Mr Merrill had found his wife's soft voice and had used it to reckon with her. Surely that was as involved as cutting your finger and tasting your own blood while waiting for a bandage.

She wandered back into the living room and hoped Betty and Julia wouldn't follow her as they usually did. She stood before the fireplace and bit her thumbnail. She would be happy if it were only the walls in this house that changed.

The only thing that was constant here was the luster pitcher with its sad and hidden autumn lights. When there were sudden moods in the house—or too much happiness—Deborah liked to gaze into the depths of the gold-brown bands and know again the unchanging sadness of that lonely day when she had, once again, after having given up all hope, been called "Mama." She rolled the little footstool to the shelf and reached for the pitcher. The handle was cool and smooth to her hot, moist palm. "Mama," she heard from the depths of the pitcher, Betty's voice, Julia's voice, only air within, yet a voice and a word if you wanted to listen.

A voice, and a word, and then a baby's cry came to her. She set the pitcher down. Glenn was crying. Off through the house where the Mean Witch could hear him. Any fat fool who was passing through the kitchen ten minutes before would now know who the Mean Witch was. Debby followed the baby-cry through the house, drawn nearer and nearer to the nursery. She pushed open the door and waited to hear Mrs Merrill scream, "Don't pick him up." She waited. When no one screamed, she let the door click shut behind her, tiptoed to the cradle, and lifted the baby. He was as hot as a biscuit and *red*! What he needed was some cool outdoor shade. Debby wrapped a flannel blanket about him. At the door she listened. When she heard no sound of Mrs Merrill, she opened the door and hurried across the back porch. The sunny back yard was no place to stop so she crossed it quickly and entered the gate to Merrill's Grove. There behind the wooden fence she was safe from the house, and under the pecan trees, safe from the late afternoon sun.

Glenn had almost stopped crying. Talking to him in a singsong Debby chanted murmur: "See the trees, see the sky, the leaves the sky. See the fence, the dog, the bulldog,

Spike. See see see. Come here Spike and see the crying baby. See Glenn cry. See the old bulldog laughing at you. See the trees. See the house. See. And see . . ." Through the fence cracks Debby caught sight of the back door opening. Mr Merrill was coming down the steps toward them.

Debby, her long skirt flaring and swirling, tiptoed in silent dance steps across the Grove and out the gate onto the back street. She listened for Mr Merrill to open the front gate of the Grove. She heard instead the car motor as he backed out of the garage and down the drive.

"See, Spike, there was nothing to be afraid of." She spoke to the neighbor dog at her heel. She had often wondered what this street looked like. She had twice before peeped through the gate, but being on the sidewalk was different, less strange. It was a whispering shady street, no cars, no children, mainly back fences and here and there a cottage. As she walked down the street Spike followed and Glenn saw with round eyes the trees and lawns she pointed out to him. The corner streets were as easy to cross as country roads and when the sidewalk ended, she walked in the street. Perhaps soon the road would be dirt, and somewhere around would be a bridge, a trail, a Secret Path, a stream, a Secret Room, and blackberries for breakfast. She held the heavy baby over her shoulder and crooned to him until he became heavier in sleep. She did not notice when Spike turned around to go home or when the sun lost its glare.

At first she walked in the shade, but as the shadows thickened and stretched, she sought out the sunny areas. Keeping in the sun was a game. Sometimes she had to cross the entire street to walk around a tree shadow. "Thisaway and thataway and acrossaway, aroundaway, and skipaway aroundaway and backaway. That's the way to stay in the sun." She crooned to the sleeping baby as she wandered down the lonesome street which was no longer bordered by back fences and barns. The road ended.

Somewhere back had she turned a corner to keep on a sidewalk? Did seem possible. Did indeed. The thing to do was turn another corner. What else could you do? Sit down and wait for night? She wished Glenn would wake so she could talk out her plans with him. She turned the corner. Her shadow pushed ahead of her up the spring-gold March-sunset street. "That woman ought to be glad this sick baby is seeing such pretty weather." At thought of Mrs Merrill she stepped faster. A store-building was in sight on the next block. Maybe somebody there would know what street she was on.

In front of the store she hesitated, stepped up two wooden worn steps, and knocked on the screen door.

"Come in," a man's voice said.

She pulled open the baggy screen and entered the heavy dusk of the store. She sniffed the air: corn meal, flour, cheese, dust, dill pickles, sweet crackers, but mainly corn meal. A cat arched and rubbed against her shoes.

"What can I do for you?" asked a newspaper floating behind the counter. It fell and there was a little white-headed, red-faced man with a great wart on his fat nose.

"Where are we?"

"Bateman's store." His voice was twilight soft and hidden by dusty breaths.

"How far is that?"

"From where?" he whispered on a wheeze.

"Anywhere."

"Ohhh," the man breathed, scratching his chin whiskers. Or maybe "Ahhh," such a low voice he had.

"We turned off the street back yonder. I think we turned

off. I was watching for the shade and then I was watching for the sun and I think we turned off. Back yonder."

"Back yonder," the man echoed.

"Do you know the way?" Debby asked.

"From where? To where?" Mr. Bateman came around the counter and tried to see her over the top of his tiny rimless smoke-clouded glasses. His breathing was louder than his voice.

"From the street we were on."

"Listen, lady." She listened while he breathed again. "Where is it you want to go?"

"Back. Back there. Back home." Fright was rising in her.

"Where is *home*?" he asked patiently.

"Home. Home is the Merrills. Do you know the Merrills?"

"Which Merrill? Three or four in town."

"Mr Merrill and her." Debby could not believe there were other Merrills. "Britt and Rebecca. And Julia and Betty."

"Ohhh. Then this must be the little one. Glenn? Born last fall. Yes oh yes, I know them. They've traded with me for years. Off and on. And you must be the new woman." He stared all over her.

"I'm Debby," she said.

"Have a seat, Miss Debby." He showed her to a wooden-bottom chair. She sat down, suddenly exhausted. "And what are you doing down here."

Wheeze wheeze sputter sputter, Debby thought listening to him breathing. If I had that much trouble, out I'd go like a wet candle. But she answered, "The baby needed some outdoor shade and quiet."

"You've come about eight blocks," he said. "Two that way. Six long ones north. Does Mrs Merrill know you wander this far?"

"She knows almost everything," Debby said.

"Oh, she is a shrewd woman. Fair dealing but she expects no foolishness. Yes, I know Mrs Merrill." He waited for Debby to speak, searching all over her face for words. Then he said, "Maybe we should let her know where you are. She may be worried before you get back." He walked to the phone on the wall. "Night isn't too far over the hills." He phoned and whispered breath into the mouthpiece. Even across the store, though, Debby could hear a high excited voice hissing out of the ear handle. He nodded yes and yes and yes at the phone and finally said yes to the shrill voice. He put the phone back together and wiped his brow.

Standing in front of her he winked and chuckled. "I don't think she likes it much. You running off with her baby."

"I didn't run off. I'm going back. Now. Right now." She tried to stand.

Gently with his outstretched fingertips he held her in the chair. "She said for you to stay here. She's sending Mr Merrill for you and the baby."

"What else did she say?"

"They've been calling all over the neighborhood. Julia and Betty are out looking. Thought you couldn't have gone far. She didn't know you had been gone long enough to come this far." He spoke gently. "Don't worry. She's a reasonable woman. Don't worry."

I've done a wrong thing, Debby told herself. People only said "Don't worry" when there was something to worry about. What was so wrong though? She watched the sleeping hot baby. Why all the fuss? Why did he say not to worry? Here was the way she lived: everything would be fine and then everything would be awful. When she had worked for the people on the mill-hill the first time she left Stonebrook everything had been mostly awful. She wondered if the

Merrills would take to hitting her. Once she would not have minded much; but now, after they had been so kind, she couldn't stand being hated again. "Everything is fine and then everything is awful."

"She's a little upset, but she'll be over it. I told her the baby was all right." Mr Bateman pushed back the blanket and peeped at the sleeping face. "Better let me hold him."

In a daze Debby let the baby be taken from her. A chain of words was being dragged through her head. She listened: "And Chicken Little ran and ran . . ." She watched the front door, waited to see the large shadow of Mr Merrill standing there, tensed to hear his loud voice shouting at her. Dusk was seeping out of the store and filling all outside. "It's getting dark early," she spoke.

"May rain," Mr Bateman said. "Clouds are due to blow in about sundown. May rain yet." He sat down heavily on a sack of flour holding the baby up and against his chest away from the bacon-salted apron lap.

Debby was so worried she had to think a long time about rain before she knew what he was saying. Rain, rain water, a shower, he was saying that there might be a rain shower. She moved to the front of the store and patted the dusty screen. A car swung around the corner. Her heart stopped, sure enough stopped, then raced as the car went past. Far up the street another car was speeding toward the store. Debby glanced back at Mr Bateman. The baby was safe. She stepped through the door, jumped down the steps, pulled up her skirts and ran and ran anywhere anywhere anywhere.

Heavy drops of rain bounced in the red-dirt; spring odors made breathing a joy, running a game. When she slowed and paused to fill her lungs, the cold raindrops pounded through her hair to her scalp and through her apron, dress, and underclothes. She stopped under an oak and followed with her eyes the red tail lights reflected in the water mirror street. Overhead thunder muffled by darkness and traffic noise no longer frightened her. Only the thought of Mrs Merrill could frighten her now. Where could she hide? A box would be a good thing to hide in if she had one. She wished that she had not seen Mrs Merrill angry. If she could recall the woman's whispering voice and sad eyes she would go back—if she could find the way. But when she tried she heard the shouting woman: "All of you!" She could not go back and face that woman. She pushed wet hair back from her face, shook water from her apron skirt, and hurried down the street. Which street it was, what hour, how far from where, she could not say.

The houses were beginning to look all alike: short walks, short drives, hedges, two lighted windows, two chimneys. Surely she was back in the mill-village. "Oh God! Don't let me be back there." What if she met up with the people she had worked for: Sadie and Buck and Sadie's brother called Baby. Baby was the one she was afraid of. Sadie had nagged at her every minute: By God this and by God that and by God my dinner when I get in from work in that damned mill and this damn fine mess and damn stupid fool and damn everything and every other word. And Sadie had slapped her one day when she didn't have dinner ready—a stinging slap that raised red finger whelps across her cheekbone and a bruise where a sharp-stoned ring had hit. Still Sadie was better than her snickering brother called Baby. He was always bragging that he was a man but a bad woman had told everyone the truth, had started everyone calling him Baby. Still he bragged and sat with his overall pants pulled up to his knees so that any decent people had to look away to keep from seeing his spidery legs where dead white skin showed through the matted black hair. "God God God what if he comes out of one of these houses."

Debby was almost ready to kneel on the wet pavement to pray, but then she saw a man coming toward her up the street, so far away he might yet be a dog. "That's him. That's Baby." She climbed a small bank at a vacant lot and stooped under a clump of giant privet, hidden from view of the sidewalk. The man passed; he walked like a drunk man, like Baby when he drank. She crouched watching, then sat down on a rusty bent gallon-can and waited for the man to disappear completely. It was Baby all right; no one could tell her differently.

He was walking cat-footed the same way he did the Saturday night he came home drunk. All three of them, Sadie, Buck, and Baby, left the house happy and singing. Debby washed the supper dishes and studied in the mirror the red finger-whelps where Sadie had slapped her. She dried her hands and went into the bedroom. She latched the door because Sadie tried it every night to be sure it was locked. "He's my husband, but he's a man. Baby claims to be one too. So don't be unlocking that door unless *I* say to." Debby took off her dress which was limp as silk with the summer heat. She lay down in her petticoat and shoes. A light cord hung empty from the middle of the ceiling. The only light slanted in from a corner street lamp where a gang of boys were throwing rocks at a swooping bat.

The mattress was dusty and the brown-ticked pillow had the odor of a scalded chicken ready to be picked. The hollering of the boys moved on the summer air, closer, closer, beneath her window, all about her, withdrew, wafted farther away, farther and farther on the summer heat, muffled, disappeared in sleep. She slept for two hours. She could not say what it was that woke her. She fancied it was the stinging dampness between herself and the mattress, the crawling sweat between her legs. She turned her head to see if the window was open. A shadow moved suddenly from the window, letting light into the room. She listened. On the porch a warped floorboard creaked. The shadow darkened the room again. She reached for the iron bed top where she had hung her dress. The dress was gone: fallen to the floor between the bed and the wall. Sadie's red and yellow flowered kimona hung in the kitchen. Debby tiptoed to the door. Light spilled into the bedroom from the open window. Whoever was on the porch could see her in her cotton petticoat. She unlatched the door and ran into the kitchen. Baby ran in from the porch. His brown, narrow-set eyes were dancing.

He reached out and pinched her left nipple between his thumb and finger. "Jiggling and bobbling around me all day." His words were thick. He was grinning a wet grin and laughing. "Jiggle jiggle jiggle." He shook her breast as though it were a dinner bell. She pushed free and held her hand to her breast which was numb for a second before it burned like a coal.

"Come on now. Don't treat Baby that way." Debby moved backward toward the door where the kimona was hanging. "Baby knows what you want." He ran his snake-tongue over his wet lips, grinning, eyes squinted and dancing, grinning. "Jiggling and bobbling and watching me. Think I don't understand?"

"Kick him where it hurts the most," she heard Thomas say. She would. If he moved any nearer she would.

He shut his eyes and wavered back and forth for his balance. He squinted his eyes. "God damn. Think like everybody else that I'm not a man? I'll show you. I'll show you." He spoke in a high voice; the grin vanished. "Bessie started that lie. Said all I could do was whimper like a baby in bed. That whore." He stopped and tried to focus his dancing eyes. The grin came back. "Hell. Throw a sack over her head and I wouldn't touch her."

Debby was startled by the idea. She turned to reach for the kimona. He grabbed her and pressed her sideways against the wall. With one hand he tore the suspender straps loose from his overalls. Debby turned her back to the wall and faced him. If she could free her knee she could kick him. He was small, boney; but he was pressing against her with his full weight. Bending her whole upper body into a shove, Debby pushed him backward. He staggered. She panted and shut her eyes for a second. Her head banged against the wall. One eye saw a green sky that cracked open into red veins which raced about her shattered head. A yellow ball danced in a purple sky. She put her hand to her eyebrow and felt the quick blood.

He grabbed her again and pressed her against the wall. Her elbows were pinned against her stomach. She scratched at his bare chest where the overalls had slipped free. He held to her hair and one ear and banged her head against the wall. "Shut up! Shut up! Hold still!" She didn't know she was screaming. She lifted her foot slowly and moved her leg between his. He quit banging her head. "That's a girl." He tried to kiss her—his wet mouth on her nose and cheek and chin. He bent slightly away from her to find her mouth. She raised her knee suddenly with all the strength she had. He fell back groaning. He came at her and she kicked him in the groins with her pointed shoe. He doubled over and vomited green.

Debby started for a mop. Someone would have to clean up after him. She opened the side door and went onto the porch to find the mop. Two men and a woman stood on the steps. There were other people in the yard.

The woman came forward and put her arm around Debby's waist. "Come on. You're going home with us. For tonight anyway." As they moved down the street pitying hands fussed and dabbed at her face and hair and torn petticoat. They walked for a block, Debby in her petticoat, to another of the stilt-walking houses that stood on the hill which was red and dusty one day, red and muddy the next. The pitying hands put her to bed and held cold cloths to her swollen eye and told her with their weary mouths how funny she was going to be with a big black eye. One of the men went up and got her dress and came back to say that Baby was asleep with his head on the table. When Sadie and Buck went singing up the road at midnight, a woman laid a cool hand on Debby's forehead and said, "You're going to stay here tonight."

And tonight where would she stay? She glanced about her at the dead leaves under the dripping privet bush. It wouldn't be a fit place to sleep even on a dry night. She wished someone would say, "Come on. You're going home with me." Perhaps Mrs Merrill . . . but Mrs Merrill was angry with her for taking Glenn out of the house. She had done absolutely nothing to Baby that time to make him angry, yet her eye had been swollen for two days. So there was no telling what would happen if Mrs Merrill ever did find her.

She climbed down the bank and stretched her cramped legs. The rain had almost stopped. A black river of sky flowed through the gray cloud-fields. A star and another one were caught like sparks on a cloud wisp. "Star bright star light . . ." She wished for a hot biscuit with butter and peach preserves on it. Still wishing she turned and walked back down the street. The wind was cool but not too cold and her clothes were drying. She walked without a plan, following any street that struck her fancy. Sometimes the houses seemed familiar, sometimes as strange and faraway as the Giant's Castle. Yet they did seem like places she had seen before. She passed a man and woman and little girl. The child stared at her and said in a loud, impolite voice, "Mother, see that little wet woman!" Cars came by often enough to brighten the sidewalk and light up the standing pools of water. Finally when she had quit noticing houses, people, and cars, and had even stopped trying to avoid puddles, a car screeched to the curb and stopped. Debby stopped, then ran into a yard where she stood behind a thick magnolia. The car horn honked.

"Debby! Debby! It's me! Britt."

She waited. The horn blew again. The car door slammed. Fast footsteps sounded and Britt was beside her holding her wrist. "Debby, we've searched everywhere for you. Every street this side of town. At least three times."

She tried to free herself. "Kick him where it hurts the most," she heard Thomas say; but then she heard Britt say the magic words. "Come on. Let's go home."

"Your Mama?"

"She wants you home. No one is angry."

Debby allowed herself to be led to the car. Once inside on the dry warm seat she was no longer frightened. They drove home, which was only two blocks away, in silence. The front-porch light was on; Betty and Julia raced out the walk toward the car; and as she went up the steps, the children pulling her by each hand, Mrs Merrill, Mr Merrill and Rebecca all stood there on the porch laughing like a bunch of crazy-fools.

Chapter 8

DEBBY lay in bed that night too frightened to sleep. Would they send her back to Stonebrook for running off with the baby? Mrs Merrill had said only: "Go put on some dry clothes," and later "you must touch him only when I say for you to." By morning, though, after a sleepless night, Debby was sick with worry and aching from a cold in her chest. She propped herself up in bed, but her eyes throbbed so she put her head back on the pillow. She waited to see what the Merrills would do with her. When she thought of leaving this place she was beginning to love so much, she was shaken with chill. Her throat ached. She didn't want to cry. Crying was for little pains you could understand. If the sky were to fall in, as Julia had read them that it did on Chicken Little, you would not cry. You could only lie, as she did now, and watch and wait. A sudden jealousy tightened her throat so that she had to open her mouth to breathe. Somebody else would polish the shoes on Saturday night, and tell stories with Betty and Julia while the shoes dried on the hearth before the fire. Somebody else would be sitting in her chair the first night Glenn could join them for bedtime stories. She had been planning how that night would be, how Glenn could sit and dream at the fire while Julia read to them. He wasn't old enough to understand reading yet, and maybe that was why Mrs Merrill wouldn't let him be brought upstairs. Now it could never happen.

When Mrs Merrill came up to see why Debby had not come down, she did not say a word about Stonebrook. She disappeared and presently Britt came in with orange juice, red-brown medicine, hot tea and three butter-toasted soda crackers. "Mama says you're not to get out of bed. She'll send Doctor Bronston up when he comes to see Glenn."

When Dr Bronston came he mainly shook his head but he did say that Deborah had only a cold which might become worse because she had not eaten the right food nor perhaps enough food for a good many years.

During that week Debby stayed in bed and Britt brought her food on a tray. He sat before the fireplace cracking walnuts on the hearth, and talked to her while she sipped chicken broth. She liked looking at the two cords which formed a dark dimple on the back of his neck. He had grown fast lately and was thin. His shoulders were still square, but very thin. There was a straightness about every move he made so that sometimes he seemed like a jumping jack Betty had got for Christmas. Pull a string and the arms jerked up in sharp angles. Pull another and the legs danced. That was the way Britt moved. Where were the strings and who was pulling them? Mr Merrill—Debby guessed. As always Britt's wiry hair needed combing. When he turned and grinned at her one lock curled down and looked from the bed like a widow's peak. His eyebrows arched sharply up from his nose, giving a wicked expression to his face. His eyes were like a cat's: blue though and not cat colored. But the pupils grew large and small, slowly, while you watched. Mrs Merrill said his eyes were like a dope-fiend's and wanted him to have them examined. His straight nose pointed down to a thin upper lip which curled easily. The bottom lip was full but well defined and belonged with the baby-cleft in his chin. Debby hadn't told anyone that Britt's chin looked like a little baby's butt. Yet that was why she sometimes smiled when she gazed at him.

She could not understand him, though, no matter how much she studied his face and words. "Debby, you know what? I believe Dad thinks I'm a . . . well, that . . . well I don't make good grades in school. Rebecca always has, and Julia will, but sometimes I think maybe I just don't have . . ." Britt shook his head and with a puzzled smile gazed at the floor. "I don't know. Dad seems like . . . anyway, what he knows he's had to learn by himself because he doesn't have much education. But he can take one of my books, read over a few pages and tell me what I'm doing wrong. Maybe I just don't have much sense." He stopped abruptly. Finally he began talking again. "They've got insurance for me to go to college on, took it out when I was a baby when they didn't have much money, just so I could go to almost any college. Then I come along and can't even get through high school. I know I shouldn't try to pass in college." He swallowed and the cords trembled in his throat. His voice trembled too. "Maybe I shouldn't even be in school now." He glanced shyly at Debby. When he spoke again the color rose up from his neck almost to the top of his forehead: "When did you quit school?"

"A long time ago," Debby said. She wasn't interested in school. She was wondering if they were waiting for her to get well enough to be sent away.

"Don't tell anybody I asked you. I mean. Just don't tell

anybody I mentioned anything about it. They . . . you know what I'm talking about. *Don't* tell anybody."

He didn't understand that soon she wouldn't be around to talk to anybody. She stared at him and the color rose again in his face. He glanced quickly away. She nodded no. He smiled gratefully to her and she knew they had a secret together. She didn't know quite what the secret was, but they had one. And Mrs Merrill would never know.

Mrs Merrill, however, did not seem interested in anything except temperatures. Her back ached she said from climbing the stairs and from nursing the sick baby. Yet she would not sit down in Debby's room. Instead she promised to send the children up when Debby begged to be allowed out of bed. Rebecca came in only one time because she was busy buying dresses, curtains, trunks and shoes to take off to college. That was all she could talk about: college college college. She would go to dances and rush parties and date until midnight and do all the things that other girls did that her mother never let her do. She could not understand her mother's fretting. She had not heard, as Debby had, about the strict relatives Mrs Merrill had been forced to live with. As far as the children knew, Mrs Merrill had had a happy childhood, as free from care as their own. Rebecca brushed Debby's hair as she talked and when she spoke of her mother the brush bristles stuck into Debby's scalp. "You're hurting," Debby said. Rebecca stopped and stroked the hair with her open palm. "Debby, let's do something about your hair."

"All right! What you want to do? Cut it all off?"

"Mama would have a fit. Let's try to fix it in some way that suits your personality. Something more sophisticated." Rebecca did like to say personality and sophisticated as often as she could. She began laughing and pressing Debby's hair into a pompador. When she finished, Debby's hair was exactly like Mrs Merrill's. Rebecca doubled over in laughter. Debby, bewildered, reached for the pins.

"Don't."

"I'm no clown."

"I know. It's just that you look so much like Mama!"

When Mrs Merrill came up with a mustard-plaster she said, "Rebecca, you shouldn't tease her." It was funny, she agreed, but the joke had lasted long enough. "I don't mind her wearing dresses cut on the same pattern as mine, and from the same material, but now this is going too far." But Rebecca, and later the other children said that Debby should wear it that way, that she looked like a little Gibson girl, a little miniature cameo. Finally Mrs Merrill said all right—provided Debby could arrange it herself. Debby knew she could because all winter she had watched while Mrs Merrill combed and brushed her own hair. She was anxious to get out of bed now so that she could begin wearing her hair in a pompador, but she was afraid that if Mrs Merrill saw her up and well she would send her back to Stonebrook.

At the beginning of the next week though, Mrs Merrill said, "Debby, you have no fever and your cold is much looser. I believe you can sit in the sun this afternoon." Was it a trick? Debby trembled as she dressed. Mrs Merrill placed a chair in the sunny part of the back yard, and gave Debby a pan of beans to string. Spike, the old bulldog who lived next door came waddling up the drive and sat by the chair under Debby's feet. Last fall while she was stringing beans, or shelling peas, or looking at pictures in a magazine, Spike liked to sit under her feet. She swung her feet back and forth so that her heels grazed the top of his head and made him shut his eyes. Occasionally he sat up straight and acted as a footstool with Debby's feet flat on top of his head. If a peddler or beggar coming up the steps put one foot on the porch, the bulldog would rumble thunder until the peddler stepped back and took off his hat.

Julia and Glenn were afraid of the dog. Julia because she was shy and frightened of everything; Glenn because the dog had once walked up and licked him in the face, then barked when Betty hollered. Debby was glad that had happened because she could pick Glenn up when Spike came near—if Betty was not around. If she didn't want Betty as an enemy she had to leave Glenn alone. Betty had always been as mean as possible; now she was impossible. Julia was the only one who could calm Betty down and no one knew how because Julia never seemed to say anything. She was growing fast and awkward and shy and it was impossible to remember her when she was not before your eyes, yet she could walk into Debby's room and Betty would quit aggravating Britt.

Actually, Britt was not supposed to go into Debby's room. He had been to summer school once, and because he was failing again he was supposed to study from suppertime to bedtime. Often though he crossed the hall and read to Betty and Debby. His voice had quit popping and squeaking and changing, but sometimes when he read to them at night he gazed into the fire and not at the book and his voice became slower and slower and slower and almost not at all. Occasionally he left the room suddenly, and if Debby followed a little later she could see him stretched out across his bed. One night she saw him shuddering and covered him with a blanket. "We're a lot alike, Debby," he said; but she told him she wasn't cold.

Britt was a puzzle. No one knew exactly what to make of that boy. The high school was always phoning to tell Mrs Merrill something. Once there had been trouble because Britt would not take an intelligence test. He had to sit in the office every day because of that, and the dean told him he couldn't have a home room unless he took the test. Debby had heard about the lockers which lined the walls of the high school and about the home rooms. She imagined that the inside of the school resembled the inside of a pigeon house. And every time a bell rang the students went running back to sit in their home room lockers, like so many pigeons in their square holes. She didn't blame Britt for not taking the test. Who wanted to sit in a box like a pouter-pigeon? She remembered that she, herself, the day she got lost, had wanted a box to hide in. But now sitting in the warm back yard, stringing beans, scratching Spike, thinking of Rebecca, Mrs Merrill, Julia, Betty, Glenn, and even Mr Merrill, she could not want to do anything except perhaps live in this house forever as they had been living for the past months. She wished Mrs Merrill would hurry and be angry with her for having run off with the baby. She suspected again that Mrs Merrill was waiting only for her to be well enough to travel.

She glanced up. Mrs Merrill was standing in the back door watching her.

"Uh oh," Debby breathed.

"Telephone," Mrs Merrill said, holding open the screen door.

"For me." It was a trick of course. She had never talked over a telephone. She didn't know anyone who would be calling. It was a made-up trick that had to do with getting her out of the house for good.

"Come along, Debby."

On the back porch in the cold shade, Debby felt clammy when she touched her hand to her cheek and then to her forehead to push back the uncertain pompador. There was a chill between her shoulder blades. She wanted first to run, then she wanted to turn to Mrs Merrill and say right out:

"Don't send me away." But since Mrs Merrill had not wanted to mention that subject yet she would wait. It was the matron on the telephone. She knew that. Already she could hear the matron's voice and see her standing there in the damp dusk at Stonebrook speaking into the dusty mouthpiece.

Debby sat down at the telephone table. She glanced up pleadingly at Mrs Merrill. "I don't know how."

"Now's a good time to learn." Mrs Merrill handed her the earpiece and pushed the mouthpiece to her face. "Say 'hello'."

"Hello," Debby whispered. She set the earpiece on the table. Mrs Merrill handed it back to her.

"Say 'hello'."

Debby cleared her throat. "Hello." She pressed the earpiece so tightly to her ear she could make out the beating of her own heart. "Hello. Hello."

"Now wait and see what they say."

Debby waited. "I can't make out any words." She said hello again. "Who is it?" she asked Mrs Merrill.

"Julia and Betty."

"It's not the matron?"

"Who?"

Maybe Mrs Merrill had forgotten that there was such a place in the world as Stonebrook. Debby would not remind her. "What do they want with me?"

"They want to talk to you."

"Why don't they come home if they want to talk with me?" Debby hung the earpiece on the hook. "I've got no time for foolishness."

"Telephones aren't foolishness. It would be a big help to me if you would learn."

"I've learned a lot." She had learned so much it made her tired all over to think about it.

"Yes. You're doing fine. But I thought you'd like to learn to talk over the telephone."

"Well, I wouldn't." Talking over the telephone would be like making biscuits: simple at first, then too much to think about. She could never learn how much flour to use for how many people. Finally Mrs Merrill had painted a red line on a little bucket which was to be kept on the pantry shelf. All you had to do was fill the bucket to the red line and that was how much flour to use. But when someone else came Mrs Merrill said to use the bucket and two or three more cupsful. Debby on two occasions took the two cupsful out of the bucket so that when the biscuits were cooked there were fewer for the whole crowd than there normally were for only the family. Now they wanted her to learn to talk on the telephone.

"It would be a big help if you could learn to answer the phone. We won't be able to keep Bertha much longer and when she leaves it's going to throw all her work on me and you."

"Bertha's leaving?"

"Mr Merrill's made some bad deals lately." Mrs Merrill enjoyed answering questions with puzzles or by changing the subject.

"And I'm staying."

"Certainly you're staying."

"God Almighty!" Debby said.

"Mrs Hall!" Mrs Merrill swayed backward a fraction. "Why do you say that?"

"Because that's what I mean," Debby answered.

"Do you have to cuss to say what you mean?"

"That wasn't cussing." She had heard cussing all of her

life and how you said a word was what made it cussing. When you were happy the way she was now you could say anything and it wouldn't be cussing. "I meant just what I said."

"Then you do want to stay?"

Debby couldn't answer; she could not speak.

"And you weren't trying to run off?"

She would have to force the words out now. She could not have Mrs Merrill believing such a thing about her. "I got lost," she mumbled.

"Before you got lost—you weren't thinking about running away when you left the yard?"

Debby gazed down at her knees and shook her head.

"That's all I've been wanting to know," Mrs Merrill said. "I was afraid I'd frightened you."

"You didn't scare me."

"I may lose my temper again, a great many more times, but you mustn't go out alone again, not until you know your way round in the neighborhood. Maybe the children will teach you sometime so you can take little walks."

"I don't want to take any walks." The truth was she didn't want to leave the house again.

"A little outdoor exercise would be good for you. I hadn't noticed until this happened how rundown you are." Mrs Merrill talked and talked about health and coloring. "If you can't learn what a balanced diet is then eat exactly what I eat. Watch me and take some, if only a little, of everything you see me eat." Deborah thought about that: Mrs Merrill ate such things as eggplant, squash, liver, and okra. Surely she would not have to eat those things instead of bread and potatoes. "We can't afford for you to be sick. For any of us to be."

Mrs Merrill led her into the living room. "All of us have to work for a living."

"I know that."

"And you don't think your work is too hard?"

She could not understand what Mrs Merrill was trying to say. She listened while the woman explained how hard it was to live in the house with a family, any family, if you really didn't like them. Mrs Merrill's own mother and father had burned to death in a house fire when she was eight years old and after that she lived with first one set of relatives and then another. She said she knew what it felt like to want to run away. She hoped Debby would never feel like that again. As suddenly as she had begun talking she quit. She stood up and left as though she had forgotten a roast in the oven. For a while Debby sat and went over in her mind everything they had said.

"She knows just what I feel like." That was a strange thing. But she knew what Mrs Merrill felt like. Dressing and brushing her hair in the very way that Mrs Merrill did, Debby sometimes stood on tiptoes to be as tall as that woman. And when Mrs Merrill had nursed Glenn, Debby had often stared at them and felt her own breast draw. Now she was to eat the same things Mrs Merrill did—and perhaps talk on the telephone.

She tiptoed to the phone table and sat down. Quietly she lifted the receiver from the hook. She listened carefully, no longer afraid she would hear the matron's voice. She waited for Betty and Julia to speak.

"Mumble fleas," a lady said. "Mumble fleas." It tickled her ears. The voice stopped and Debby laughed. The voice became louder so that she had to hold the receiver away from her ear. "Mumble fleas!" There was a clicking noise and a new voice said, "Special Operator." It was Betty of course, playing grownup.

"This is Debby."

"What number do you want please?"

"I don't want anything," Debby said, glancing about the house. She had everything she wanted, almost. She set the receiver back in its cradle. From that moment on, the days passed like seconds; weeks, minutes; months, days; and a year and another and another.

Chapter 9

EVEN though Debby wanted each day to be exactly like the day before, Mrs Merrill was always making changes. It was summer again and Rebecca was coming home, so the curtains in her room had to be taken down and washed. Nothing could remain the same. Even the potted plants had to be reset. In the Grove, sitting on a box under the fig bush, Debby rubbed Spike's head with her outstretched foot. Mrs Merrill was leaning before a pile of rich black dirt. Flowerpots rolled about her when she moved. Britt was bringing white sand in a shovel from the greenhouse. Julia was playing with Glenn on a canvas spread under the pecan trees. "Ready for two more." Mrs Merrill set a begonia and a Christmas cherry on flat ground and wiped the dirt from the new green paint. "Let's start on the ferns now." Betty and Debby stood up and started toward the house. "Just one each. Don't try to carry two."

The ferns were large. Betty in faded blue overalls, too small for her, hugged the flowerpot to her stomach and wrinkled her nose when the fern fronds tickled her face. Debby carried a large maidenhair fern that was always being lent out for school plays, commencements, and parties. Some of the ferns were never brought back. Mrs Merrill was suspicious of women who couldn't grow their own flowers. Frequently a woman would come to the door early on Sunday morning and say in a desperate voice: "Mrs Merrill, I need help. I'm responsible for the altar flowers today and you seem to be the only person in town with any in bloom." Mrs Merrill handed the woman garden scissors and watched from the window while the yard was stripped of every flower. "Sometimes," she said, watching from the window, "it seems that all my life people have just taken me for granted."

Debby kicked open the gate and set the maidenhair fern before the kneeling woman. With a knife Mrs. Merrill sliced the hard dirt from the pottery. Then holding up the streamers, as though they were actually hair, she pounded the side of the pot against the ground, turning it slowly and carefully. Then abruptly she slid the container from the cake of hard dirt and roots. She set the fern upright, just as though it were in the flowerpot, and let them all observe how the yellow roots had twisted and matted into a net. She said the flower could be free now to grow; it was like taking off a tight-fitting shoe. Then slowly, while they gathered about and breathed hard on her, Mrs Merrill grasped the roots, digging her fingers deeper and deeper into the tangled mass. Finally and quickly, jerking her elbows back, she tore the flower in two. "Mama!" Julia said. Mrs Merrill again explained about the roots being pinched by the small flowerpot; but Julia, clearly, was not comforted.

Debby and Betty made two more trips to the house. On the second one Betty said, "Rebecca's coming home tomorrow."

"I know it," Debby said.

"She'll probably have a big fat head."

"How come?"

"Just because she got on the little old dean's list and Britt has to go to summer school."

"What makes you think that?"

"That's what Britt says. He doesn't want her to come home."

Debby said, "Well I certainly want to see Rebecca." Mrs Merrill read her every one of Rebecca's letters. Usually at the end they said: "P.S. Give little Debby my love." Or "Tell little Debby I miss hearing her trotting about over the house." A great many times Mrs Merrill forgot to read this part until Debby said, "Didn't she say anything about me?" Then Mrs Merrill would take the letter from the envelope and turn through the pages and say, "Why I must not have seen this. She says, 'I think about Debby often and I certainly do want to see her again. I know she is a big help to you now that Bertha is gone.'" Once the letter said, "How did we ever get along without Debby?" Debby bent her face and smiled into the depths of the fern.

"What are you laughing at?"

"I'm just that full!" Debby said.

"You look full," Betty said and punched with one hand at Debby's stomach.

"Now don't you start punching me again. You hold on to that flower."

"You're getting a pot belly."

"A flowerpot-belly?"

"Debby, you're batty. What makes you so batty?"

"I was born that way, I reckon."

Betty peered oddly into her face.

"I was just teasing you," Debby said.

"I don't like to be teased." They walked up the drive to the back yard. Betty was still squinting oddly at her when she asked, "Debby, you know what year this is?"

"It's Saturday. I know that."

"But I mean what year?"

"Is it some special year?"

"No. I just mean what do you call this year."

"I suppose you can call it anything you want to."

Betty told her what year it was, then unexpectedly ran on ahead. Debby wondered what the hurry was. At times Betty couldn't be good enough to her; and yet again she would move across the room and stare brazenly. Julia never came as close nor moved so far away. Betty was holding the gate open. "Come on, Fatso, I'm waiting for you." Debby was out of breath when she put the flower down. Mrs Merrill told her to sit in the shade and rest awhile before going after another. She sat down again and worried Spike with her toe.

Betty picked up a broken broom handle and threw it across the grove. It landed on the canvas in front of Julia and Glenn. "Betty!" Mrs Merrill rocked back on her heels. "That might have put his eyes out! Don't ever let me see you do such a thing again!" Betty sauntered over and kicked the gate shut. She picked up the broomstick again and hit the branches of the pecan trees. There was a tinkling of glass as though there were a family stirring their iced tea among the leaves.

"Stop it! You're going to break my cymbals." Julia had made an odd-thing in Daily Vacation Bible School. She had tied little rectangles of glass with silk thread to a wire potato masher. On the handle she had pasted a piece of adhesive tape with these words written on it: "I have become as a tinkling cymbal." Britt had teased her for three days about the noise the glass made when moved by the wind. That was why they weren't speaking to each other now. He had called her into the kitchen and showed her a cup of water with a thimble in it and said: "I have become as a sinking thimble."

The tinkling music thinned and stopped. One of the pieces of glass spun idly throwing out a blinding light. Debby held up her hand to shield her eyes. Quietly, Betty came and stood in front of her and rubbed the stirring hair back from her forehead. "Debby, you've got pretty hair."

"I know it," Debby said.

She did not feel that her hair was really hers since Rebecca had taught her to wear it like Mrs Merrill's.

"You're my little girl," Betty said. Debby grunted in amusement.

"Nobody better not bother you while I'm around," Betty continued.

"Go on. Who you think you are?" Debby didn't like to be treated as if she were a baby. "I'll look after myself." She pushed Betty away, which ordinarily would have started a wrestling fight between them. But today, Betty allowed herself to be pushed. She went over to the gate and stood, every now and then turning to look solemnly at Debby. She came back finally and sat down beside her. "Debby," she said, "are you *real* sad?"

"There's nothing wrong with me," Debby looked straight ahead. "You go on and leave me alone." She didn't like all these questions Betty was beginning to ask, and just when they had been getting along so well together. School was what did it. Let a child start to school and first thing you knew it was learning how not to be friendly.

"I know how to spell your name," Betty said, trying again to be the way she used to be, "want me to tell you?"

"I want you to leave me alone." There was a lump in her throat and she couldn't understand why Betty was making her so uncomfortable. At that moment the car came up the drive. "He's here!" Debby announced.

Julia and Betty raced to open the gate. Betty opened it,

and turning suddenly, pushed Julia backward. "Betty Merrill," Julia said, "I hate your guts." Julia stood in the Grove and scanned the yard. Then unexpectedly she too ran, her braids thumping against her back. "It's Rebecca. Mama. Here's Rebecca!" Mrs Merrill stood up and brushed her hair with the back of her dirt-covered hands. Britt turned and went back into the greenhouse. Glenn, alone on the canvas, reached out and picked up the little box Betty had brought home from DVBS. In it was the round half of an egg shell with tall silk grass growing out of it and on it the printed words: "And some fell on fertile ground."

They came back in; Julia and Betty each holding to Rebecca's hands. They were all laughing, and even Mr Merrill when he appeared in the grove did not look as worried as he usually did of late. Everyone talked at once: "Why didn't you tell us you were coming classes out early the house is a mess because no exams in English and Daily Vacation Bible School weren't looking for you but the train got a gold star that was just awful curtains aren't up yesterday we were just resetting them DVBS no blight this year or cut worms and Mae Jenkins has got mumps and is like this and little Glenn I wouldn't have known him Rebecca my cymbals up there up there Rebecca stand up Glenn Rebecca and no this isn't a new skirt it's the one I wrote you about the same girl from Barnwell I'm exhausted." Rebecca was trying to see everyone and talk at the same time. She had lost weight Debby thought, or else it was that long skirt and full waist and the way her hair was curled. "And little Debby!" Debby grinned all over herself. "How's my little ole chum?" Rebecca patted her shoulder.

Britt came out of the greenhouse with a shovel of sand. He let Rebecca kiss him on the cheek. "Hiding from me?" she laughed.

"No," he said, his voice unusually deep, his back unusually straight. He was trying to talk like a man, but Debby thought he sounded more like a Yankee. "I was getting some more sand."

"We don't need anymore. That's all we're going to do today."

Glenn sat back down and watched Rebecca while holding the egg shell cupped in his palms.

Betty picked up the broomstick and looked at the cymbals. Julia was listening to Rebecca. Betty held the broomstick behind her, ready to swing it out in a wide arch before turning it loose.

"Who's this young man you keep mentioning?" Mrs Merrill asked.

"I told you, Mama, I'm sure I wrote you. He doesn't care anything about me. I know he doesn't."

"Who is he? Where's he from?"

"He's, well, his name is Raymond Anderson. He's from Atlanta. Not that it makes any difference. He, he just asked me to a dance. That's all."

"Is it?" Mr Merrill asked. The sunlight caught on his gray temples and Debby wondered: Reckon Mrs Merrill is mad because his hair is turning gray and my hair is turning gray and her hair is staying coal black.

"I was in the Infirmary that week end and couldn't go. He doesn't care anything about me. He goes with a dozen girls."

"Then why did you keep mentioning him?"

"He's just nice. That's all."

Debby waited for her to say that Raymond had a good personality and was sophisticated. But when Rebecca didn't apply her two favorite words to him, she knew that Rebecca's world had changed.

Rebecca turned on her heels and waved her arms. "It's so

good to be home. And back here. I can't get over the way the children have grown."

Silently Mrs Merrill sought her husband's eye. They regarded each other a moment. Rebecca talked on, her voice full of excitement and stubborn gaiety. "I don't think I could have stood school another day. It was so hot there. And the food, we finally got so we couldn't eat anything except the salads and . . ." Her eyes were full of tears. "It's just wonderful to be home. Look at Glenn. He's staring at me like he doesn't even know me." They all were. "And the pecan trees! Now that I'm finally home," she said, still trying to talk above the silence, "nothing . . ." She ran suddenly from the Grove, leaving them to study the last fern with its pot-bound roots which must be pulled painfully apart before they would grow again.

Britt laid down the shovel and said, "I'll go see what's wrong with her."

"Leave her alone," Mrs Merrill said.

Mr Merrill stood up. "Come help me with the baggage." Britt and Julia followed him.

Betty, who had stopped her aim, squinted again at the prisms of glass tinkling in the pecan tree above the canvas. She glanced at her mother and then at Glenn. He had pulled the grass out from the egg shell and now was separating the half-sphere of mud.

"Glenn!" Betty screamed and ran to the canvas. Glenn ducked his head so that only his sand-colored hair could be hit. He held the grass behind him. "Give it to me. Give it to me."

"Don't. Don't. Mama. Debby!"

Betty wrenched his arm to the front and pried open his tight fist. The grass was hopelessly crushed. "You darn little squat-face!" Betty snatched the mud and grass and rubbed it over his face, holding his head so that he could not slip away. "See it. See it."

"Mama! Debby!"

Mrs Merrill had been intent on separating the roots of the last fern. Without looking up she said, "Betty, if you don't leave that child alone I'm bound to whip you."

Betty was satisfied now. She stood up and leered at Glenn's muddy face, wet cheeks, and hate-filled eyes. He ran to where his mother was kneeling.

"Mama, look!"

Mrs Merrill lifted her head. "Go get Debby to clean you up. Mama's hands are dirty."

Glenn, crying louder, stumbled over to Debby who was sitting under the fig bush. "Debby, will you?"

She picked him up. Even though Mrs Merrill had said he was too big for her to lift she carried him into the yard. Betty dashed out from behind the car screaming and waving the broomstick: "Put him down. I'll hit him if you don't. I'll kill him dead." Debby stood him down and together they ran across the back yard and up the steps. When she turned to latch the screen door she could see Betty writing in the dust on the car fender. And through the open gate she could see the kneeling woman tamping dirt about a fern which someone would take from her as soon as it was big enough to be of some joy.

Chapter 10

ALL THAT summer Rebecca thought about nothing but Raymond; and Julia thought about nothing but following Rebecca around. It was a peaceful time with Rebecca planning, planning, planning, but never telling Mrs Merrill anything about anything. But this morning at eight o'clock a special delivery had arrived from Raymond saying he would be here tonight. Rebecca of course had to tell Mrs Merrill who, surprisingly enough, was not angry. She had merely said, "Don't worry about the dinner. Just go see about your clothes and get some rest."

Now Rebecca, after having looked at all of her clothes and chosen a yellow linen dress that would be bright against her tan, was taking a sun bath in the middle of the back yard. She was stretched out on her back reading the letter from Raymond. Julia, skinny, in white underpants, was waiting for her to finish. Debby was ambling in the back drive, kicking at half-buried pieces of glass. She was looking for a marble. During the game the night before, played on the figured carpet in the back living room, she had lost all her marbles to Betty and Glenn. They played for keeps but they kept their winnings together in a walnut jewelry box Mr Merrill had given Debby for Christmas. Each night they sorted them out again from memory, but if the night before you had at least one left, you could always claim several more. But if you didn't have even one, the children were sure to remember. All she needed to get back in the game was a measly little old marble. But she had kicked the drive until her shoes and the hem of her long skirt was dusty. Spike followed up and down the drive, nuzzling against her legs whenever she paused.

"Think of it," Rebecca said, half to the summer sky, half to herself. "He'll be here tonight. Then I'll know for sure."

"What?" Debby asked. During the summer Rebecca had developed a peculiar habit of beginning a conversation at the tail end. She would sit at the table thinking to herself, then suddenly come out with an alarming conclusion: "Britt, you should buy a white V-neck sweater." "When I get married I'm not going to be caught without whipped cream." "Don't you just love the smell of banana oil?" By working backward they learned that Raymond had a white sweater; that Raymond liked whipped cream, not only on sundaes and in cocoa but also in his coffee; and further that he had dyed a pair of shoes with polish that smelled like banana oil. He had been embarrassed because everyone in the class wanted the windows raised—everyone except Rebecca.

"I wish we could have had the house painted," Rebecca breathed heavily.

"Is that what Raymond does? Paints houses?" Julia sighed. She sighed every time Rebecca did during the summer and was just as fretful when a day passed without a letter from Raymond. Next to Jesus Christ, Raymond had become the most important part of her life and when she could no longer bear the hateful torments of Betty, she either picked out hymns on the piano or begged Rebecca to read aloud from her growing stack of letters. Julia's daydreams were upsetting to Debby because the child spoke in such awed tones of both her Saviors. Half the summer Debby had been rather expecting Jesus Christ to come riding up in a white sweater.

Rebecca rolled over on the blanket and brushed her hair up from her neck. She was already as black as sin, but still not dark enough she said to wear the yellow linen dress.

Julia turned over and pointed her sharp shoulder blades at the sun. She was a painful pink and on top of her shoulders and on her forehead were liver-colored freckles. Her big front teeth were hard to conceal and looked natural only when she was chewing nervously on her bottom lip. Everyone said it was a shame Julia's teeth were beginning to protrude. Everyone said she had been such a lovely little girl.

"Debby," Rebecca called, "is there any vinegar here I can rub on my back."

"I'm not going to have anything to do with you." Debby clearly did not approve of so much nakedness. If it hadn't been for the desperate need of a marble she wouldn't even have stayed in the same back yard with such a sight.

"You're a little prude."

"You're the one." Certainly Rebecca was as dark as a prune and if she didn't quit baking in the sun, she was going to be every bit as dried and wrinkled.

Julia went to the house for vinegar. She would have fetched snake skins if they could have made Rebecca more attractive in Raymond's sight. Julia was a faithful handmaid. When she grew up she was planning to marry her sister's oldest son who would be named Elisha. Or if God made Rebecca barren and unable to beget a son, Julia intended, she told Debby, to be a foreign missionary in Nashville, Tennessee. In the meantime her devotion to her sister was such that all summer they were tortured by the new moon, the full moon, the evening star, the mimosa puffs, the odor of honeysuckle, and sometimes by seemingly nothing more than a gentle breeze foreboding an early autumn.

"Debby, do you want to know a secret?"

Debby hurried over to the blanket without looking at Rebecca's copper-brown legs. "What kind of secret?"

"You won't tell?"

"I don't tell everything I know."

"Promise."

"Hope to die."

"Not to Mama. You swear you won't let her know."

Debby crossed her heart and swore.

"What, Rebecca, what?" Julia came hopping painfully across the backyard, a tumbler of vinegar sloshing in her hand.

"Nothing. Be quiet."

"What was Debby crossing her heart about?"

"The vinegar. She promised not to tell Mama."

"Tell another one!" Debby said.

They could not pry the secret from Rebecca now. She hugged herself and rolled over on the blanket. She smiled at the sky. She grinned at Debby and Julia. She hummed a tune and sang bits of a song. She smiled again and hugged her lovely secret closer to her, so close in fact that Debby was worried for fear that one of Rebecca's breasts would pop free like a rubber ball and go rolling downhill.

Everything was a secret these days. A storm was swelling in the house. It differed from other trouble in that no one mentioned or denied its slow, certain approach. For somewhere, long back, they had faced the matter before and dispelled it. Until this summer. Fury could be avoided, Debby realized late in July, only if Rebecca and Mrs Merrill leveled pistols to each other's heads and fired two volleys.

"Tell us the secret. Tell us, tell us, tell us," Julia begged as she rubbed the remaining sharp-scented vinegar on her own freckled nose. "We've promised." Rebecca scanned the blinding white clouds and held her bare arms toward them.

"It's nothing. Just something I think's going to happen." She waited, smiling at them, then whispered, "I may get married when I go back to school. I think Raymond's going to propose tonight."

Debby trembled inside as though her heart had suddenly swung loose and turned somersaults in mid-air. The storm cloud would soon burst.

"See why you've got to keep quiet. Mama'd throw a fit. Oh Lord! you've got to keep quiet. I'll kill you if you tell."

It would happen, Debby knew. Mrs Merrill would find out.

"She won't let me out of her sight if she guesses I'm even thinking about marrying before finishing school."

Mrs Merrill had rather have a dead daughter than an uneducated one, Debby thought.

"None of this would have come about if I'd stayed home. God, when I think how she used to scare those poor little boys who came around here. She's not as bad as she used to be, but Julia, you've got to get away. Sooner than I did. Julia, whenever she starts talking to you about men or about . . ."

Debby went back to the drive. She did not like to hear Rebecca talk about her mother. Debby was confused by such talk because it was as though they saw two different women, one hard and cunning and jealous, the other strong and understanding and kind. Surely if Mrs Merrill were the woman Rebecca claimed, her father would not enter the house each night saying, "Where's your mother? Where's your mother?" and would not leave on those infrequent occasions when she was away saying, "I can't bear this house when it's empty. I'll be over at the McAllister's. Call me when she gets back."

But perhaps, and the idea thrilled Debby, she is what Rebecca says. And if she is. . . . She dared not finish the thought in words, but in her mind she saw Glenn running toward her: "Debby save me. Save me." Dark in the house, dark in Debby's mind, Mrs Merrill stood.

A shining bit of glass, striped blue and white, shone when a gentle breeze ruffled the ground ivy under the pecan tree. Debby ran to the spot, and holding her breath, not daring to wish, she sought through the leaves and found the marble. She was in the game again. Surely this was a revelation to her that God knew what she was planning and would help her. It wasn't much of a plan. All she wanted was to be able to take Glenn up to her room. But Mrs Merrill always said "No, you have the other two." And Betty always said, "You bring him up here and I'll kill him in his sleep." But she had found a marble and she would find a way.

She wished that she could find a way to help Rebecca. All afternoon she worked with Mrs Merrill on the dining room, polishing the silver, shining the crystal, washing all the gold-rimmed plates that had been collecting dust in the china closet. Then when everything was clean and shining, the table was set for only two people. Rebecca and Raymond would eat alone. The idea was shocking to Mrs Merrill. She thought it meant Rebecca was ashamed of her family. She thought Raymond would think it peculiar and that perhaps the family did not like him. Finally she thought it meant that they were entirely too familiar for unmarried people. Each thought led to an argument in which by shouts and whimpers Rebecca had to wear down her mother. "I'm not ashamed of you, any of you. I want him to meet you all. That's one reason he's coming here." "You can show him without eating with him that you do like him. Just be friendly and natural. You don't have to stay with us every minute. We want to be together alone for at least that long." Deborah and Julia looked at each other. Did people propose in a dining room? "What is so intimate about eating alone with someone? He takes me out to dinner at school. We eat alone then. Oh, certainly there are other people around in the restaurant!" Mrs Merrill was finally worn down. Her chin trembled and she said, "If that's the way girls do now, well all right. It's just that I've never had a daughter grow up and I don't know, I don't know, and when you don't it does make you anxious. If Mama had lived until I was a little older, I'd know how to do. But living around with relatives I had to be so careful of my name." She was tired now. "All I want is for you to be happy."

By the time Raymond arrived, shortly after sunset, Rebecca and Mrs Merrill were both as nervous as witches. Then Bertha didn't come to serve supper; then she did finally come in time to serve the dessert. Mr and Mrs Merrill met Raymond before supper. Afterward the children went in one at a time, then Deborah.

She was proud of the way Mrs Merrill was talking to Raymond. She didn't notice that he was not leaning back comfortably in his chair. She did not notice how he had his feet lined parallel and how he did not cross his legs. She did see that Rebecca was actually on the edge of her seat leaning forward as though to be between Mrs Merrill and Raymond and that she interrupted Mrs Merrill and put her sentences into different words. Mrs Merrill was asking him about what type work he had been doing this summer and when he said he had not been working she seemed rather surprised. Each time Rebecca interrupted, Mrs Merrill's next question would be in a lower voice until finally everyone was leaning forward to hear what she said. On some words her voice trembled and finally she leaned back and tried to smile at what the others were saying even though you could tell she wasn't hearing a word. She glanced at Betty and Julia and they knew to say "Good night." She glanced at Debby and Debby stood up. Mrs Merrill then glanced at Rebecca as though to be glanced back at, but Rebecca was staring at the rug. Mrs Merrill stood up. She had regained her voice, "We've enjoyed having you, Mr Anderson. When you're passing through again, do stop by to see us. And I'll see you again before you leave tonight. Good night." Raymond was standing like a park statue. Rebecca smiled awkwardly at her mother. Debby, without having said a word the entire time, waved good-by from the door.

In the back living room Mrs Merrill undressed Glenn and dressed him for bed. Debby went up to cut on the lights for Betty and Julia while they undressed and got to bed. She came back down after an hour of arguing with Betty about the trunk which the child claimed she was going to take and raise rabbits in. Mrs Merrill was sitting quietly, not even fanning herself. She had been crying. "The supper was terrible. The steak was tough and even the salad wasn't too good. The mayonnaise was oily." They had even taken time that afternoon to mix homemade mayonnaise.

"I thought you'd gone to bed, Debby. Past your bedtime."

"You said I could stay up tonight. He's just going to be here one night."

"We aren't going back in there," Mrs Merrill said. They sat without saying a word while the water gurgled out of the tub. Mr Merrill came to the door and asked how late she was going to sit up. "Until eleven. I'm going to let her stay out past ten-thirty tonight." Mr Merrill said good night. "Debby," Mrs Merrill said, "you need to go to bed. You've worked hard today."

"So have you."

"But she's my daughter. There's no reason for you to take such an interest. Not to the point of working hard and then sitting up half the night."

"It's hot upstairs. That tin roof just throws the heat in my window." Deborah was determined to see the storm.

Promptly at eleven o'clock Mrs Merrill walked into the hall and said, "It's eleven o'clock, Mr Anderson. We don't want you to miss your train. We've enjoyed having you and I know Rebecca was glad you could stop by." Rebecca explained in impatient tones that Raymond's train was not leaving until six o'clock. "Rebecca usually has to be in at ten-thirty," Mrs Merrill explained to Raymond politely. She returned to the back living room. At eleven-thirty she went out again and said good night in such a way that he did not tarry longer. Debby followed Mrs Merrill into the living room when the front door clicked shut. Rebecca stood at the door and watched until Raymond disappeared up the street beyond a clump of giant privet, his rapid footsteps echoing back duller and duller, then not at all.

Silence held for a moment.

Then slowly, with a bitterness in her voice and a sharp flash of hatred in her eyes, Rebecca turned to her mother. "Are you satisfied?"

"What have I done wrong now?" Mrs Merrill asked as though she had not already been crying about the tough steak and the oily salad. She was plainly shaken by the remark.

"Asking him to leave. Mama, I could have died. He looked so odd. He'll never come back."

Mrs Merrill's chin trembled, the tears began. She steadied herself, gripping the back of a chair, with knuckles white. She moved behind it as though to ward off the words that were certain to be spoken. But Rebecca, glaring at her without mercy or compassion, with no trace of pity or of tenderness, slowly crossed the room and ran up the steps. For all they knew Raymond might never come back, and now Rebecca was gone. She came back down the steps the next morning, but she was not the same person the rest of the summer.

Chapter 11

At sunset on a warm evening that autumn a lonesome bell rang out in the neighborhood. The Merrills froze standing. On the wide street, cars slowed, and old man Theo Clark who had been out taking his constitutional paused to say that he had never heard the bell before in all the days of his long life. Mrs Merrill went down to the boxwood hedge and talked with a group of women who were out looking at the graying sky and listening to the bell which every fifteen minutes—Mr Merrill timed it—rang for a full minute.

Betty could not be persuaded to go find out what the ringing bell meant because she had been tree-sitting all afternoon and had sworn and hoped to die if she set foot on ground before dark. She explained to Mrs Merrill that if there had happened to be a convenient tree next to the one in which she was sitting she could swing over from there to it and so on to the roof of the next house and then into another tree and another to a second roof, but that she just couldn't see her way clear to come down out of a perfectly good tree. Julia never sat in trees, let Julia go. Mrs Merrill stood at the tree trunk and glared impatiently at Betty who climbed out on a creaking limb. There was something wonderful to Betty in being taller than her mother and out of reach. She often explained to Debby what a fine feeling it was and how someday she would figure out a way to get Debby up in the tree too. They had thought about letting the laundry basket down by a rope, but they didn't have a rope. Britt often sneaked out food to a friend of his who lived in a tree. There were plenty of empty houses but the trees were full. Debby was delighted and sometimes prayed to God Almighty for a rope so that she too could live in a tree.

Doom doom doom. The graying sky echoed back the bell noise and dipping swallows fluttered nervously, darting swiftly into the dark trees. More whispering women joined the group at the edge of the yard. Debby stood out of sight behind Mrs Merrill and listened to the guesses: the Ward was testing a new fire bell? the president of the United States was dead? Revolution? The Baptist Church? No for it had no belfry. Only the small Spanish building behind the Catholic Church had a bell tower, but there had never been to their knowledge a bell in it. They talked and waited for the hapless noise.

Debby tiptoed away from the crowd and went up to Britt's room. Since Julia had become so studious and religious she would not always talk to Debby; but Britt appreciated visits. Each night since he failed summer school he was ordered by his father to go study. He could not even sit on his bed until after 9:30. Debby pushed open the door. Britt turned from his table where he was unwinding rubber strings from the inside of a golf ball.

"Debby." He acknowledged her presence. She stood in the doorway and waited until he said, "Come in." She stepped inside. No one would know she had broken the rule about Britt's room.

Why sometimes did it hurt her to look at Britt? Was it because he was thin and because his head was handsome and fragile? The square smile hurt, the dark eyes. He moved quickly, nervously, slammed doors, raced the motor, drove like a madman, cussed to himself, and said over and over and over that he would not stay in high school after his class had gone. He would quit and work full time. He didn't want college. He didn't want charity. He didn't want to be pitied, loved, or touched. He was glad when Rebecca left for school. He avoided Betty. Julia, he tolerated, except when she prayed for him.

"Debby, what's the bell for? What bell is it?"

"Nobody knows. It's awful. It makes me cold all over."

"If they'd let me go, I could find out."

Debby knew why Britt could not go out. The day he failed summer school he did not come home. At midnight he was found sitting on the floor in the bathroom, sick. The ovenish upstairs reeked of hot sour liquor. Mr Merrill tiptoed through the house opening windows that squeaked and whispered to Debby not to say a word about Britt to Mrs Merrill. He washed a ragged cloth in cold water and wiped the dew-beads from Britt's forehead. He helped Britt into his room and onto his bed. Debby followed with a pan of water. Mr Merrill sat on the edge of the bed and bathed Britt's face and neck and knobby collar bones.

While he bathed his son, Mr Merrill asked questions. He even grinned when Britt turned gray with chill. He promised that Mrs Merrill would not know. After a while Britt sat up and talked: "I knew you'd all say I didn't try to pass. That I didn't study. Wasted my time. But that's not so. I tried. Daddy, I tell you I tried. Well all right I won't talk loud but I tried. I'd pretend I wasn't studying so if I did fail. Did you know I failed? Yeah I failed. I tried and I failed. I failed and I tried and failed. I don't mean I tried to fail, I mean I tried *and* failed. That's different. You see that? Yes sir, but do you see that? Yes sir, I'll shut up but just say do you see that? Because if you don't then that's the difference in you and me. See? If I say I failed to try that means I haven't got any damn sense and that's what I mean. I mean I hadn't got sense enough to be in school. When you were my age you were out working for a living. Here I sit and let you work yourself crazy. Hunh! You didn't know you were crazy did you? You act like a crazy man sometimes. You used to . . . just let me tell you this . . . you used to act like you owned the world. Big R.M. Merrill. Big Shot. Big Cars. Local Boy pulls self up by Big Boot Straps. Lord how you used to . . . all right just let *me* talk a minute . . . Mama telling you to save money and you throwing it away. Look at you now!

"That's what I call funny. You're licked without even turning your hands. Helpless. O.K. O.K. we won't talk about you. Who you want to talk about? Debby? Let's talk about Debby? O.K. we'll talk about me. What you want to know? I'm seventeen and haven't earned a damn cent in my life. Tomorrow I'm getting a job. If you can't support this family, I'll show you how. Daddy, I'm going to help you. You never have had any help from anybody. Poor ignorant. . . . Don't push me back. I'm just going to pat you on the back. See, I try to love people and they push me away. Is it because I'm dumb? Tell me. You won't hurt . . . I love people, but I'm just so dumb and we're so poor . . ." Britton turned over and quit talking. Mr Merrill and Debby watched while he went to sleep. Since that night Britt had not been out of the house after dark because he would not promise that he would not be sick again.

Tonight as he listened to the bell Julia came to the door.

"Mama says I can go find out if you go with me, Britt."

They left the house and a half an hour later Julia returned alone. Britt had gone downtown. In the fog of twilight Julia's face was pale white, her eyes bright with excitement. She was out of breath and while she panted she covered her teeth which were in braces with a cupped hand. It was awful, the thing the bell was ringing for; but she could not tell them until her breath came in smaller swallows. Once more the bell rang out and darkness which had hovered over the town settled on the neighborhood. Debby watched the yellow-eyed houses across the street stare blankly out at the night. Two eyes upstairs, the door was the nose and the sidewalk was the tongue licking out at the street.

Julia was choking on stubborn tears. The bell was ringing because the Poor Claras were hungry. For five days, five nights the nuns had been praying for food. Tonight they had divided their last crust and their strength was failing. Julia cried now and her wet face shining from the window lights seemed as far away as a moon of fox fire in a swamp. Why, she kept asking, hadn't the Poor Claras looked at the pie. Mrs Merrill explained that if they had no food they had no pie. But Debby knew the pie Julia was talking about. In the *Book of Knowledge* was a circle which showed by big and little slices that God in their particular state at their particular time was over half Baptist and less than a sliver Catholic. Tonight the nuns had divided that last thin slice of pie.

The Poor Claras were starving. Julia wanted to carry them all the cooked food in the house. Mrs Merrill's voice was low as a grave: "Julia, you mustn't let your sympathy run away with you. These are hard times but we've got to look after our own kind first."

"But Mama, they're hungry!"

"They'll eat tonight. We aren't the only ones who heard the bell."

"They'll starve."

"No. They won't starve." Mrs Merrill sitting on the top step turned to look at Julia on the porch. How calm the woman's face was; how untroubled, how near to stone. "We'll all live through it. I've lived through worse times."

"They're hungry."

"There'll be people who hear the bell tonight who'll be better able to help them than we are."

"I saw the little nun. She was at the door talking. Let's take them some food. Please, Mama."

"No, Julia. This week they'll have plenty. We've got to look after ourselves."

"But what about the leftovers. Can't we take them?"

"There won't be any leftovers by tomorrow noon. We cook just as much as we can spare and we haven't thrown out a bite in two years. We cook too much, I know that, and I intend to as long as we are able. There's Bertha who comes by two and three times a week. And old Uncle Ben comes begging, and the washwoman's little niggers. That's as many as we can do for. Maybe next week when others have forgotten."

Julia stood lost on the porch. Her wet cheeks were burning red with anger and grief. She had never murdered, stolen, or committed adultery, but the cold glint in her eyes did not honor her mother. What she said seemed to have nothing to do with the conversation. She spoke without emotion as though it were an old fact: "You don't love me, Mama. Jesus does." She walked slowly into the house waiting for an answer, a denial, a single word. She paused at the door while Mrs Merrill leaned forward to speak but then instead sank backward against the post without having said a word, as though nothing had occurred here on the porch. Julia let the screen bang shut.

When there was excitement in the house or neighborhood or when there were any unexplained changes in the events of the day, Debby's sleep was troubled by dreams that blended the familiar with the awful, and a fear haunted her sleeping mind. Tonight the bell—whether heard or dreamed—echoed through her sleep and Betty called from the tree: "Up here Debby. Taller than her taller than her." While Mrs Merrill—how odd Mrs Merrill looked, unsmiling, unbending, hard and distant and tired—stood with a broom in hand. A Negro man was saying: "Any old cold bread?" He reached out a shaking brown hand with a withered pink palm. It touched her arm and fashioned itself about her wrist in a bracelet. She pulled away and Britt's voice said, "Debby, don't be afraid."

She opened her eyes. Wavering in the late moonlight by her bed, Britt was tugging at her wrist. "Wake up and talk to me, Debby. I'm afraid. I'm so afraid. Come talk to me."

When Debby sat up, Britt staggered, caught on to the bed and clung there while Debby hastily wrapped herself in a blue bathrobe Rebecca had left for her. She led Britt across the hall to his own room, shushing him against noise, supporting him against a fall. He fell across the large bed and giggled while she tried and finally succeeded in lifting his feet to the bed and removing his unpolished shoes.

"Debby, old girl. I've been out tonight. Free as a bird. No studying, no books, no caring a good goddamn how dumb I am. How poor we are." He sat up and focused his eyes on her as calmly and seriously as an entirely sober man might. He lowered his voice in a thin whisper. "Know what I started to do?" She listened while he told about drinking so much of this and more of that, about starting over to see the superintendent of the city schools, about phoning all of his teachers and telling them to go to hell. He had also phoned, or so he said, a girl named Sally and told her to quit speaking to him if she really believed he was as dumb as she had told Bud Stimmel.

Debby's sanded eyelids fought the light from the student-lamp on the table. Dusty outdoor odors from the grass rug tickled high in her nose and Britt's whisper tickled deep in her ear. The small room whirled as the eyelids sank slowly, opened suddenly to see again the cocoon tree in the corner. To her sleepy eyes the thousand cocoons tied to the bare branches of the poplar saplings were as blinding as the glare from Christmas candles. She looked for relief to the mantel wall where two crossed swords made X on the space. X marked the spot, Betty often played, where all her enemies lay dead. She wondered who Britt's enemies were.

"Debby," he said, and his tone was in that of an answer. Had she spoken aloud? "How would you kill yourself?"

"Upside down," she answered for that was a fine joke she had with Betty who played at committing "sideways" and afterward lying dead on the rag rug, presenting a problem to Debby who knew that to step over a growing child would be to stunt its growth.

"I wouldn't. Women take poison. Men shoot themselves."

"You haven't got a gun."

"I wouldn't shoot myself. And I wouldn't jump. Like the Scandinavians. They jump. There are better ways than jumping."

"Like what?" Debby was interested but she didn't want to raise her head lest she shake out all the sleep and be left sitting as wide awake as the glaring lamp.

"I'd, well I wouldn't jump. Jumping's no good. I'd like to . . . know what the Russians do. They cut their wrist.

Go to bed with a book and an apple and cut their wrist. Let it hang off the bed in a bucket of warm water till they bleed to death."

Debby watched while the throbbing blood ebbed from a sad Russian, leaving the arm skin wrinkled and deflated as an empty balloon dangling from the edge of the bed.

"A hypodermic of milk into this vein. The insurance company'd never know what happened. Blood clots."

Debby watched the cocoons that dangled and that, in the cool breeze, spun gently on their silk cords. The cocoons were open at one end in ragged, gaping holes—except for a few small shriveled ones that would never hatch forth the powdery dull moths which at certain times during the year blindly beat their silly wings to powder against the window screens, their soft, ripe-heavy bodies beading the wire with tiny eggs. Here was a mystery; for Britt who showed affection for no one in the family, except occasionally for Julia, guarded his cocoon collection like a mad man. Debby had seen him sit an entire afternoon watching a moth embroider the screen with eggs while all the time the fluttering wings beat silently and dumbly into powder. Britt explained to her how wonderful it was that they came out of the cocoons and found mates. He explained how hard it must be to get out of a cocoon and how hard and sharp the outside world must seem to the soft creatures.

He talked on and on; his waving hands cast flying shadows on the wall. He was ashamed because he had only a nickel each day for lunch and couldn't go through the cafeteria line. He would buy a bottle of milk or cinnamon buns and stand out on the steps back of the gym to eat. He was angry because someone had put a note in his locker saying, "Why don't you get a haircut?" and he had walked all over town trying to find a barber who would still give Mr Merrill credit. He stayed by himself; he had no friends; he was miserable; he wouldn't mind dying; he wouldn't care a bit if he died in a car wreck. He wouldn't blame the nuns if they killed themselves instead of ringing that bell.

"I'm glad it wasn't no fire bell," Debby interrupted. "They scare me."

"Why?"

"Supposin' it was this house?"

"What would you do?"

"Burn up, I reckon."

"Now, Debby, talk sense. What would you do? Say you woke up and your room was full of smoke."

"Open the window I reckon."

"Then what?"

"Wait till the smoke cleared out?"

"But if the house was on fire the smoke wouldn't clear out. So what would you do?"

"I'd run down and tell your mama."

"Suppose the steps were on fire." Britt propped himself unsteadily on his elbow and his eyes focused uncertainly and oddly at a point a foot in front of her face.

"Let's not talk about such." Debby was frantic.

"We've got to. It's important. Now if the house were on fire and the steps were burning and you couldn't get down them, what would you do?"

"Die. Burn up."

Britt told her that she should first try to come to his room, or, if Rebecca were at home, her room; but if Debby were alone she should tie the sheets end to end, fasten one end to the bed and the other throw out the window, forming thereby a rope to the ground. "Now, Debby, tell me what you would do if the house were on fire."

"Just what you said."

"What did I say? Word by word."

"If the house was on fire," she watched the billowing smoke and through it saw flickers of orange, "I'd call you and Rebecca." She waited for his nod of approval. "Then I'd tie the sheets and bedclothes together."

"Right."

"And see that the knots were strong."

"Good."

"And I'd tie one end to the bed."

"Good."

"And throw the other end out the window."

"Fine!"

"And that would be a rope to the ground."

"Perfect. Then what?"

"Then I'd run down the steps."

Britt fell back on the bed and exhausted himself with a sigh. "Go on to bed, Debby. I'm sorry I woke you."

Debby stood in the door and looked back at the moon-bright room. The cocoons were hanging as still as death from the tree. Britt's arm swinging over the edge of the bed beat nervous circles in the air. He sighed again and rolled over in the bed, the white sheet winding about him, protecting him from her curious, wondering eyes and from the chill which had come unnoticed into the night air.

Chapter 12

As SHE opened her eyes, her heart stopped, one two—a choking in her chest—shook violently, sank fluttering to her stomach. She slid her hand from under the warm pillow and felt with her fingertips the throbbing hollow between her ribs. The square of window was black against the faint grayness of the walls. The vast emptiness within her was cold and terrifying. She slid her hand out through the icy sheets for the nape of Thomas' warm, solid neck. Her hand grasped nothing and her heart pounded. Death was in the room as certain, as enveloping as the darkness. Thomas was gone. He was gone. There was no one left in the house. A reflected light determined one corner of the slanted ceiling and she was awake again, knowing what bed she lay in, what house this was; knowing that she was awake before dawn because a train—its violent puffing echoed now through the frosty night—had screeched out, splitting the darkness wide. In her dream she had seen a flash of light and heard the noise.

Exploring with her feet the icy distances of the bed, bringing them back again to the warm nest, reassuring herself in this way and by the steady, audible rhythm of her breathing and the throbbing of her heart, that she was still Deborah Hall and still alive, she listened to the silence of the Merrill house. It was like the silence of no other place and was the presence of blended noises rather than the absence. A bare branch scraped as always on the roof, but tonight she heard Britt turning over in his bed, again, silence, again, silence, again. A fine silk thread of yellow light shone under the hall door. Britt would not stay awake in the dark. He, too, then had heard the train's anguished cry. Under the silence was a muffled roar, perhaps wind in the hall, air in the attic, perhaps voices of the dead who once had lived here, who talked incessantly, who were waiting only for the right knob to be turned for their words to become clear, distinguishable, without static; perhaps the thoughts of the Merrills, bouncing around, resounding, yet blended into silence: Julia, you must get away from Mama I'll not burden them forever because Jesus loves me and you don't we'll be rich Debby save me save me Debby when we have the candy store and they're so poor so poor so poor Hoover we've a lot of work to do today where's your mother where where where no time for play so as long as I live you have a home at two times four at six percent Mrs Merrill Mrs Merrill Mrs Merrill. The huge box springs rumbled on Britt's bed and the voices were again wafted away by the stirring air.

Her hand, which would have curved around the firm warm column of Thomas' neck, paused and in it was the memory of the sharp bristles along the hard chin bone, the soft beneath, the rising adam's apple, the hollow between the collar bones where often his chin moved down suddenly and caught her fingers in a trap, of the escape to the back of the neck where the smooth warm shore ended abruptly at the forest, of his coarse voice trembling the question in his throat as her fingers slid up through the hair at the nape of his neck. The sheets were cold and her hand came back to her, still unclosed.

"Thomas." If he turned to her . . . again the slanted ceiling of this room which was in Mrs Merrill's house. An ambulance howled through the night. The train bell clanged.

If only Rebecca had not plied her with questions during the summer, she might not now be remembering Thomas. Rebecca was actually afraid of men. At least Mrs Merrill had accomplished that much by keeping a sharp eye on the living room and the front porch. Rebecca asked such frightened questions that Debby could not explain the way things had been between herself and Thomas. "You love him and he loves you and it's the best kind of play a body can play." Everything was simple if you just had fun and did what you wanted to and not what somebody else always said not to. Rebecca could not seem to understand. She talked of shame and pain and labor and disgust and brutes.

She tried to tell Rebecca about a certain day she remembered better than any, but Rebecca stopped her. She thought of it again tonight. It was midsummer, the day she stepped into the nettles. They had not been married long, she remembered, because Thomas was still coming up from the field in the middle of the morning to help her get started on the housework. They made the bed, drank coffee, and he heated the dish water and began dinner while she swept and dusted. Then he went back to the field for an hour. In the afternoon he came up again, and sometimes, she followed him back to the fields and stayed with him till sunset.

"I've been helping you with the house," Thomas said, and she knew without looking for dimples in his hollow cheeks that he was love-laughing and mocking. "You think you can help me in the fields."

"No," she said. She could mock too.

"No!"

"That's right."

"No! Did you say 'no'?" Thomas could always make her laugh. She followed him to the field and during the heat of the afternoon they hoed the cotton, digging around each plant, scraping weeds back between the rows, Thomas a whole row to her half. Her hands blistered early and the blisters—fascinating little white mountains with fingerprint terraces she could have studied all day—burst and the water ran out. The skin tore off and the burning pink beneath smarted in the red dust-grime from the hoe handle.

"What's the matter? You aren't quitting on me?"

Then she dug faster, ignoring the pain in her hands and the growing pain in her back. The sky when she looked up suddenly was black with heat and the willows whirled past on the horizon. She steadied herself on the hoe and wiped her wet forehead with the hem of her apron. Lucky she had remembered to wear an apron because she had on nothing under the dress. She watched sweat drops, heavy as quicksilver, roll down the short brown calves of her legs and streak her dusty red ankles and feet. It would be a fine thing to go wading. She watched to see if Thomas would stop at the end of that row. It would be a glorious thing if he turned and said, "Debby, my girl, let's go wading."

At the end of the row Thomas said, "We're half through."

Another row and another and another and then it didn't make any difference. The glare, the heat, the pain in her back, the awful smarting of her hands became the entire world and there was no such thing as a stream where a body could wade and refreshen up.

"Listen," he said as they stood toward sunset in the shade of the willows. "Listen." A katydid was calling to its mate. "Ninety days till frost." Deborah shivered—whether from his husky whisper or from the mention of frost, she couldn't say when he asked. "You're tired, maybe," he said and loosened her grip on the hoe handle. She stood with her back to him and wondered at the sunset while he kneaded her shoulders. "Poor little Debby's tired," he said, and he picked her up and began walking across the field. The hard blue line of his chin and jaw saddened her, and when he swallowed and the hard sharp hill rose in his throat and sank again, Deborah fancied her heart was behaving in the same way.

"I can walk," she said when the pain of watching him was too much. They did not speak as they entered the south pasture, their long shadows sliding ahead of them up the hill. If she didn't speak she would cry. "I'll race you home!" she shouted. He made a false start and she fled toward a thicket which might be a short cut. She heard him running close behind, then: "Not that way! Nettles!" She stopped and turned to him sobbing.

"Did you touch any," he asked.

She shook her head, no, sobbing without shame.

Again he picked her up. "Debby, Debby, you're plumb wore out." At the house he set her on the steps. "Don't move," he said. While he rattled in the kitchen, kindling the fire, heating water, she saw again the blue hard chin and once more the mountains shimmered in tears. She watched as he drew water and filled the big tub in the yard. He stood on a feed sack and dropped the towel-cloth from around his thin waist. Naked in the sunset he was a grand red sight. With her eyes she fondled every part of him while he covered himself with soap-clouds and washed them away. He dried himself as though it were the skin and not the water he wished to be shed of. With the towel-cloth tied around him again, he rinsed the tub and filled it with hot water from the stove and with cool water from the well. "I'm Debby and that's Thomas." But it did no good to explain to herself. In the field when he was carrying her in his arms, it was like walking on his legs and when the lump rose in his throat it was her heart that rose and sank there. She was hopelessly confused, infinitely sad. The distant mountains swam before her and were dissolved in tears.

"Your bath's ready."

Deborah remained motionless. Thomas dragged her to her feet. He turned her around and unbuttoned the small, cloth-covered buttons. He unfastened the apron and let it fall. He put his arms about her waist and walked her to the tub. He was smiling and she couldn't help smiling back.

"Raise your arms."

He peeled the wet dress off over her head. For a moment he looked at her, then buried his lips in the hollow of her neck. With his lips still on her and his arms about her waist he lifted her into the tub.

His voice was hoarse and trembling. "Sit down," he said.

He bathed her face and neck. As he ran the soft cloth over her back he kissed the nape of her neck, his sugar bowl. Her shoulders rounded and she shivered. Slowly his hands moved under her arms and over her breasts, the soapy water warming them. Now it was that she knew the direction of her grief and its source. She shut her eyes and gasped repeatedly as he bathed her breasts, and softly, with his fingertips, the nipples.

"Stand up," he whispered.

He washed her feet, her ankles, her calves, and then the back of her knees where she couldn't stand to be touched. "Thomas." And then they were on the bed and oh oh oh and again and again and again.

The katydid droned on, and the mountains, no longer

shimmering, huddled calm and dark against the faint glow in the graying sky.

The train bell no longer rang; the ambulance had howled off to silence in the darkness. A hush filled the Merrill house again. Off in the distance a factory whistle was blowing. Dawn was quivering. "Deborah-deborah-deborah debby-debby-debby thrace-thrace-thrace" a lone catbird called from a bare branch of the mimosa. A pale gray light filled the room with late winter and despair. "Smile, smile for me, my own little playpretty." And he kissed her in each dimple. "Show me my rosebuds." And on the nipple of each breast. She threw the heavy covers back. The rag rug was damp and chilled. The floor before the dresser was burning cold, and the mirror itself was like a sheet of blue ice.

She smiled timidly, somewhat hopefully. The dimples were two deep wrinkles. With the tips of her fingers she touched the graying, plaited hair. She could not let Thomas see her thus. Impatiently she tore at the throat button of her flannel nightgown. It rolled on the floor, and as she glanced down she saw her bare bosom, the two sagging breasts hanging like . . . she turned her back to the mirror and clasped the gown together with rough, freezing hands. If Thomas should come today, oh he would be mad at her for letting such a thing happen to her, his playpretty. She turned again to the mirror and, standing close, looked at her lips as Thomas would look at them. Bending nearer she shut her eyes and pressed her lips against the glass in a cold, hard kiss. Her mouth parted from the frosted image. She did not have strength enough to move her head away; for leaning with her forehead against the glass, she had allowed herself to admit what she had always known: Thomas was dead. She stood back and saw where her nose had touched the mirror, leaving a greasy spot. And that, she knew, was all that was left of Thomas.

Chapter 13

THE house, like a turtle, had drawn unto itself for the winter. Deborah sometimes felt sorry for the house, having to sit outdoors all year round, snow, rain, sleet. She liked to think about having enough money to build a great big barn over the entire yard with some kind of roof that on warm days would open out like a sewing machine top. Then the house would not have to huddle unto itself.

It was not the house's closing up, windows, doors, each room to itself, that she minded so much. It was the fact that with the beginning of cold weather the Merrills themselves seemed to draw into their private worlds where she could not reach them. In summer she could hear the children skating up the front walk and could run to the front door in time to latch the screen. She would stand there and argue with them. "Take your skates off. No, Debby is not going to let you in. Your Mama don't want you in here with your skates on. No. I'm too busy to bring you the machine oil. You get it yourself. I'm dusting." And then when she would start back through the house for the machine oil, Mrs Merrill, deep in another part of the house, invisible, would call as though she had seen every move. "Debby, don't get my machine oil. Don't wait on them. If they want something in the house, make them take their skates off." Then back at the door, she would argue another fifteen minutes that she was too busy to be waiting on fool children.

And in the cool of the evening she could sit on the bench, Spike under her feet, and referee Capture the Flag, deciding whether a person had said "Cawcawcaught" three times before the enemy tore away. Or if the game were Kick the Can, she would sit on the bench and watch where people hid, then point out the hiding places to Betty or Julia if either happened to be It.

The hiding games were the ones that made her so excited she could not help much with cooking supper. Long before dark when the children were hiding, Mrs Merrill would come to the door and say, "Debby." Debby would follow Mrs Merrill back to the cool sitting room where they would talk, slowly, softly, about nothing in particular, merely enough to keep the outside sounds from making her want to run and shout. "Bushel of wheat, bushel of rye, all not ready and tomorrow, Debby, bring down that other petticoat bushel of clover." It was a summertime song sung before twilight, a perfect counterpoint: the strident, unbridled chant without, the slow sad voice within, rising, rising, rising to the crest which was never reached.

Now, in winter, there was no twilight song, nothing to hold the family together. Mr Merrill was a turtle with a newspaper shell. Sometimes his head popped out at the top to announce solemnly that Roosevelt had doom doom doomed.

Usually Debby thumbed through the magazines, searching for the chubby-cheeked little girl who stood by a plate of soup large enough to swim in. The pages of the magazine were slick and cold, but the colored pictures were rough and warm to the thumb. Debby liked to wonder how the little girl could lift the huge spoon. But more than likely, she wouldn't use a spoon. She would probably lean across the large flat rim when no one was looking and lying prone, drink the soup and maybe even fall in head first. Near the little girl there was always a poem. The type though was so small that to Debby it looked gray and lacy, little ant tracks on the page. She would hold her thumb at that page while she waited for Julia and Betty to finish their lessons and read her the poem. She couldn't talk to them while they studied.

Tonight though was different from other winter nights and she was glad. At twilight when she went to the porch to bring the ferns in, she had seen the Negroes, who usually straggled along in uneven groups calling back and forth to each other, hurrying toward Negro Town in close, silent little bands. A young Negro boy with hard leather heels ran clackety-clack-clack down the street. None turned their heads to look at Debby, and it was strange because there was no storm coming up the sky.

Then Mr Merrill came home to supper, excited with a story of how a white woman had fought off a Negro man in her cellar when she went down to fire the furnace and how they had the Negro man—or one just like him—in jail. Mr Merrill said lock the doors and lock the windows.

Britt said, "You think there'll be a mob."

"No," Mr Merrill said, "they've probably moved the Negro by now."

"Where to?"

"Rogersville. Maybe even to Georgia."

Britt had been reading all afternoon as calm as you please. He had not complained even once that on this, his one afternoon off from the grocery store, he was not allowed to leave the house. Usually on his afternoon off he argued that he was being treated like a drunkard, but lately he seemed satisfied to read away the time. Now at supper he was talking excitedly, almost it seemed to Debby, wildly.

"What if a mob did gather? Would the sheriff fire on them?"

"I don't think that'll happen," Mr Merrill said quietly.

"Which? A mob or the sheriff shooting?"

"Neither."

"Say it does though. Say a mob does gather. Will the police try to protect the Negro?"

"Britton," Mrs Merrill spoke, "quit bolting your food. You've plenty of time. You're not leaving the house tonight."

"Who said anything about leaving the house?" Britt's eyes were flashing and dancing. "If it were a white man . . ."

"It wasn't a white man," Mr Merrill said with firm finality.

"It was a man though." Britt lay his fork down and dreamed at his plate with steady eyes and a curious grin. "You know," he said, "I know exactly how it feels to be lynched."

Debby turned toward Mrs Merrill because that, she knew, was who would speak next. Mrs Merrill had almost nothing on her plate and she wasn't eating that. "Britton, you're trying to get yourself and the rest of us upset. Now let's not have any more talk. It has happened and we can't help it."

"It's the Negro I'm thinking about."

"If you've got to think about it, think about the poor white woman."

There was no talking to Britton, not when he was in a mood. You could tell by the angry way he cut the meat that at the moment his concern was entirely for the Negro, and that he probably wouldn't care if every woman around were grabbed and ruined.

"Did you bring the begonia in? It was by the swing."

Deborah had forgotten the begonia. She pushed back her chair, her hands waving in preparation of speech. "I'll get it now."

"No. Finish your supper. We'll get it later."

"Is the front door locked?" Julia asked.

"Yes. The house is all locked. Now let's stop worrying. We can't be responsible for anything that happens outside."

"Can't we?" A strand of muscles showed in Britt's cheeks.

"We'll do the best we can. Other people will have to take care of themselves."

"If they call out the State Guard . . . would they call out the Guard if a mob gathers?"

No one tried to stop him from talking.

"Think how you'd feel there, waiting, knowing they were going to drag you out and lynch you."

"He should have thought of that before."

"I'll bet the window on the staircase isn't locked," Julia said.

"I know exactly how it would feel to be lynched," Britton was seeing something beyond the kitchen wall, something out past Merrill's Grove. "I was in the third grade, the year I went to Katie Powell."

So that's what he was seeing: Katie Powell Grammar school. It sat back on a tremendous green lawn and there was a railroad track between the lawn and the street. Britt had shown her the school the morning after the train wakened them in the night. The piercing whistle was from the train and not—Debby often reminded herself—from the woman who was killed that night. They said she had driven her car up on the lawn behind a boxwood, then when the train came near, she drove out on to the tracks. All that was left of her was a foot, still in the shoe, and some doubled insurance. Mr Merrill said that was one way of getting through the Depression, a very fast way. Britt was fascinated by the scene and went back three times that day. Debby had not liked the sight of all the greasy newspapers and of the scattered chunks of automobile tires. She turned and looked at Katie Powell which had been a fine home but was now a school.

"It was at first recess," Britt was saying, "you remember where the little graveyard is, between the grape arbor and the boxwoods on the far side of the school. At first recess, I was in the third grade and a boy named James Donald and I crawled under the boxwood looking for a bird nest. We saw the bird fly in and we thought there was a nest in there. We weren't supposed to go past the gravel walk because in spring that was where the jonquils came up. But we slipped over there and when we got on the other side of the boxwood there was this little iron picket fence enclosing the little cemetery. James was in the fourth grade and he said he wanted to see who was buried there so we climbed over the fence and stood up on the big stone tablets, just like two big chests sitting up on the ground. They were wet and there was moss on the brick sides that held up the tablets. Then there was a whole row of little baby tombstones and over in one corner was a square marble that looked almost new and had engraved on it: 'Dickie, A Bird.' "

"A yellow bird?" Glenn asked.

"It didn't say. It just said, 'A Bird'."

"An old buzzard, maybe," Debby said to Glenn. They liked to sit together on the back steps and watch the buzzards soaring in huge lazy circles.

"Sounds like something old Miss Katie might have done.

Buried a buzzard," Mr Merrill said to Debby. She lowered her head quickly as she always did when Mr Merrill spoke to her.

"Go on," Mrs Merrill said to Britt, "you were in the graveyard." She had quit eating and was listening as politely as if her son were a complete stranger.

"But we weren't supposed to be in there and when we started to leave James climbed up on the fence and jumped down all right," Britt continued. But when he climbed over he ripped a hole in the seat of his pants. They were black serge ones and they fit too tight anyway. When he and James got back on the playground James told everybody where they'd been and that Britt had ripped his pants. Britt sat down on the fire escape. They all ganged around and tried to make him stand up. They were tugging at him and he was hitting back when the bell rang.

Between that recess and the next he said he missed every question Miss Feltus asked him because all the boys in the class were staring at him and he knew they were just waiting for next recess. He claimed that was when he started being dumb in school, but Mr Merrill assured him he had always been dumb.

At the next recess, well sure enough, a gang started chasing him the second he got down to the bottom of the fire escape. He ran, lord how he ran. He was out of breath just remembering it. Debby was out of breath listening. He crawled up under a little building that had been a kitchen for the big house. Under there he hid behind the chimney, but they saw him. He saw the whole gang, third and fourth and even fifth and sixth graders, great big boys, surround the building. "I'll bet some of the same ones are up at the courthouse now, ready to surround the jail. Boy it'd be fun to take a machine gun . . ."

"Did they get you?" Betty asked.

"They got me." Britt said. Two big boys had crawled up under there after him. He waited. He didn't even move. They dragged him out by his heels and the other boys stood him up and beat the dust out of his pants hitting him as hard as they could. That was when he started fighting back. He scratched and kicked and bit, but it wasn't any use. They had him outnumbered. They started dragging him toward the schoolhouse where they were going to lynch him. Everybody in the whole school was in the gang by then, and they pushed right past two teachers who didn't even try to stop them. Went right on talking to each other. "There was nothing I could do." Britt glanced about the table at the masked faces as though he had not been talking out loud. "How long does it take a mob to gather?"

"If there were going to be one, it would already be under way."

"Debby," Mrs Merrill said. The two women stood up and began clearing away the dishes. "Julia, you and Betty get started on your lessons. Glenn finish eating. I want you to be through with everything on your plate by the time we're through washing these. Debby, before we forget, you'd better bring in the begonia."

Britt followed Debby into the dining room. "I'll go with you."

"I'm not afraid."

When she started in with the begonia, Britton said, "Debby, don't tell them I'm gone." She watched him run down the walk and get in the car. So he'd had the keys all during supper!

She wanted to go directly back into the kitchen and say, "Britt's gone. In the car." But he had asked her not to and it would only worry them all so she was silent as she dried the dishes and set the table for breakfast.

About nine o'clock, it must have been that late because

the children were in bed, the phone rang rang rang. Had somebody seen their son, Robert? Was he with Britt? No, Britt was upstairs in his room. There were rumors of a mob. Yes, they would send Robert home if he came over for Britton. Yes and thanks for the news because it certainly wasn't a good idea for anybody to be out if anything were going to happen—especially young boys. Well, they were hoping to send Britt to college next year. They had moved the Negro everyone believed. That was good. Still with a mob you couldn't tell what. They'd keep an eye open for Robert. And come see us sometimes.

It was then they discovered Britt had left in the car.

"Ten-forty," Mr Merrill said, winding his pocket watch for the third time since the telephone call. "He's not back yet." Mrs Merrill had long since quit pretending to sew. She left the room. Through the half-open door Debby could see her standing with a sweater shawl-like about her neck, watching car lights blaze up the street, the small red lights shooting after, and then darkness again. Debby went and stood with her on the porch.

"Go back in Debby. You'll catch cold."

"I'm not cold."

"It's your bedtime. It's long past your bedtime." Mrs Merrill's voice was hardly louder than the rustling of the winter shrubbery. "Debby, you've got to start learning to take care of yourself. We never do know what's going to happen. When I'm busy, when I've got a lot on my mind, I can't always remember to see what you're doing. It'd ease my mind a lot if you'd learn to take care of yourself."

"I get along all right."

Mrs Merrill shivered and lapped the sweater sleeves across her chest holding the cuffs under her arms. "Why does he have to do this way? We've done everything we could for him. Up until the Depression he had everything he wanted. If I could only be sure the other children would have half as much I could be happy."

A car approached slowly. Mrs Merrill stepped out from behind the column to the edge of the porch. The car drove on. Mrs Merrill leaned against the post. "Why do I deserve this?" She asked the night, for she certainly wasn't talking to Debby. "When Uncle Lee used to drink and I'd be so scared, I always said if I had a son that would be the one thing he shouldn't do. And Blessed God, if it isn't the only thing Britton seems determined to do. Lord knows I've tried to raise my children so they'd be of some account. Now, I don't know."

"Allan's a good boy." Debby said, comfortingly, and then she realized again that Allan was her own son, not Mrs Merrill's. "And I like Britton too."

"You've been good to the children, Debby."

Debby smiled to herself and shook her head slowly as though the little compliment from Mrs Merrill was too big and rare and precious to be understood in a moment. She wished Mrs Merrill would go back inside where it was light and warm. Why was she troubling herself on the porch simply because Britt was out of her sight? Britt was a big boy now. And he wasn't a husband coming home late.

"It's the colored boy they're going to lynch," Debby hoped Mrs Merrill would understand and quit worrying.

"I know, Debby. But Britton's too sympathetic. He lets his emotions run away with him and if he starts drinking . . ." She turned abruptly toward the house. "Who's he talking to?"

Mr Merrill was at the telephone. "Yes, well I'm glad Robert's at home anyway." He hung the receiver back. He picked up his hat and started out the door.

"Where're you going?" Mrs Merrill asked.

"Nowhere." Mr Merrill tried to pass her.

She grabbed his arm. "Don't answer me as if I were a fool!" Mrs Merrill was quick with anger. "Where're you going? Answer me sensibly."

"I'm going out to get Britt."

"Is he with Robert?"

"Yes," Mr Merrill said. Nervously he put his arm around Mrs Merrill's shoulder. "No. No, he's not with Robert. Robert's at home. He saw Britt uptown in a restaurant."

"Oh," Mrs Merrill said weakly. She let herself be kissed on the forehead. "And the lynching?"

"There's a good bit of excitement, I understand."

"If he's been drinking—and I know he has—don't say anything to him. Let's not fuss at him this time." Mrs Merrill held the door open. "Just bring him home." She shut the door behind her husband and walked over to the hearth. "Debby, go on to bed," she said gazing into the fire which was burning and crackling like hell itself.

Utter black dark and the telephone was still ringing as her feet touched the floor and her hands groped toward the chair for her cape-collared winter coat. Only God Almighty Himself would be ringing a telephone that long and loud at an hour like this.

"Hello. Yeah! Hello!"

Debby stood barefooted at the head of the steps, the coat around her shoulders. A painful light was shining up from the staircase pit.

God, Debby remembered from Betty's Sunday School lesson last Sunday, had called Sammy when the lad was twelve. Maybe He was calling Britt now. Britt was seventeen, but they were on a party line.

"Hello. Yes, this is Mr Merrill."

He'd better say "Yes, sir," if he doesn't want to get struck black dumb-dead by a bolt of lightning, Debby thought.

"All right. Yeah, I do have a 32 Ford. . . . Black. That's right. Yeah. I don't know. I'll check and see. Would you mind repeating that number? I say repeat the number. No one in it. Oh. Oh. Yes." The receiver clicked. "Thank you."

Back in her room Debby held a burning match lest she wake Betty while looking at the clock. The little hand pointed to one and the big hand hung not quite straight down. So it was after one, how much after she couldn't say because the long hand did not really mean the numbers it pointed to. Nevertheless, it was a late time for a telephone to be ringing. Something was wrong. She looked for a crack of light under Britt's door. He would explain it to her. He was never impatient with her as the others sometimes were. There was a cold black line under Britton's door. Then she remembered. He had run off with the car. A Negro was going to be lynched.

"Debby, standing there barefooted!" She heard it as plain as if Mrs Merrill had really said it. "Debby, you've got to learn to take care of yourself. We never know what's going to happen." She went back to her bed and put on her stockings and the high-topped shoes, the little metal tips of the strings tapping smartly against the leather as she changed the strings from hand to hand, zig zag zig zag zig around the metal hooks. Well, Mrs Merrill needn't worry, Debby thought, I can look after myself. It was true. When there was doubt about what was to be done, Debby could stand perfectly still and hear Mrs Merrill's voice as real as life telling her what to do. While she laced the shoes she heard Mr Merrill calling the bus station for a bus time and another number for a taxi. The front door slammed. The house was silent.

Cautiously Debby went down. Mrs Merrill, still dressed, was standing before the fire where Debby had last seen her. Nothing had changed except the time. There was the door through which Mr Merrill had only a minute before gone to find Britt. In a twinkling Mrs Merrill would turn and say, "Go to bed, Debby." They had lived through this moment before. Maybe it would go on and on and on, forever repeating. Maybe Mrs Merrill would never move away from the fire, morning would never come, Mr Merrill would continue walking down the walk, and Britton would never return. Something awful had happened to all the clocks in the world and so they were doomed to stand here forever in this scene that never changed.

"Go on back to bed, Debby."

Was it a dream? Surely all of this had happened before. She was simply dreaming now. Without speaking she walked to the door. She turned back to scan the room again. Suddenly the sheath of ice melted and Mrs Merrill was free to move. The clocks were ticking once more, the pattern broken.

Mrs Merrill's face was wet with tears, white and pinched and red with grief. "He's gone, Debby." She sank to the floor and cried into the sofa cushion. "They've found the car. Smashed to pieces." Her muffled sobbing was like laughter, yet sad and bottomless. "Oh ho ho. He's gone. He's gone. He can't be alive. I know it. I know it." It was wild and without end. "Britton, oh, ho ho. My poor boy." Debby watched the collapsed woman being shaken and shaken by these horrid laugh-sounds. Debby wanted to sit on the sofa and let Mrs Merrill cry on her knees. She wanted to pat her on the head and say, "There, there." She wanted most of all to cry with her. But she knew Mrs Merrill would push her away. No one could touch Mrs Merrill with pity; no one ever had.

The wind . . . a ghost . . . Glenn pushed on the hall door. They came into the room together, battling the close heat, the blind lights, and the unsteady floor. "Mama, I'm afraid."

Bewildered, still half-asleep, he stood in the middle of the room and his eyes were vague with unfinished dreams. His bare legs, thin without baby fat, disappeared under the outgrown flannel nightgown. The top frog had torn loose and the delicate collar bone formed a blue hollow with his shoulder. His straight brown hair was uncombed, rumpled with sleep so that it looked curly. That was why he had appeared a ghost, Little Britton, when the door cautiously opened.

"Mama."

Debby waited. Mrs Merrill would take him in her arms and bury him beneath her. Mrs Merrill, her hands clutching the sofa cushion, wept on without ceasing.

If he were half-asleep, would he know? Debby picked him up and sat down in the rocking chair, making a pillow of her arm. She warmed the bottom of his feet with the palms of her hand and squeezed them together. "Shhh."

"I woke up," he mumbled.

"Go back to sleep," she whispered.

"A mean old witch was chasing me. She had a whip in her hand. A peach switch like Mama uses."

"Shhh." She put her hand lightly over his mouth. "Debby's here now."

He watched the fire with eyes that grew smaller and smaller until they were completely shut. He rolled his head on her arm and buried his face in her breast.

Debby studied Mrs Merrill. Her fingers, still desperately

clutching the cushion, were red, the knuckles white. The neat, polished hair was slipping loose and one coil fell to her shoulders. Crumpled on the floor, Mrs Merrill no longer seemed large and tall and unbelievably strong. Debby watched the fire grow small, felt cold seeping into the room, heard in the far distance a rooster crowing. She nodded.

When she opened her eyes, Mrs Merrill was no longer crying. She was crawling up onto the low footstool at the hearth. She sat dumbly watching the fading flames, shivering as though she would never be warm again. She stared with an expressionless face at Debby. Her voice was flat and dull. "What do you do?" She stopped for a deep breath. "When you fail at the one thing you think God put you on this earth for?" An immense gasp came involuntarily from the center of her being. "I always said my children were going to know what it was to have a mother."

Glenn turned, his face in the light.

"When you fail." She gasped and tears jelled in her eyes and her chin trembled. "I've tried. God." Her voice was rising. Glenn struck out with his arm and groaned. "Maybe I didn't try hard enough." She buried her face in her hands and laugh-noises filled the room. Her hair was tumbling down her back. "Maybe I tried too hard!"

"Mama."

Debby stood up. He would want to go to his mother now. "Mama."

The sobbing broke. Mrs Merrill, still bending over, dried her face on the skirt of her dress. "I've tried to teach them right from wrong. I've whipped them when it'd break my heart to do it."

What was Mrs Merrill talking about, Debby wondered. Didn't she know children were made to play with and snuggle up to and love and love and love? She hugged Glenn closer to her.

"What's he doing up?" Mrs Merrill blew her nose. "Put him back to bed." She moved closer to the fire and leaned her head against the mantel column.

"Can I take him upstairs?"

"Take him," again a deep gasp, "anywhere." Her eyes filled and her cheeks became wet. "Maybe you can do better with him than I can." With not enough pride left to cover her face, she sat leaning against the mantel, crying without shame. "Take him. Debby, you've got to help me."

Debby did not wait to see if Mrs Merrill would change her mind. She had wanted almost too long for this moment to come. She closed the door and, hugging Glenn strongly to her, climbed the stairs.

"You're going to be my little boy," she whispered into Glenn's ear.

"That tickles," he said. "Do that again!"

"You're my little boy."

She knew what they would do. They would get under the cover and build a warm nest and tell bedtime stories and all sorts of Secrets.

They were at the closed door of Britton's room. Deborah hurried past. Tonight it was unpleasant to think of that room with the bare tree on which hung the hard, empty cocoons.

"You're my little boy," she whispered again, and they laughed softly together as they went into her room. "Look at the moon. See the moon there in the tree." At last a bare limb had reached out into the sky and captured the moon.

The sobbing downstairs sounded like doodley-squat.

Chapter 14

WITH Glenn sleeping cuddled into a ball at her back Debby dreamed that night of Allan Hall. When she woke in the late winter grayness she had to bend her face kissing-close to see that it was not Allan there in the bed with her. The happenings of the night before were confused and except for the fact that here, at last, Glenn was in the room with her, it was possible that nothing at all had occurred. As she dressed she convinced herself that she had only been dreaming. Even now she was not sure she was awake, because Glenn's being in her room belonged in a dream. Before she left she peeped at the face on the pillow again to make certain Allan Hall had not come back.

In the kitchen Mrs Merrill was sitting alone at the table, holding a cup of coffee with both hands, both trembling. Her eyes were red but she was not crying. "I do wonder what ever happened to Allan," Debby said turning the damper on the stove. "What?" Mrs Merrill asked absently. "I say I wonder what ever happened to my boy." Mrs Merrill breathed a shivering breath, "They found his car last night, turned over in a ditch near Rogersville. Britt hasn't been seen. All the papers say is that the Negro is safe. Mr Merrill's gone down now to find out about him." Debby cracked an egg and poured it into the frying pan. "It's just put me to wondering about my boys, Grover and Allan. I do wonder what's happened to them." Mrs Merrill seemed not to hear for a while, but then she said, "We've been selfish not to try harder to find them. We'll try again. I . . . I didn't know what it could be like to lose a child . . ." She didn't look as though she had another tear left in her, but she did—several, in fact.

Mrs Merrill had been crying all that cold night but even so she cried that day until four o'clock when Dr Bronston arrived to give her medicine. She told Dr Bronston what a sweet, sensitive, sympathetic, shy and misunderstood creature Britton had always been. The doctor held her by the wrist and talked to her about relaxing and about giving the children more freedom in all matters that did not concern their health. "They're going to grow up," he said, "in spite of everything you can do. I'm not worried about their physical health, Mrs Merrill. I told my wife once when you phoned to say Britton had stepped on a nail that I could almost tell by the tone of your voice what the child's temperature would be.

"And I've told her a dozen times that if more mothers were as sensible as you, my work would be easier. Think of all the times I've had only to listen to you over the telephone to be able to tell you what to do. Without ever seeing the child. You would have been a wonderful nurse. But children aren't invalids. Not unless you want them to be. It is not their health I'm talking about."

Dr Bronston was still there talking when the phone rang: Mr Merrill saying he had found Britt. Everything was all right. Britt was not hurt but he did not want to come home. Mr Merrill was going to let him stay and find a job. For a few minutes Mrs Merrill cried like a loon, then lay quietly on the sofa staring at the rug. Dr Bronston closed the curtains. He said to Mrs Merrill, "Try to sleep," and to Debby, "Keep the children out," and aloud to himself, "With her blood pressure that high I don't see what keeps her from having a stroke."

When he left, the gray-green twilighted room was as quiet as a muffle. In the chimney ashes glowed red, shifted, powdered, fell. In the hall the grandfather clock was going "Big Doc Big Doc Big Doc," and occasionally rumbling. The children had eaten lunch next door and there were no child noises about. A small gray mouse peeped out from behind the brass coal bucket, darted to the center of the hearth, stopped dead, moved cautiously to the other side and poked its nose at the straw in the little hearth broom. Mrs Merrill was holding the mouse in sight as though it were the very little animal that had been gnawing at her heart.

"I've been a fool." Mrs Merrill sat up suddenly and let her feet hit the floor heavily. She stood up very straight and stared into the mirror, twisting her hair into a smaller, tighter coil, stabbing it with hairpins.

"Uh oh," Debby thought, "we'll have seven years of hell."

But the year which followed was unusually happy for everyone except Mrs Merrill. The children did just about as they pleased, except for certain things. Mrs Merrill seemed afraid to speak to them. She found a list of books in Rebecca's desk on how to raise children and every week sent Julia to the library for a different book. Instead of sewing, patching and mending, in the afternoons Mrs Merrill pored over the pages. With utter weariness she laid down one book after the other. For a while after she had pushed away the last book, there was a possibility she would cry, but her voice was hard and clear. "If you don't have much education, Debby, there's not much use in trying. I don't know what they're talking about." Then she went into one of her quiet spells, the kind she had when letters came from Britt who wrote that he was never coming home to be a burden to them and again to say that he was in the CCC. If it had been a mouse gnawing at Mrs Merrill's heart before, it was a spotted beast now. She worked, she sewed, she visited the neighbors only when they were in trouble, she figured and planned unceasingly with Mr Merrill about bills and money. But also—Debby listened for it as they worked together in the kitchen—she sighed frequently and now after her quiet moods, she had headaches that blinded and deafened her.

"Go be Debby's little boy," she would say when Glenn leaned against her bed or grabbed her skirts and aprons. "Go be Debby's little boy." And since Mrs Merrill said it herself, there was no harm in Debby's saying: "You're my little boy."

At first Glenn said, "I'm not your little boy." But then after they had told stories under the cover, night after night, and snuggled warm together, he did not mind her claiming him. When others in the family mentioned Glenn and Debby, the two glanced at each other and thought about their warm Secrets. Sometimes Glenn turned suddenly away to his mother. But Mrs Merrill ate on without raising her eyes from her plate, as though she had not heard a word spoken. It was a glorious year.

With Britt and Rebecca gone, the house was quiet at night. Mr Merrill was losing the last of his temper and his sudden loud voice—still frightening to Debby—with the last of his money. In the evenings if it were winter, they sat in the back living room, Mr Merrill talking every now and then about money, both of them dreaming into the fire. Betty and Julia studied until Julia drowsed off and Betty then began making paper airplanes that often sailed straight into the fire, waking

Mrs Merrill for a moment from her dream which she never told. Glenn and Debby played marbles on the rug patterns. If the grown people weren't watching her, she knelt to shoot, spanning the way Betty had taught her. But if Mrs Merrill was watching, or even likely to, Debby sat politely on the floor, her legs drawn up under her long skirts, a lady at a picnic. She did not mind Mrs Merrill telling her how to work, but she knew more about playing than Mrs Merrill did any day.

In warm weather they took chairs into the yard and Debby and Glenn would lie in the grass and look at the stars; or Glenn wandered off to catch lightning bugs to put in the fruit jar which Debby held for him. In summer Betty played under the street lamps with a hollering crowd on skates. When she came into the yard she was usually too tired and wet-hot to bother Glenn. She stretched out in the grass and if anybody paid any attention to her she rolled back her eyeballs and pretended to be dead.

Julia never sat with them in the yard very long. No one ever noticed exactly when she wandered back into the house where she was completely out of their minds. Mr Merrill watched Julia more than he did his other children and laughed lately only at her graveness, when she was going to a party and waltzed before the mirror in an organdy dress with puffed sleeves and a sweetheart neckline. She would pause and straighten her shoulders, filling the bodice with breast. Before Rebecca's engagement was announced, Julia had walked round-shouldered as though a sweater were harsh against the tender new rosebud breasts, or as though she were embarrassed by what was happening to her. Since then however she had not been able to stand straight enough. She pointed them directly at you. Debby had made a deliberate effort to stare at her. No matter how long you fixed your eyes on Julia you couldn't remember a minute later what she looked like. It seemed to Debby that she never really saw the girl and when she thought of her it was as a baby in a white nightgown afraid to go to the light switch. Even when you tried to see her you were more apt to be seeing the hazy light on her blonde hair, or the nervous fluttering of her hands. In the same way you never heard her until she quit talking. Then you heard the echo, much louder than the timid wavering voice itself.

The only time any of the family seemed to notice her was when she was not there, and then it was not Julia they noticed but the fact that Betty and Glenn fought constantly with no one to keep peace between them. "She was a beautiful little girl," they had been saying for years, as though that little girl had died. It never occurred to anyone to say, "She's grown into an awkward child." Lately though they had taken to saying, "She is going to be a lovely woman." It was as though childhood had been unbecoming to Julia.

When she tried to read she huddled up on the sofa and went promptly, efficiently into a profound sleep. At the table she studied her food for small worms and other unwholesome things that might have dropped out of the air. She sent in coupons and got back seven shades of blended powder, a star wheel for telling fortunes, a tiny lipstick in an aquamarine tube, and her hand writing analyzed. ("You," the letter said, "are a determined person. Your aggressive personality will win you an enviable place in your profession, but unless you learn to conserve your vitality, it will also win you many enemies.")

She would go to the phone, whisper a number two or three times and say, "Margie, they came. The pictures of Gary Cooper. Did yours?" No one ever saw Margie and Mr Merrill was certain Julia called a blank number where there was no phone. Debby could imagine what the blank number room was like. It was perfectly square with white walls and white woodwork. The mirrors and pictures were turned toward the wall. The furniture was white and marble-topped. Above a small table was an electric wire sticking out from the wall. A bell under the table would ring and Julia's voice would fill the place. The lights flickered, dimmed. Then there was a nickel click and the room was again bright, square and silent.

Julia wasn't the only one who talked to herself over the phone. After every one of her headaches, Mrs Merrill went to the phone and talked to people about Allan Hall. She called orphanage homes and welfare places and asked them to write letters to other orphanage homes. Debby listened to these conversations but she knew they were make-believe in the same way that Julia's were.

One night, however, Mr and Mrs Merrill talked in whispers while Debby and Glenn shook the lightning bugs out of a wet fruit jar. Mrs Merrill was watching her, she could tell even though she did not lift her head from the game. She waited and knew exactly when Mrs Merrill would speak. She wasn't prepared, though, for what Mrs Merrill said: "Debby, we got a letter today. It's from a woman who says Allan is working on their farm."

"Who is Allan?" Glenn asked in the long silence that followed.

"Allan is Debby's son."

Glenn drew away from her, reaching out his arm to take the fruit jar from her lap.

Debby didn't know what to say. She wanted to go on playing as though Mrs Merrill had not spoken. Glenn moved toward his mother but stopped and glanced back at Debby. "Here's another lightning bug," she said, palming one that was crawling up her dress. Glenn did not move.

"Do you want to see him? He's happy there and he doesn't want to leave, but I thought, and the woman thought, you should see each other. The woman says they're going to be passing through here twice before Christmas and that they'll bring him even though they can't rightly spare him. But if you want to see him I'll write the woman."

Debby watched Glenn, and then, releasing the lightning bug that flew away without so much as blinking once, said: "If he wants to see me."

Glenn sat down in the grass and began whimpering about a splinter in his foot that had been hurting him all day long.

Chapter 15

SHE could not talk to Glenn about Allan. He wouldn't listen. In the months that followed she tried to make him forget that Mrs Merrill had invited Allan for a visit. Glenn though would not forget. He asked a thousand questions without mentioning Allan's name: "Why do you live with us? Did you used to be my mama? Are you my Mama's mama? If she goes away will you be Mama then? Will you ever grow any taller? When you get grown are you still going to live with us? Will you take me? You aren't ever going to leave me, are you?" But finally he asked: "Do you love us better than you do your own children?" She could not find an answer to this question. Maybe that was why Glenn moved over to the bed that Betty had left when she moved into the room which Britt had left. If they couldn't whisper and talk about everything there was of course no point in sleeping in the same bed.

Debby couldn't say though that she didn't want to see Allan. She didn't know. She had last seen him, thin, brown, barefooted, running across the field, frisking in a lamb dance before Nurse Janet. Now a hundred years later he was coming back. It happened on a Sunday morning. Mr Merrill came to the kitchen door and said there was to be a surprise for her, and Mrs Merrill sent her up to comb her hair and change into an afternoon dress. When she came back down, Mrs Merrill was waiting for her at the foot of the stairs saying that Allan was here only for the day but that he could come back at Christmas time. Neither he nor the people who brought him knew anything about the other child.

"Allan?" Debby turned to run back up the stairs.

"Allan Hall! Your son, Debby." Mrs Merrill grasped her by the elbow. She pulled away.

"Debby."

You go croak, Debby thought. Mrs Merrill didn't even understand her own children, much less Allan. Debby certainly didn't want the little old ragged, wormy-looking boy back. Now she would have to go out and pick berries to keep him from crying. And then when he and the baby fretted late at night nothing would keep them quiet, not even tying flour sacks about their empty bellies. She allowed herself to be led into the long living room.

Allan stood planted at the distant end, his back to the bookshelves. He was short and heavy with long arms hanging haplessly from thick, sloped shoulders. He was dark from the sun and his brow was furrowed with deep yellow wrinkles. Debby's hand clutched Mrs Merrill's skirt, the fingers pulling folds of cloth into the wet palm.

Through the shadows of the room she could see Allan lurching toward her in his heavy, shuffle-foot gait. Quickly, he seized her in a crushing bear-hug and cried "Mama, Mama." His tears fell hot on her neck, and tears from her own eyes rolled involuntarily down her face. They stood rocking in the center of the room, blind to the walls, to the Merrills who appeared and disappeared at the doors, deaf to the muffled weeping in the house and to Mrs Merrill's words from the dining room, "Leave them alone for a little while."

She was aware only of the strange odor as he pulled her head to his chest. It was like the smell of hay or of the broad plank floors where grain has been stored and been covered with dust. She wondered where he had been sleeping. The odor was not from his clothes for they smelled faintly of kerosene. "Mama," he cried, and as she wiped her wet cheeks against his rough shirt she sniffed to discover the secret of the sweet-musty odor which seeped through from the broad chest of her son. "Mama, I found you."

"Have you been sleeping in a barn?"

He didn't answer. He didn't talk much good when the Merrills were gazing at him from the doors or from the very room. But that afternoon, upstairs in her room, with no one about and a fire going, he talked fine. He shut his eyes when he spoke and pointed his chin more or less in the direction of the ceiling. He said the weather had been nice and she agreed that indeed it had. Then for a long time he sat there with his eyes closed. She shut hers too, until he spoke again. He said, "It's been nice."

"What?" she asked. Twelve years had passed.

"The weather," he said.

"It sure has," she said. And there had certainly been a lot of it.

He closed his eyes and turned blankly toward the heat of the fire. After a while he said, "It's nice here too."

"The fire?" she asked. Maybe he meant this room or the Merrills.

"The weather," he said.

"It sure is." She wished Mrs Merrill were here to see how much he knew about the weather. And oh, how wonderful it had been when he said "Mama" and wasn't talking to Mrs

Merrill! If he stayed around long enough Mrs Merrill would be trying to get him to call her "Mama," but now then he just called her "Mrs Merrill," as though she were a perfect stranger and no more kin to him than a lady baboon.

"Sometimes," he opened his frightened little eyes as wide as they would go, which wasn't much wider than a buttonhole, "it isn't though." After letting her in on this startling secret, he promptly shut his eyes.

"No, it isn't." She didn't know what they were talking about because she was busy exploring the possibility of his calling Mrs Merrill "Mama." She could not determine exactly what kin he would be to Mrs Merrill or what claim that woman would have on him. Debby wanted him to leave now, this minute, while he was still hers.

"Mama."

She knew he was only voicing a memory.

"Mama."

It sounded the way she had been waiting to hear it.

"Mama."

The tone had changed with rising excitement. He too knew how it sounded, how long they both had waited.

"Mama!"

There was an urgent rising inflection. It hurt her to see him sitting there blindly saying her name to himself.

"Mama!"

Alarm was in his voice.

"Yes."

"Where is the privy, Mama?"

She showed him the bathroom and how water ran into and out of the tub and lavatory, and how the toilet flushed. They laughed at the noise of so much running water. Then when all the noise had gurgled dry, she went outside and waited for him. She waited and waited. Mrs Merrill brought up a heaping plate of icebox cookies and told her there was coffee on the stove, milk in the refrigerator. Debby watched Mrs Merrill go downstairs, then listened again at the bathroom door to the running water. She hoped he wouldn't disappear completely.

When he came out he said, "It's fine."

"Yes," Debby said. It was indeed a lovely day for this time of year.

"You just turn the knob and water comes out."

He could swallow a cookie in one bite. She showed him how to nibble around the edge until they became smaller and smaller, from fifty-cent to dime size, then not at all. When he chewed that way, little bites, foam built up in the corners of his wide mouth and reflected the fire light. They rocked and rocked. He was in the big chair she had begged for Glenn. It was as peaceful as a grave being here with Allan. He didn't ask a thousand questions. He seemed to be staring at her through his thick eyelids. There he sat in Glenn's chair. She wondered where Glenn was this afternoon. She hadn't seen him all day. He probably wanted to come to her, but he wouldn't because Allan was here. She wished Allan would leave, that he would never come back. No she didn't. She wanted to torment Mrs Merrill by showing her who it was that he called Mama.

When they couldn't eat any more cookies, Allan picked up the dish and went to the bathroom. One at a time he dropped the cookies in, flushing the toilet after each. Julia sailed like a bird out of Rebecca's room and down the steps. Then there was laughter downstairs. Debby didn't care. They were having fun, more fun than the Merrills. They worked together, Allan dropping the cookies, Debby flushing the toilet. Then they went downstairs, as Mrs Merrill had said to do, and each drank a cup of coffee, and then a glass of milk.

Mrs Merrill came to the door and said, "They're waiting for you" and she meant some bareheaded country people who were parked in front of the house in an old Ford truck with a steaming engine. Allan untied a bucket from the hood and came back into the yard where Debby helped him with the intricate spigot. She was glad that Mrs Merrill stayed on the porch and watched while he unscrewed the cap—a regular service station man couldn't have done better—and poured water into the radiator. As he tied the bucket back in place and turned to jump up on the truck, he waved. The gesture, the high-flung hand, the casual smile, were so familiar, so like Thomas' she could have screamed with pain.

As Debby started up the walk, slowly, her head down, Glenn came around the house. He put his hand on her skirt and they walked up the steps together. In her room she gave him four cookies she had hidden from Allan and they sat down before the fire to talk about Christmas. As they talked they forgot that such a person as Allan Hall had ever been there. "I'm going to give three Christmas presents this year. One to your Mama and one to you." She didn't tell him that the third present was for Allan. Mrs Merrill had said, "Give Allan the handkerchiefs I'm making, but you mustn't give me anything. There's not a thing you can give me—except to help me get through Christmas."

"What are you going to give Mama?"

"You won't tell."

He crossed his heart.

"Some elastic to make garters out of." She had given Julia the money to buy the presents with.

"What are you going to give me?"

"A . . ." she almost told him. "A surprise."

They began the game again. "Will I like it? Is it alive? Is it big, little, fat, thin, square? Does it make a noise? Is it to eat, play with, wear?" Finally she opened the trunk, and took the brown bag from the tray. "It's a pencil." It wasn't an ordinary pencil though. It was a foot long and as big around as the top of a catsup bottle. It was red, white and blue, flecked with gold and silver. There had never been anything like it in the house before.

"And what are you going to give me?"

He grinned sheepishly. "I haven't got anything yet, but I'm going to give you something." Then quickly he added, "Let's see if it'll write. Write us something on this bag."

"You write it."

He drew heavy black lines on the paper, chewing on his tongue which was sticking out the corner of his mouth. When he looked up and saw her watching him he grinned. She knew then that it would not make any difference if Allan did come back again.

Mrs Merrill came to the door; she had a way of appearing always at the wrong time. "Debby, you've got a big strong boy." Glenn started over to show his mother the pencil, then stopped and hid it behind his back. Mrs Merrill asked: "Did Allan say anything about coming back?"

"Just at Christmas time."

"He didn't mention coming back after that?"

"Not that I remember."

"Well, if he doesn't mention it, don't you, unless you really want to see him." She hesitated. "Now if you really want to see him, well of course you can . . ."

Debby wasn't sure. Something though was troubling Mrs Merrill.

Mrs Merrill cleared her throat and finally spoke, "He didn't mention Julia did he?"

"No, he didn't mention anybody. Why, did Julia want to see him?"

"No, no," Mrs Merrill opened the door. "It was just that I didn't like the way he watched her."

"He was probably just trying to see her," Debby explained.

"Anyway," Mrs Merrill said, "let's not mention his coming back after Christmas unless you're particularly anxious to see him."

Debby watched Glenn who looked as though he were going to follow his mother out of the room. "I'm not anxious to see him," she said, and waited to see if Glenn would leave.

Chapter 16

SURPRISES were coming in bunches now—like bananas. First Allan came and then a letter from Rebecca saying Raymond and his family wanted to come and meet the Merrills, Julia was off visiting for three days and now, Jingle Bells, Christmas was almost here. The house smelled of pine and cedar. And it looked a sight: holly sprouting out from behind picture frames, mistletoe from chandeliers, and a live tree growing in a brass bucket in the living room. Silly wasn't the word for it, but they carried on like this every Christmas, because it was Jesus Christ's birthday. Sunday, two days before Christmas, Allan came back, just as he and they had said he would.

He brought a paper sack which held a long flat box wrapped in holly paper and tied with a red ribbon. On the bow was a lovely corsage of patent leather holly leaves with glass berries. Debby and Allan were upstairs alone when he gave her the package. "My goodness!" she said; that's what Mrs Merrill would have said. She shook the box and listened to the clatter. "Gloves, I'll bet you got me some gloves." She rattled the box again. It sounded like marbles but that was the buttons hitting together. "I'll bet they're warm mittens."

She certainly did need some gloves. She didn't want little thin gray suede dress gloves. She wanted some of those big blue and yellow canvas ones like the garbage man had. He let her try them on one day and the big wide stiff tops came almost to her elbows. They had leather palms and were the nicest things ever—exactly what she needed for bringing in coal and wood. All the thin little gloves on the back porch safe were about worn out, all ragged at the fingertips. She rubbed her thick fingertips over the shiny patent-leather leaves and over the little glass berries. "Aren't they pretty," she said. "And I know to my heart it's gloves."

"No it's not!" Allan was beside himself with joy. He tore the paper bag the present had been in. "It's beads!"

"Beads! My goodness! I can use some beads."

"Open them."

"Not yet. It isn't Christmas."

"Open them anyhow."

He placed half of the paper bag on the updraft and watched it float out of sight up the chimney, then the other half. "Debby," she could hear Britt saying in that strange, sad voice, "would you know what to do if the house caught on fire?"

"I haven't given you your present yet. You wait here." She went downstairs and asked Mrs Merrill to wrap Allan's present. Mrs Merrill was grating coconuts for the cake which wasn't to be a fruitcake this year because a fruitcake needed a lot of things in it that weren't in the pantry. Mrs Merrill dusted her hands and wrapped the present. In the box were six white handkerchiefs as big as dinner napkins. Mrs Merrill, way last August, had got on the streetcar one day and ridden out to the Parthenon Cotton Mill and bought a big bundle of white scraps for twenty-five cents. She marked off blue squares, holding the pattern this way and that, and cut out an inch stack of handkerchiefs. She rolled and whipped the hems at night while she talked and figured with Mr Merrill about selling insurance instead of stocks and about not being ashamed of going down into Negro Town to sell ten cent policies. He said even the Negroes laughed now at the way the wrecked car rattled, but Mrs Merrill sewed and talked as quietly as if her husband had merely said he was tired of breathing. On the six handkerchiefs for Debby to give, she embroidered a white "H" and that stood for "Allan" Debby remembered as she went up the steps, holding the box of handkerchiefs. Allan had the door open, waiting.

"I'll bet it's a harp," he said.

"It's handkerchiefs."

"Handkerchiefs," he said.

They sat in the two chairs before the fire with the presents in their laps. It was a sunny December day, not much like Christmas weather at all. Debby studied the package in her lap. No matter how long she stared, it would never be gloves.

"Who would have thought you would give me a present!" she said gaily. But then the room was quieter than ever.

Allan closed his eyes. "The people I live with. She said I ought to get you something."

"Beads?" Debby asked.

"She said beads would make a nice present."

"Wasn't that thoughty of her!" Debby tried again to make the room sound Christmasy. Allan sat with his eyes closed, his hands not touching the box in his lap. Debby waited for him to open his present. When he kept his eyes shut, she began worrying the corsage on her box. She found the little wire and uncoiled it from the ribbon. The corsage came off and she held it in the flat palms of her rough hands.

"Merry Christmas!" she said.

"Me too," Allan said.

Debby wished Rebecca were at home. Rebecca knew how to make a houseful of Christmas. She wasn't coming home though, Mrs Merrill said, until after Christmas and that was when the coconut cake was for. Rebecca was spending Christmas with Raymond's family and then they were all going to come here—Rebecca, Raymond, his family, all of them were going to spend a day with the Merrills. That was why there was so much work to be done. "Don't work yourself to death," Rebecca had written, "but I do hope everything can be nice."

"I wish you could stay and meet these folks that are coming," Debby said. "You could help us entertain them."

"I'm not much of a hand at meeting folks," Allan grinned at her with his eyes closed.

"Rebecca is thinking about marrying that boy."

Allan didn't answer. Debby slid the ribbon over the corner. "Aren't you going to unwrap yours?"

"I suppose so." He broke the string, clawed the paper off, pried the box open. He fingered the white embroidered "H." "Handkerchief," he said.

"Handkerchief," Debby said, "and for 'Allan Hall.' "

He touched the handkerchief gingerly, with great respect now that he understood that the "H" meant his name. "I sure will keep these," he said, "right in this very box."

Debby unwrapped her package. The beads leapt up and spilled over the sides, white, purple, gold. The white beads were on a long string and were carved to resemble the kernels of chinaberries. The purple and gold beads were on a shorter string. The purple beads were square; the gold beads were round. Debby sniffed them. They had a good brassy odor.

She stood before the mirror and slid the beads over her head. She wore a square apron, a black dress and Britton's big sweater with the heavy collar. It had originally been white but when Britton left, Mrs Merrill dyed the sweater black for Debby. Since then it had been washed so many times it had faded out to a dull purple, and the collar, where it rubbed against her neck, was almost white again. Debby let the beads hang on the outside of the buttoned sweater. The white strand hung almost to her knees. The purple and gold ones barely reached around the heavy collar. While Allan burned the wrappings and ribbons, Debby pinched her cheeks and patted at her graying hair which was twined into a tight coil on top of her head. The light from the grate made a shaggy halo of the broken hair which had escaped from the braids.

A fire bell was ringing.

"Always always always," it was Mrs Merrill's voice coming to her from the back of her mind, "hold paper down with a poker till it burns." Allan had watched while the two parts of the paper bag drifted up the chimney, and while the glowing tissue floated upward.

The fire truck was still far away, but coming closer.

"What would you do if the house caught on fire?" Britt's voice. Her own voice: "Burn up, I reckon." His: "The sheets, the sheets, the sheets."

The fire truck, still far off, was louder.

"We've set the house on fire!"

"O.K. Let's do!"

"The sheets," she grabbed the cover off her bed. "Help me."

He grabbed the cover off Glenn's bed.

"You shouldn't have let the paper go up the chimney."

"Here's some more." He picked up the remaining tissue present paper. "There's plenty left."

"Tie the corner together." She couldn't control her fingers.

They tied the sheet corners together while the siren roared nearer.

"Tie this end to the bed," Debby was shaking so she could hardly raise the window. What in God's green name would Mrs Merrill say? "Debby, you've ruined my house! Look at it!" That's what she said about cakes.

She unhooked and pushed the screen. It fell and caught on the shrubbery, by the driveway. A man on the pavement stopped and watched. He was holding a Christmas tree. "He's seeing the fire," Debby thought. She could not move.

"This end's tied to the bed."

"Throw them out." They watched the sheets unfurl to the driveway. Two more people, a man, a girl, both laden with packages, stopped. Three more people came running up. "It must be an awful blaze," Debby whispered.

They stood in the window and watched a crowd gathering in the street. They leaned out to see if there were any people directly in front of the house. A man ran up on the porch next door. He banged on the door.

The siren was screeching now.

"Let's go!" The howling of the siren had her heart pounding. They ran out the door, down the stairs.

"The house's on fire! House's on fire!" she was hollering.

"Fire! Fire! Fire!" Allan had a huge voice.

They ran down the steps, through the house, out the back door. At the gate to Merrill's Grove they stopped. Mrs Merrill was running down the steps, drying her hands on her apron. As she ran, in quick little steps, she glanced over her shoulder at the roof. A man bounded up into the side yard and held the end of the sheet. "Come on," he screamed.

"Here they come, here they come." Allan was panting.

The fire trucks roared nearer; with an unbearable fury

they passed the house. "Here!" the crowd hollered. The trucks screeched to a stop, backed up, the engines pounding.

"Bring a ladder!" The man in the yard yelled to a fireman who was running toward the porch with an ax. He turned back. Two firemen hauled a ladder off the truck. They raced into the yard.

"Lord, they're going in my room!" Debby said. The ladder was leaning against her window and a fireman was crawling up. She and Allan ran to the side yard and stood behind a bush. "Oh my trunk," she said. The black elastic and the grand pencil were in the trunk tray, and the many colored box she was going to put Mrs Merrill's present in. "They'll burn up, sure as anything." There wasn't a flame in sight though. Only a thin line of smoke trailed off from the chimney.

"Where's the fire?" The fireman hollered from Debby's room.

The fire chief glared up at him, then at Mrs Merrill who was standing at the foot of the ladder. "Where's the fire?" he asked.

"Who called you?" Mrs Merrill's voice was trembling. She was watching the bush behind which Debby and Allan were standing.

"Why," the fire chief wavered, "Bateman's Grocery Store." He turned to a fireman who was holding the hose. "Who turned in the alarm?"

"Bateman's Store," the fireman said weakly. "That's where they said."

"Then what are you doing in my upstairs?" Mrs Merrill glanced quickly away from the bush where Debby was standing.

The chief politely removed his helmet and scratched his

head. "Joe," he yelled. The fireman stuck his head out the window. "What're you doing up there?"

"Looking for a fire," Joe said.

"I hope they don't find one," Debby said, "because I'm certainly not dressed to go to a fire." She lifted the beads over her head and tucked them neatly away in her sweater pocket.

"Any signs of one?" the chief asked.

"Yonder!" the fireman answered, pointing at the horizon where a cloud of black smoke was boiling up from the treetops. It was Bateman's Store all right.

"Back on the trucks!" the Chief yelled. As the fireman ran toward the trucks, the Chief looked suspiciously at Mrs Merrill. "Lady," he said, "just one thing. What are those sheets doing hanging from the window?"

"Drying," Mrs Merrill said, her face expressionless.

"Oh," the Chief said. He raised his helmet in a farewell gesture as he backed respectfully away.

"You're stepping on my boxwoods," Mrs Merrill said sternly.

"Sorry," he said, retreating faster. "Sorry to have caused you any trouble."

"Don't mention it," Mrs Merrill said flatly.

The chief ran and jumped on the truck which was already moving down the street. Debby and Allan stepped out from behind the bush and watched the trucks roll away and the crowd thin out. There simply wasn't any way of knowing what people were going to do next—especially firemen.

Chapter 17

EVERYBODY liked the fire. The upstairs and roof of Bateman's store had burned rapidly, but the downstairs had been saved by the tardy, shamefaced firemen. The stock was watersoaked and the labels washed off of almost every can in the store. After the insurance man had settled his claim, Mr Bateman called his customers and invited them to come in and buy at ridiculous prices. Mrs Merrill borrowed a twenty dollar bill from Debby. She and Betty went down with a wheelbarrow which Betty brought home stacked high with bright silver cans. Paper labels were slapped across some at crazy angles. She unloaded the wheelbarrow on the back steps. Before Debby and Glenn could tote all the cans to the kitchen, Betty was back with another wheelbarrowful.

"Debby, you ought to see that place!" Betty had been the source of all the news, and now, with pride, she hitched her fingers in the straps of her tight-fitting overalls. "Water two feet deep all over the floor. People walking on a gang-plank made out of twenty-five-pound bags of sugar. Right down the middle of the store. Mama's sitting on the counter with Mrs Bateman and Mrs Butts. She lets me do the wading. Robert Butts was wading barefooted for his mother but he cut his foot on a jar of pig's feet that busted. Biggest mess you ever saw. All the Negroes in town are standing on the street waiting for the white folks to get through buying. Mr Bateman's laughing and having himself a time. Mama's bought this much more stuff. We got it set in an orange crate on the meat counter. Here, Glenn, you and Debby divide this." She poured him a double handful of candy-covered blow gum. "I got all that for a penny. Not counting all this I got in my jaw."

"Let me give you some money to get us some more stuff." Debby had spent little of the money she had been paid in her early years at the Merrill's, but lately Mrs Merrill had let her buy a few things, always saying, "I don't know how, but we'll pay you back someday."

"Can't wait! Can't wait! Got to go!" Betty ran down the drive, the wheelbarrow bouncing before her. She was a real show-off when she got into those overalls. And with her hair shingled like a boy's, she didn't act natural in anything else. During the week, when she wore dresses she was like an awkward cripple, but on Saturdays, everyone might as well scatter.

"Biggety little devil," Debby said. Betty was getting too mean to think about. Mrs Merrill, for instance, had known roughly what was in the cans when she bought them, but by the time Betty had thrown them in the wheelbarrow, joggled up the street at breakneck speed, and rolled them out on the backsteps, pickled beets had turned into big hominy.

After that day the meals were interesting if not especially appetizing. One day they had three different kinds of sauerkraut when what they had hoped for from the size of the cans was green peas, tuna fish, and dessert peaches. During the week that followed the neighbors often came or sent empty cans with a word saying what was likely to be found in one of that shape and size. Luckily, Mrs Merrill had brought home two sacks of cans herself. She put these in a safe place in the butler's pantry because she wanted to be sure of having a nice dinner for Raymond's family.

"Everything has got to be nice then. It has *got* to be," Mrs Merrill had said a thousand times. She put aside certain clothes that weren't to be worn until that day. She and Debby washed the woodwork in the living room and dining room. She made Debby a new dress for the Andersons' visit because she was afraid Debby might spend her remaining money foolishly instead of for clothes. The afternoon before the Andersons were to arrive she sent Betty and Glenn down for haircuts. That night Mrs Merrill walked around and around the dining room table with a letter from Rebecca in her hand. She would mutter: "I wonder if she meant this dish. I wonder if she'll think the candles are tall enough." Finally she said, "I've done the best I can," and cut off the light.

Debby of course slept like a hunted rabbit all night, waking by jumps and starts. At daybreak she was sitting in the kitchen waiting for Mrs Merrill to come and get her started, tell her what to do, and what to do next. Glenn could not understand why she could not stop and play with him, just for a little while, as she did every morning. She didn't even have time to peep out with him to watch the company coming up the walk. He came back and told her about how dressed up the Andersons were.

"I won't know how to act around them," Debby said later while Rebecca was showing the Andersons the town, "if they're that dressed up."

"They're just people, Debby. Don't be fooled by all their

talk and clothes. When people aren't sure of themselves they have to hide in fine clothes and brag about their grandfathers, who, if the truth were known, probably weren't worth shooting. You can usually tell what kind of families people come from without their telling you. I like for people to be proud of their first names, not their last." Mrs Merrill finished grating the coconut and began opening a can. She stopped and sighed. "This has *got* to be diced fruit." It was and she finished making the ambrosia. She slapped Glenn's hand when he reached for a pearly yellow-green grape. He turned so red with anger that Debby thought his hair might actually singe. Tears stood in his eyes and she waited for them to go sizzling down his face, but he pressed his lips tightly together and glared.

"Find a place for this in the refrigerator. As near the ice as you can." She handed the dish of ambrosia to Debby who found a place on top of the ice which was certainly near enough. Before she closed the refrigerator door she grabbed out the grape and slipped it to Glenn. He set it on the table and wandered uncertainly out of the room. Debby put the grape in her apron pocket. Maybe he would eat it later, maybe she would, but at the moment she could not eat anything. She had heard so much about the dinner that by the time Raymond and his family came back from sight-seeing with Rebecca, she had lost all interest in food. Half-heartedly she scraped the celery, pausing to study the coarse blond curls that stuck to the wet butcher knife.

"You're tired, Debby. Go on upstairs." Mrs Merrill sighed as she opend the oven door.

"I didn't say I was tired."

"You are though. Go take a good bath while the water's hot. And then rest a few minutes before dressing."

"You're the one what's tired."

"I'm going to stop in a minute. Just as soon as Bertha comes to finish up dinner and get her dishes ready for serving."

While the tub was filling, Debby opened her trunk and found the half-full bottle of bath salts, given to her by one of the sweet-smelling ladies at the home. With effort she opened the rusty top. The sticky lumps of pink purple crystals had lost none of their odor, which was every bit as lovely as funeral air. She rummaged through the boxes and ribbons until she found the square tin box of bath powder and the bar of lavender soap with its disappearing rose shape. She had been saving the bath salt, powder, and rose for an occasion.

For a week now she had thought that perhaps the dinner party might be the occasion. This morning when she had caught a glimpse of Raymond, his mother, father and a sister, or maybe an aunt, all elegantly dressed, she had been certain that this was the day for finery. "Rebecca won't have any reason to be ashamed of me," she said happily. This morning the shining white cloth, the glittering goblets, and the soft gleaming silver which milkily reflected red from the flowers, ribbons, and fire had stirred an uneasiness in her. "There're so many knives and forks, I won't know what to eat with," Debby said. "Aren't you going to eat early with Glenn?" Rebecca asked. Debby waited for Mrs Merrill to answer. "She's worked hard and she's going to eat with us." There was firm finality in Mrs Merrill's tone. "It doesn't make any difference to me," Rebecca was crawfishing, "I merely thought there'd be less confusion if there weren't so many at the table."

"Debby," Mrs Merrill said, "let's you and me eat in the kitchen then. She can tell her fine friends she's ashamed of us."

"Oh, Mama. You have to take everything so personally. I said . . ."

"You said you thought Debby was going to eat in the kitchen. Well she's not. She's been working like a slave for three weeks getting this house clean. I had to stop her from washing windows on the coldest day. She's been thinking about nothing except this dinner, and she's going to sit at this table if not another soul does." Mrs Merrill whirled through the door into the butler's pantry.

Rebecca smiled and kissed Debby on the forehead. "Certainly you're going to eat with us. Mama misunderstands everything." That's what Debby loved about Rebecca: she was the only person who would stand her ground with Mrs Merrill. Rebecca could make everything seem fun and like a party. Even Mr Merrill who rarely spoke now was talking again and had had a haircut. Debby wished Rebecca would stay at home. Then the house would not be full in every room of the sight and sound and air of Mrs Merrill.

Still thinking about Rebecca, Debby poured the bath salts into the tub and filled the bottle with water to swish out the stubborn crystals. She ran her fingers through the pink cone of salts—a goldfish castle—and spread them out to form a carpet on the bottom of the tub. By the time the crystals had disappeared the water was pure perfume. She shut her eyes and breathed through her nose. The odor was so wonderful, so nearly like the one she had wished for, she was afraid to open her eyes again. There was only one thing more it needed, and if she had not already undressed, she would go fetch it. Vanilla. A dash of vanilla would make the bath perfect. Before Mrs Merrill allowed her to wear a little perfume on Sundays, she had been in the habit of dabbing vanilla—or lemon extract, depending on her mood

—behind each ear and on her upper lip. She had become partial to vanilla.

She lowered herself into the warm water. The bath was not as comfortable as she had expected. Some of the crystals had remained hard and sharp; some had melted to paste. Lying in the tub with the bar of rose soap almost floating off her navel when she breathed, she thought again of the grand dinner party. Raymond's father would turn and say, "And who is the sweet-smelling little lady down at that end of the table." Raymond's mother would say, "Doesn't she smell sweet!" Rebecca would be proud then, but she wouldn't let anyone know. She'd lower her eyes to her plate and remark casually, "Oh, that's Debby. She always smells that way." She would pat her foot and answer, "You all smell good too."

Again she remembered the picture she had glimpsed through the dining room door. It was practically a dream, it was so strange, so remote, and so beautiful. She had seen the people Rebecca would live with the rest of her life. That was a big thing to see. Here Rebecca had always been in this house with her mother and father, sisters and brothers, and then she had gone off to school and met Raymond. Now she was going to marry Raymond and his family would be her family. And she, Debby, herself, had caught a glimpse through the door of Raymond's family, which would be Rebecca's family. The oddness of growing up and changing families came to her with a sudden, bewildering sadness. Only the happy happy fact that she had been allowed to see the people who would be Rebecca's people, softened that grief.

Mr Anderson, Raymond's father, had been sitting in a chair smoking a cigar. He was as stately and white headed as those men who sit against red walls on the slick back-covers of magazines. Mrs Anderson, in a dark green dress, with a heavy gold chain about her neck, reminded Debby of a green parrot she had once seen chained to a perch, but when Mrs Anderson laughed and spoke, it was with a bold voice, hearty and as Rebecca had said, "Horsey." The aunt, strangely enough, had a long horsey face but she laughed and talked with bird noises. Debby had often noticed that people's voices frequently got in the wrong bodies. During the morning when she remembered the scene, she rearranged the voices, so that Mrs Anderson both looked and sounded like a bird while her sister, Eveline, had the face and the speech of a thin horse. While Debby had been tiptoeing around in the dining room, she had listened to the living room conversation: first the booming words of the Andersons, then the soft, whispering Merrill voices.

"Up and at 'em!" Debby sounded Betty's battle cry. She would not allow the Andersons to overwhelm the family. She sat up suddenly and scrubbed her arms and back with the putty-soft wad of lavender soap. It quickly disappeared. She sank under the water and washed the flesh-colored foam off. It was a shame to let such fine fragrant water go down the drain. Reluctantly she pulled the stopper up, wishing while the water gurgled out that she had a trunk full of frosted bottles to preserve it in.

Half-dry, she slapped at herself with the pink-gray powder puff from the square tin box of bath powder. She poured a tablespoonful of it into each palm and doused it under her arms and breast—with just a dab for the navel. "Uhmm, uhmm, this is glory!" she said aloud.

Mrs Merrill had told her exactly which underclothes and black petticoat to wear, which gun-metal hose, and low shoes, so she had no choice in these. With a frown she slid the plain, tailored black dress over her head. It fit perfectly even without a belt. She remembered how delighted Mrs Merrill was at having found the remnant on a bargain counter. "Debby, you couldn't want nicer material." Debby said, "I know it," but actually she knew the cloth could have been finer. It could have been bright red.

While her face was still damp, she slapped it with the soft puff until a cloud of powder started her to sneezing: one, two, three, four. Often she sneezed as many as twelve times before quitting. Everyone in the house usually stopped and counted out loud. Today they would be too busy entertaining Mr and Mrs Haughtybell. The powder settled and gave a nice frosted touch to her shoulders. Debby considered leaving it there to brighten up the black dress, but finally brushed it off. Her face was white except for her nose which was red from sneezing. She repowdered it with a delicate touch. Her graying hair blended nicely with the blank white face. She could not avoid smiling at her own deftness. "I'm handsome enough to be sat up with and buried," she said.

At the idea of death she realized what was wrong with the dress. It was a shroud, tailored for a corpse. A fleeting thought disturbed her about Mrs Merrill and death and why Mrs Merrill had made a dead woman's shroud for her to wear to an important dinner party. She searched for the thought to study, what the meaning meant, but her mind was again calm, her steady eyes studying the smooth white face, as pretty and soft and white as biscuit dough.

She let her hair down and twisted it around into a loose afternoon-do, with a bobbing pompadour. At the little v-neck with the collar like an open shirt's, she pinned the small gold pin, two snakes fighting, a grapevine growing, or whatever the gold tubes represented. It didn't make much of a show.

"Miss Debby. They say come." Bertha was holler-whispering from the stairs.

"All right, Bertha." Debby whirled elegantly before the mirror, glancing over her shoulder. She opened the door. "I'm almost ready." How wonderful that had been, to have a servant call and ask you to present yourself. She laughed and felt reckless and ladylike.

"I can wear all my jewelry," she said and even her voice sounded to her like someone's, not hers.

She opened the walnut box where she kept her marbles. The beads were there as shiny as ever. She slid the purple and gold strand over her head, then the white ones that reached almost to her knees. The white beads dangled so wildly when she moved that she tucked them under her belt and let them hang in one double straight line down her skirt. She opened the box again and picked out the hollyberry corsage with the patent leather leaves. She had never felt so dainty in all her life as when she pinned the corsage on her left shoulder. She wished Bertha would call again while she was patting the leaves into place so that she could tilt her chin, arch her throat and call back, "Yes, Bertha."

She lifted her skirt as though it were very long with a heavy train. It did not matter that her knickered knees were showing, for there was majesty in the gesture and in the stilted, yet swaying gait by which she descended the steps and, lowering her skirt, entered the noisy dining room.

Yellow light shone softly from the white tapers, from the oakwood fire and through the fading silk curtains. Fires danced in the gold-leaf mirror over the sideboard, from the silver chafing dish and the water goblets, and ran in liquid lines around the diamond shaped patterns of the punch bowl centerpiece, piled high with nuts, apples, oranges, grapefruit and holly. As she shut the door, the candle flames bowed to her.

The click of the doorlatch was all that was needed to shatter the ringing cutglass laughter. They had been standing in a circle, a Merrill, an Anderson, a Merrill, about the table, their hands lightly touching the carved grapes on the curved backs of the rosewood chairs. Now with fixed grins they arranged themselves as though for a photograph, to see who had entered the room. They stood absolutely partified—as still as if they had seen a real wild-haired, wild-eyed photographer standing there. If she'd had a black cloth to hide under she could have taken their pictures a dozen times before anyone stirred.

"Ahem!" coughed Mr Merrill.

Debby, pleased, fingered the purple and gold beads at her throat. Mr Merrill hadn't known she could look like this. She wished Glenn were here to see her.

Mrs Merrill in a molasses-slow walk moved toward her across the room. "This is Mrs Hall, Debby, who's been with us for a long time. Mrs Anderson, Miss Whitmire, Mr Anderson, and Raymond."

Debby nodded to each. She had been planning to say, "How do you do?" but her throat was too dry for that. She tried to catch Rebecca's eye to see the pride in it, but Rebecca was staring at her plate which, from the expression on her face, was full of snakes. She wouldn't raise her head; Raymond was watching her.

When they sat down to the table, Betty and Julia, who had been placed on opposite sides so they couldn't whisper, glanced across at each other. Then a terrible thing happened. In the middle of the company-blessing which Mr Merrill was reciting, the two girls giggled. Debby reached under the table and touched Betty's knee. Betty opened her eyes, which were wet with laugh-tears, and burst out into loud laughter. She pushed back her chair and ran from the room.

"I'm sorry," Mrs Merrill said. "Betty is . . ." But no one was listening. Julia was acting strange, holding her napkin up to her mouth.

"Julia," Mrs Merrill said. Julia dropped the napkin. She was as serious as a baby. "Excuse me," she said.

Debby glanced about the table. She smiled at Miss Whitmire. That woman answered back with a nervous, uncertain smile. Rebecca was still watching her plate, and Raymond was looking at Rebecca. Mrs Anderson was fluttering a napkin trying to get it into her lap. Mr Anderson sipped water. Debby had never seen such dull people. They didn't even know they had come to a party. She had worked hard to clean the house, wash the woodwork, and if they wouldn't be sociable, she would. Mrs Merrill had said, "Don't mention the food," but she had to talk about something to end the silence and begin the party. She smiled down the table. "I'm simply ravished!" she said.

Mr Anderson choked on water and turned the goblet over as he set it blindly on the rim of his plate. Then everybody talked at once and laughed, not politely, but really.

They can thank me, Debby thought, watching Mr Anderson drying his eyes, for starting the party. She intended now to eat and listen, but if anyone wanted to tell her how sweet she smelled she would say "Thank you." With immense pride she let her eyes follow the line of the magic circle about the table: Anderson, Merrill, Anderson, Merrill, a purple bead, a gold one. The dinner party had at last begun. She wished that Glenn could be here with her so that later they could tell each other about it, talking, whispering and laughing about everything, waiting for sleep and dreams and another happy morning.

Chapter 18

GLENN had never seen snow before. Oh, two or three times there had been some mixed in with rain, and once damp flakes which sank immediately into the ground. But never in the six years of his life had the back yard and Grove been dazzling white. He stood on a chair at the kitchen window, Debby beside him. How in the world could she get him dressed if he couldn't leave the window for a second? Already Mrs Merrill was scraping the toast which Debby had forgotten to watch.

"Debby Debby Debby." He pounded on her shoulder.

"Look, but don't kill me."

"Snow snow snow."

She caught his hand and held it from beating her. With her arm around him she kept him from dancing off the chair.

"Where is the lavender snow?" He peeped around the window sill. "And the pink snow and the red snow."

"You won't see that till sunset."

"You said it would be blue and red and white and all colors." His voice trailed off into nothing as he breathed clouds on the windowpane.

Why had she been so anxious to wake him? Now he knew as much about snow as she did and there was precious little left for him to ask her about. What would take the place of all the questions? How could she fascinate him into staying in the kitchen with her? "Glenn, see this flour coming through the sifter? That's sorta like snow." "Debby, if we threw flour everywhere would Betty think it had snowed?" "If we put flour in the icebox and then took it out would that be snow?" "If we chipped up some ice into little old bitty pieces, say in the meat grinder, would that be snow?" "Is snow like dandruff?" "Is it kinda like a cold sheet?" "When it melts does it look like milk like ice cream?" "Does it taste like vanilla ice cream?" "What does it smell like?"

She wished now that she hadn't wakened him. Mrs Merrill had made her wait until the kitchen was warm before allowing her to bring Glenn down. She had stood him on the chair and then quickly let the shade flap up and around.

At four that morning she had casually opened her eyes; some noise, or perhaps the complete, dead silence, had disturbed her sleep; and before she turned her face toward the window she knew she would see snow. Silver lights, lavender shadows haunted the room, she gazed peacefully, the white pear tree was heavy with snow-blossoms. Since the beginning of winter she had promised Glenn a world such as this, a world he could not imagine because he had never, as she had, seen one.

Pushing off the heavy covers, she slipped her feet to the floor and, pulling the coat around her shoulders, tiptoed over to where Glenn was asleep in Betty's outgrown bed. He was on his stomach, his arms stretched out under the pillow as though he were holding his head on a tray and would, in a minute, holler "Join-The-Baptist or they'll kill you too."

She reached out her hand to touch his shoulder. "There is snow on the ground. It snowed during the night." Through the muffled quietness she heard Mrs Merrill whisper: "Don't wake him, Debby. He's a growing boy." Her hand paused. It had been almost two years since she brought him upstairs, but always when she was with him she heard Mrs Merrill telling her what to do, what not to do. If she and Glenn could leave the house, be out of sight and sound of Mrs Merrill, he would belong to her. They had talked about running away, but since January he had had to go to school every morning except Saturday and that was her busy day. She let her hand drop to her side and, shivering, went back to bed.

She tried while watching his sleeping face to know what it would be like when he saw the snow. Maybe he wouldn't believe it was real and in that case no one could persuade him to stay at the window. There had probably been ten people more stubborn than Glenn in this world, but she didn't know who they were—Chinamen probably. Everyone else in the house could button buttons as well—or almost as well—as she could. Yet he would not let anyone but her help him dress. "You don't know how!" He would kick at Mrs Merrill. "That's not right!" He would tear the buttons off. Then he would get slapped.

He wouldn't cry though until he got choking red-faced mad. Sometimes he came sobbing into her room with the startling news that he was going to cut off the heads of all his family with an ax. Of course he couldn't handle an ax, so Debby always suggested a butcher knife. Then, in bloody talk with gray brains spilling, they would discuss the advantages of various weapons: Ice picks, monkey wrenches, saws, hammers, nails; until, drying his cheeks with the backs of his hands, Glenn suddenly laughed and grabbed her around the neck. "You're going to cut off my wind," Debby would play at loosening his arm grip. "I'm going to love you to death," he would say grimly. She wished they could be alone now, free to look at the snow as long as they pleased and without Mrs Merrill listening to every word.

"Yonder? Why are the fenceposts white on that side?"

Mrs Merrill glanced over their shoulders. "It's the direction from which the wind was blowing."

"Why aren't they white all over?"

"I just said: the wind was blowing from that direction."

"Debby, what does she mean?"

"She means the wind was blowing that way."

"Oh," Glenn said and made lip prints on the breath-stained window.

"It's a strange thing you can understand anything Debby tells you and nothing I say." Mrs Merrill was hopping-mad. "Get ready for school."

"Now Mama, I'm not going to school!"

Mrs Merrill raised her eyebrows and stared at him through the top of her glasses. "I'd like to know the reason you're not!"

"There's snow on the ground and I'm not going to school."

"You most certainly are!"

"Now Mama, I'm not! It'll be all melted by the time school's out."

"You're going to do as I say." She touched his arm and he began screaming: "I'm not! I'm not! I'm not!"

Debby waited for him to come home from school, fearfully watching for a milky sun in the pewter sky. She hurried to the front door when she heard the children screaming. Glenn was high-stepping it across the lawn, a howling Indian. He stomped up the steps and, as part of his homecoming ritual, handed her his tablet and books, unsnapped the helmet cap.

"We had a snow fight." He was red and out of breath.

"Who's we: Johnny and Pete and Win?" She and Glenn talked about people Mrs Merrill had never heard of.

"No. They were on my side and we won."

She helped him off with his coat. "And Debby," he whispered. They were in the living room. He kept his eye on the door.

"What is it?"

"You won't tell."

She crossed her heart and held up three fingers.

"Hope to die?" he asked.

"Hope to die," she said.

He motioned for her to bend low. "I found a place for us to play this afternoon. No one knows about it and it's back of the boxwood by the little graveyard and nobody's been there. Not any tracks."

"She's not going to let us go streaking way off to Katie Powell schoolhouse."

"Yes she will."

"She may let you but she's not going to let me."

"She promised that if I went to school you could play out in the snow with me this afternoon."

"She didn't mean that far."

"We won't tell her. That's what you promised."

After lunch and the dishes, Mrs Merrill stood at the backdoor and said, "Wait a minute. Let's see how you're dressed." Glenn had his leather helmet, gloves, scarf, dry socks and was ready. Debby held her breath. If she had to go upstairs and change, Glenn might very well leave her. She moved up for inspection. Mrs Merrill rebuttoned the top button of the cape collar. "Let's see what petticoat you've got on." Debby raised her skirt several inches. "Is that the thickest one you've got?" Who, Debby would have liked to know, would think about petticoats when there was snow on the ground? Surely only someone taking leave of senses, or—she saw the thin red trees in Mrs Merrill's eyes—someone coming down with a deaf dumb blind headache.

"This is the thickest I've got," she said, and to herself: "on." You could do anything if you didn't say all the words out loud. Betty had taught her that back in the days when they were partners in the candy business.

"What knickers do you have on?"

"The thick ones." She crossed her fingers hopefully.

"All of your knickers are the same weight. Have you got on the ones with the new elastic?"

Glenn was in the middle of the back yard, dawdling toward the Grove. If she had to stop now to change knickers, he would be gone.

"Come on, Debby." He kicked a flurry of snow.

"The good ones," she said.

Mrs Merrill opened the door.

Debby stepped much higher than was necessary, like a cat prancing in paper boots. As she pushed open the Grove gate she turned back to see the black holes her shoes had . . . Of all things! Mrs Merrill was on the bottom step gathering snow! She patted it into a ball and, laughing silently, threw it at Debby and Glenn. It was almost more than Debby could bear: the sudden revelation that for the first time in her life Mrs Merrill was being a little girl. Debby wanted to run back to her, and Glenn did, patticaking a snowball as he hurried toward her. Mrs Merrill ran up the steps, sheltering her head from the expected snowball. She reached the door safely and when she turned to fasten the screen, she was once more tall, dark, grown, fifty years old, and weary.

"Come on out, Mama. Please Mama!"

Glenn stood at the backsteps dancing with joy and surprise.
"No. Mama's through now. Go on with Debby."

"We'll stay here if you'll come out." You would have thought she had thrown gold at him, or chocolate-covered peanuts.

"You and Debby go play. I've got to sew some on Rebecca's wedding dress."

"Please Mama! Just for a little while?"

"I feel a headache coming on and I've got to sew. Run along."

Glenn, showing off, ran plowing through the snow, through the gate into the Grove. As Debby turned to shut the gate she saw Mrs Merrill still standing dark and alone in the door. Debby was suddenly ashamed of the hate that had been building up in her while Glenn was begging at the steps. She wished she could return to the house and not slip off to the schoolyard. "Come on," Glenn hollered from the backstreet. Mrs Merrill was waving good-by.

It was a bare, cold world, full of strange shadows, odd shapes, and delicate interlacing designs. The Grove, the streets, the schoolyard were etched with intricate purple shadows from the overhead tangle of dark limbs, creaking mysteriously in the still air, shaking down small gifts of snow that vanished even as they fell. The nearest voice was a hundred miles away.

"Through here." Glenn pushed a way between the slick boxwood leaves and the rough homemade-brick wall. They straightened up in a little garden that was hidden by the boxwood, the wall, another line of boxwood, and a green latticed fence. In the corner was the graveyard, speared off by iron pickets. Tracks, obviously made by a very earnest little dog, probably Spike, who was thinking only about getting home and getting his feet warm, hemstitched the exact middle of this secret place.

"Tell you what," Glenn said as though he had brought her here to say expressly this and not to play in the snow.

"What?"

He glanced quickly away from her and gazed awkwardly about the garden. Finally his eyes glazed and he stared at the snow-covered tombstone which someone had thought to put over the grave of a little bird. He kicked the snow but did not move his eyes, nor his hands which were rigid at his sides. "Let's play like you're my Mama."

A chilling wind was rattling a broken lath on the latticed fence. The treetops bounced against the low gray sky which toward the west was remembering pink. She waited to hear Mrs Merrill's voice shrieking on the wind; but the lath slapped, slapped, slapped and stopped.

"And play like I'm your little boy." His voice was tense and pleading. "And we'll build a snowman and that'll be Daddy."

"All right," she said. "I'll be your Mama and you be my little boy."

"But I'm not really your little boy," his voice was defiant, yet weak and uncertain, "am I?" He put his arm around her hips and pressed his face against her side. His voice was so tense he could hardly speak. "I mean we're just playing-like, aren't we?"

A drawstring was pulling her throat shut and she could not answer. She bent quickly and cleared a space for the cold snowman.

Chapter 19

WORK work work work work, that's what a wedding is." But when they finished cleaning up the church for Rebecca's wedding and before it was decorated, Debby was going to marry Glenn. She had promised him five times that morning.

Dust from the pipe organ sifted constantly onto the choir seats. She dusted them again. The empty church echoed the children's voices: loud, high, hollow. From the choir loft the clear windows were as clean as if a big cat had licked them. The stained glass ones sparkled even though they had not been touched. A tree branch cast a shadow on the lamb which seemed to cuddle softly in the arms when the wind blew softly and to wrestle when the wind blew harder. A tiny red ruby of glass had fallen out of the lead casement when she was washing the adjoining window and from time to time as she dusted, swept, and washed, Debby took the glass, a drop of blood, out of her apron pocket and studied it and wondered how anything could be so red.

"THIS IS the wedding maaarch, Da da da Da da da DA DUM." Betty sang out from the back of the auditorium. She raced full tilt down the aisle and stood before the altar in her blue shirt and rolled-up khaki shorts. "Here. Marry me. I want to get married. Yeah. I do. I do. I do. Certainly he does. He's lucky to get me. I'll beat the devil . . ." She glanced meekly around, she was in church. "I won't ever let anybody hurt him. Thank you. How much I owe you? Here's a quarter. That's all it's worth. Come on here. We got to go on a honeymoon." She raced herself down the other aisle, screeching like a banshee, a married banshee.

The windows were washed; the floors and carpets swept; the sheets tacked in place, ready for the fern; the tall white wicker baskets were clean and waiting for the gladioli which a curb market lady had promised for bright and early in the morning; two rolls of white cloth, furnished by the church for the price of laundering, were lying at the end of each aisle, to be unrolled for the bride to walk on. They had been working since nine o'clock that morning. They sat down now to see how well they had done. Debby, Julia, and Glenn sat together. Betty stretched herself out in the pew ahead of them and was only a loud voice. They would have gotten through much faster without Betty because they had all had to help her. She had decided at noon, without telling anyone, that she was going to shine the pipe-organ pipes. "They shine like pennies," she said when they discovered her. She had polished four of them up as far as the side holes. The part she had done was, as she said, bright as new pennies, but above the side vents the pipes were as dark as old kettles. The only thing to do was to polish all of them as high as the vents. There were forty-eight of them.

"There's no way I can think of to cover up that mess," Julia said.

"I think they look good," Betty raised up on her elbows. "They look like great big mechanical pencils with shiny metal tips."

"I gave you a big pencil one time," Debby said.

Glenn frowned. "What did I do with it?"

"Lost it I reckon. Either that or give it away."

"I didn't give it away. I bet I know where it is."

"Where?"

"In your trunk."

"Mama'll think of some way so it won't show," Julia said.

Mrs Merrill had come around to the church to bring their lunch and to help Mr Merrill tack the sheets in place. She had had to rush back to finish covering the buttons for the wedding dress. Rebecca had the silly idea that she wanted covered-buttons all the way down the back to the waist even though it had a nice secret zipper on it.

"Debby let's me and you have a rehearsal," Glenn grabbed her thumb. "You promised."

"Debby's tired."

"You promised."

"Just once."

"Julia, you said you'd play for us."

"It's going to be beautiful." All spring Julia had talked about the wedding and about the lovely white cloth, the dress, how to decorate the church, and how she would walk when she was a Junior Bridesmaid. She walked that way now to the piano and began the Wedding March.

"Not yet. Not yet. Come on Debby . . ." They hurried out to the door.

"I'll be the preacher." Betty picked up a song book and ran to the altar. She waved her arms as though she were conducting an orchestra.

Glenn reared back, held his breath. Debby watched him start off. "Come on," he whispered. Then he came back and held her hand. They started together. He was holding his breath again and trying very hard to be like his father.

Julia watched them over her shoulder. "You're marching too fast." They weren't marching at all: they were running. Glenn slowed to baby steps. "Hurry up," Betty yelled. "Got to go preach a dead man's funeral."

They turned from the aisle and marched to the altar. The music stopped. "Do you, Deborah Deborah Hall take this man here to be your awful wedded husband?"

"Yes," Debby said, nervously. She was trembling.

"I do," Glenn whispered. His hand was hot and wet.

"I do," Debby said weakly.

"Do you, Randolph Glenn Merrill, take this woman." She stopped. "Julia, you say 'this lady' don't you? 'Woman' means a Negro lady."

"Not when you're in church it doesn't," Julia began playing the Rosary.

"Do you, Randolph Glenn Merrill, take this woman to be your awful wedded wife?"

He sighed as he frequently did when he had been holding his breath, waiting to speak. They waited. Suddenly he sat down heavily on the floor. "You ruined it." He was hollering at Mrs Merrill who had been standing, for no telling how long, smiling at them from the choir door. "You ruin everything."

He stood up and began running furiously down the aisle. "You ruined everything, everything!"

"Well now! Who's that hot-headed little fellow?" The voice boomed out from the side door. A young man—Debby glanced twice—it was Britt. But Lord, who would have known him the way he was dressed all in khaki, the way he had filled out, his face still dimpled, but leathery and brown, his neck solid, his hair cut short as a thumbnail. In two long steps he was in the aisle. He caught Glenn and swung him into the air, high overhead. "Temper temper temper. I've got a little temperbox for a brother." Glenn fought vainly against his brother's broad chest and thick arms, then gave himself to the luxury of defeat. "Did you bring me what you wrote you had for me?" he asked in a baby voice.

Julia and Betty stood awkwardly, near the altar, watching. "He came just after lunch," Mrs Merrill said. "Aren't you going to kiss him." Britt came forward carrying Glenn under his arm, on his hip, like a sack of meal. He let Glenn slide to the floor. He placed both hands, square and red, on Julia's shoulders. "Julia," he said and kissed her on the forehead. Julia pressed her face into his starched khaki shirt and hugged him about the waist. She freed herself and turned away. "Julia," he said again. "And Betty." Betty quickly held out her hand. "Of all the little tomboys!" He refused her hand. "No siree, you're going to kiss me too." He lifted her and kissed her neck. Betty was as red as the glass. "Put me down," she said meekly. He *had* been away if he couldn't remember that Betty didn't like for anyone to touch her, and no one but Debby had ever dared lift her. He set her down and tousled her hair. In return she half-hugged his waist, slapping him on the back.

"And little old Debby!" When he said that, her heart stopped beating. He picked her up and whirled around three times—her feet were flying through the air in a big circle. She grasped his firm warm neck and held her breath. "How's my little Debby?" She grinned at him and couldn't say a word.

"Mama," Britt said, "you've done a good job with these. They look healthy to me."

"Your money's helped," she said.

"We'll pull through all right. Dad and I together should be able . . ." He set Debby down. "But this is a wedding. No time for worrying." He stood back and squinted his eyes to see how the church would be when decorated. Debby could study him now. So he had been paid for changing this much. There was not a sign of the brown curls on his close-cropped head. His forehead was deep-wrinkled from sun-frowning, and there were untanned laugh wrinkles about his eyes. His lips though were thin and grim and his entire face and bearing had lost the angular grace and boyish charm she had remembered. He was broad and thick, and something none of the other Merrills were—coarse. He almost reminded her of Allan. His voice was harsh and full of ugly "r" sounds. He said "wed-ding" and "tall-king" and sounded like the spring snapping on a screen door. His hands—she couldn't believe the roughness of his hands—were solid thick callouses.

"There are to be white gladioli in the baskets and fern and ivy on the sheets." Mrs Merrill paused when she saw the bright tips of the pipe organ. She glanced quickly at Debby. "And my ferns on the ledge there before the organ."

Britt shook his head. "It won't do."

"It'll appear better when the flowers are here. They'll make all the difference in the world."

Britt was thumbing through his wallet.

"And the candles. We've got . . . how many . . . forty something tall white candles. We can't put them up in this heat. They'd bend right over." She watched Britt's face anxiously. "Candlelight makes everything beautiful."

"How much would a florist charge to decorate?" he asked.

"They'd rob you! All churches are this way the day before a wedding."

"How much?"

"Britt, be sensible. Nobody's going to be counting the flowers. We just want a sweet *little* wedding."

"Mama, I know Rebecca. She may tell you that, but it'll

kill her to have a tacky wedding. You know how proud she is, how those haughty Andersons already try to make her feel."

"We've talked it over. We called Griffin's florist and then decided to use whatever money we had on clothes. That's what we did: bought clothes."

"How much did Griffin want?"

Mrs Merrill sighed. "He wanted twenty-five dollars. Thirty if he brings in the two big palms Mae Watkins had at her wedding."

"That settles it then."

"Britt, do you realize what twenty-five dollars . . ."

"Do you realize what a wedding means to a girl like Rebecca?" Britt hollered. Immediately he was embarrassed. "I'm sorry Mama. I've been saving since Christmas to give Rebecca something nice."

"I'll bet she hasn't written to you twice."

Britt chewed at the corner of his lower lip. "When we were little we got along. This'll be my wedding present. Just don't say anything about it until after the wedding. Let her think it's going to be just as you all planned it."

It was the next day at the same time, late in the afternoon, that they peeped out the front windows and watched the dressed-up neighbors going down the street to the church, gathering in whispering groups, poking at each others' dresses, pulling at belts, adjusting neck lines, tilting hats, and glancing uncertainly at the closed door of the Merrill's house with the three shiny cars parked in the driveway. Rebecca had not come downstairs yet, and she wouldn't let anyone except Julia in to help her dress.

Mr Merrill's hair was almost as white as his linen suit. He pulled his watch chain and studied the gold watch as he marched, shoulders back, up and down the long living room. He had once seemed gruff and frightening to Debby, but now by the side of Britt he seemed small and as soft spoken and gentle as Julia.

"Do I look all right?" Debby smoothed the white silk-voile dress over her hips. She and Mrs Merrill were wearing dresses cut just alike from the same material, even though Rebecca had objected to the idea. But then Rebecca had had another idea. "It'll be all right because you won't be sitting together." Rebecca had explained that no one could be seated within the family ribbons after Mrs Merrill had been seated. "And you see, Debby, I need you to help me at the church with my veil. You'll be sort of my godmother. Then you can sit in the back." Debby had heard Mrs Merrill and Rebecca arguing upstairs later. Rebecca had finally screamed: "It's my wedding and I'll have it like I want it. You remember the dinner party. Nothing like that is going to happen at my wedding." Debby enjoyed hearing that girl have her own way.

Julia came almost floating down the steps in her white organdy dress. She lifted the bouquet of baby-pink rosebuds over her head and fussed with the streams of satin ribbons. Betty sat with her ankle on her knee, apparently disgusted by the whole proceedings. "Don't wrinkle that dress." Betty stood up and shook the skirt. She put on the blue silk jacket which kept the transparent bodice and lace petticoat from showing too much. "Hoc spit dog," she said to no one in particular. Then she turned to Glenn. "Don't you look cute?" she mocked.

"Yes I do," he said defiantly. He wouldn't move in his white linen suit and white shoes, not even to touch the bow and arrows Britt had made during the winter evenings in camp.

Through the dining room door Debby could see Britt

bending and turning before the mirror over the sideboard. At ten o'clock that morning he had tried to get into a white suit he had bought before he joined the CCC. Even without a shirt the sleeves were so tight he could hardly slip his arms out of them. Mrs Merrill wanted him to phone and borrow a suit from one of his friends but Britt claimed he didn't have any friends in this town and that he certainly wouldn't borrow a suit from the damned college snobs he had known in high school. So now he stood before the mirror in Mr Merrill's everyday seersucker suit. It was too narrow across the shoulder and chest, too big around the waist and when he stood straight or walked you could see almost all of his white silk socks that looked muddy because of the brown ankles showing through.

He breathed in and lowered the belt on his hips. He leaned over to see about the trouser length. Mr Merrill's collar was also too small for Britt and even though he didn't have the top button fastened he kept stretching his neck and twisting his chin from side to side. He hadn't been certain that he could be home for the wedding and so he had not been included as an usher. Rebecca had said that if he did come—and she thought it was too long a trip—he should enter and be seated with Mrs Merrill.

"Fourteen minutes, the Wedding March starts in fourteen minutes," Mr Merrill called up the stairs. Keeping out of sight Rebecca called back. "Send Mama and the first car on." "Good-by," they all hollered good-by as though they would never see Rebecca again. Mrs Merrill turned suddenly from the door and went to the foot of the stairs. "Can't I come kiss you good-by?" she half-whispered. It was a strange tone, a strange request for Mrs Merrill—perhaps it had something to do with Britt's coming back, alive after all.

"Now Mama, don't start getting weepy. It's so awful to see mothers crying at weddings," Rebecca said, still out of sight. "Please try to act like Mrs Anderson. Like we're somebody."

Mrs Merrill stepped up a step and craned her neck. "I love you," she said to the stair well. Glenn tugged at his mother's hand. "Come on. We're late."

The first two cars left. Debby waited in the front seat of the third car. The veil was on the back seat and beside it the bridal bouquet of white roses, white satin ribbon, white baby's breath, and lilies-of-the-valley. Mr Merrill came out the door and held the door while Rebecca came through holding her skirt high. Debby had seen Mrs Merrill poring over the dress for so many months she couldn't tell whether it was pretty or not. Rebecca sat alone in the back seat and Debby could see her black hair and fine eyebrows in the little car mirror. At the church they rushed up the steps. Julia trembling noticeably was starting slowly down the aisle, an Anderson cousin in a white linen suit was going down the other aisle. Jane somebody, the maid-of-honor, was whispering with Ray's young brother and then they took their places at the doors, smiling back at Rebecca as she passed. The church was trembling with music.

Britt was standing in the side parlor.

"Why didn't you go in with Mama?" Rebecca whispered.

"I'm going to sit in the balcony," he said.

"Britt?" Rebecca seemed puzzled. She looked down at his body which was almost bursting from the tight suit.

"If I don't get to the reception . . ." he held both her hands. "I just wanted to wish for you all the happiness you can get . . ."

"Britt, don't make me cry." Rebecca pulled her hands away. "We're grown now, you know."

She turned to the mirror and with deft, practiced motions, fastened the veil exactly in place. She paused a moment as Britt went up the stairs to the balcony. "He can sit in the balcony for all I care. He just wants people to feel sorry for him." She smiled at herself as she lifted the bouquet. "He had the same chances I did. He knows he's out of place here." She practiced being solemn, then happy, with lips closed, then smiling radiantly.

"What am I supposed to do?" Debby asked. From the door she could see Jane and Ray's brother reaching the huge palms, crossing, past the altar, turning slowly to face the audience.

"Debby! I'd almost forgot you. You're to see if my veil is straight and then you're to take a seat just inside the door. "I'm depending on you not to let me stand . . ." The Wedding March began. Rebecca pressed her stomach firmly with her free hand and shut her eyes. Mr Merrill slipped his arm through hers and steadied her. Rebecca talked on weakly, yet with determination, as though in a trance, "up there with my veil all wrinkled. Is it all right? You won't let me stand up there with a wrinkled veil will you, Debby?" She was as white as the flowers. At the door they stopped to begin again, in step with each other, in time with the music.

Hardly moving at all they started down the aisle. A few smiling heads turned around, quickly, then back to the front. The women stopped fanning, a hush was drowning out the music. Someone coughed. Debby tried to find Mrs Merrill's head in the front rows. All the hats were alike at this distance. She watched Mr Merrill and Rebecca; they were walking faster now; she would let them get a head start. So far, she was glad to see, the veil was behaving fine, lifting a little in the breeze but that was pretty and bridesy. Debby patted time with her foot and stepped out. If she stared at the veil she wouldn't be afraid. She was walking too fast, just as she had yesterday when she almost married Glenn. She had trembled more yesterday than she was now. The music had a calming effect she thought. She took baby steps and stayed a nice distance, four feet, behind Mr Merrill and Rebecca. "Debby!" some ill-mannered fool whispered as they passed the family seats. She knew better even if they didn't. She had heard Julia say you shouldn't turn your head to the right or left. Mr Merrill and Rebecca were rounding the corner by the palm. Debby hurried her pace. She was at the altar almost as soon as Rebecca had taken Raymond's hand. "Everyone's practiced this except me and Rebecca and we did just as good as anybody," she thought. The veil seemed in perfect shape to her, except perhaps for one small fold.

"Dearly beloved . . ." the preacher began. Debby leaned forward and gave the veil a quick yank and a shake. It was perfect now. "Dearly beloved . . ." the preacher began again. Debby turned and tiptoed away. Rebecca had said for her to sit on the back seat. As she started down the aisle Betty reached out and grabbed her dress by the hem. They had made room for her in the family pew. She sat down between Betty and Mrs Merrill. "Dearly beloved . . ." the preacher said a third time staring nervously at Debby. When he saw that she was not going to move again he continued, "we are gathered here in the presence of God . . ." Everyone was coughing. Julia lowered her head and stared at the floor. The boy beside her was red and was laughing into his folded handkerchief. Some people didn't know how to act at a wedding.

"Did I do all right?" Debby whispered.

Mrs Merrill reached out and held Debby's bare hand in

her own gloved one, patted it, and then squeezed it so tight it almost hurt. Was this the first time Mrs Merrill had ever touched her? The candles were flickering softly in the still air; the music was low. Nothing had ever been so pretty. She had never been so happy. To think that she, Deborah Hall, had been in a wedding!

Chapter 20

THE nickel was gone! Before breakfast she had arranged it just-so between the ivory celluloid pin tray and the ivory celluloid powder box which was the roundhouse when she and Glenn played trains. The money was for a special purpose. That summer each Monday morning, Mrs Merrill counted out six nickels from a knotted handkerchief which was kept in the bottom of the Grandfather's clock. "Debby, it is a sin that I can't give you more than this. Someday we'll pay you all your back wages, every penny we owe you. He . . . it's the best we can do this year." Debby answered: "I don't expect anything. I don't want you giving me anything," then to herself, "except the nickels." For it was a fact that spending the five cents was the dreamed-of part of the day.

After lunch and the dishes and the dining room floor and the chairs back to place, she would take her bath and put on whatever clothes she and Mrs Merrill had talked about during the dish washing. By that time Glenn would be upstairs at her heels, to the closet, to the trunk, following every step. "Get out from underfoot. What're you hanging around here for?" As if she didn't know, pretending she didn't really care where he might be.

"What're you going to buy today?"

"What're you talking about?"

He stood at the bureau sliding the nickel across the scarf with his fingernail. "With this?"

"Who said I was going to spend that. I'm going to start saving my money."

"What for?"

"Going to build me a house."

"A house!"

"Yes sir. A house."

"You mean a big house? To live in?"

"Big enough for me." She had borrowed the dream from Mrs Merrill who often at night when Mr Merrill was too tired from worrying to read would talk about selling this place and building a house in the Grove, and having enough left over to pay their debts. Every envelope in the leather mailbag hanging at the side of the mantel had house plans drawn on them. "See here, Debby," Mrs Merrill would say to her on the long dark winter afternoons, "this is the way the house will be. Kitchen here, door here right into the dining room. No drafty pantry to walk through. No step-up step-down." The first house Mrs Merrill drew had only room enough for the family until Betty anxiously asked where Debby would sleep. In that second Debby remembered the lye-soap, pee-pee smell of Stonebrook. She shuddered involuntarily. "My goodness. We can't forget Debby," Mrs Merrill said, although it was plain as a goose that she could. But obligingly she drew in another room.

Debby watched Glenn worrying the nickel back into place. "You want to live with me?"

He was silent a long time before mumbling: "According to how far away."

"I'm going to build me a house in the Grove, facing out on the Back Street. Is that too far?"

"You know when this nickel was made?"

"1928." That was a good guess for nickels.

"19*18*."

Pennies were made in 1935. She knew that.

Then they would discuss how they were going to live in the Grove house, and what they would eat in the middle of hot summer afternoons: lime sherbert, banana pudding, lemonade-tea with enough-sugar-to-ruin-your-kidneys, hot dogs, that fluffy pink stuff—cotton candy! She would prolong the talk by cleaning out her trunk; polishing the furniture with an oil you could smell way up in your head between the eyes and in the very center of the forehead; straightening the closet; rewinding the hundred little coils of wire which she had collected because they would be just the things to hang pictures on if you ever had that many pictures to hang. All the while the nickel would be there before them, making almost any of their dreams seem possible. Now it was irrigably gone.

She searched her apron pocket, the pockets and handkerchief rags in her black-purple sweater. She peeped under the bureau, into the wastebasket, under the andirons. She dragged over a chair and touched a spot on the picture molding. Well, somebody might have put it up there—Betty with her everlasting chewing gum which was the best glue ever.

Betty, that was it, Betty had got her nickel. Maybe they were going back in the candy-business. Buy three pieces for a dime and sell them for five cents each and the one you didn't sell you could eat. Betty had been paying her no heed lately, up at dawn, into overalls, back for lunch, hot, red-faced, tired, gulping milk, talking with a mouthful of bread, brushing back wet bangs over her ears like a boy's, and out the door—

slam! She'd come back at dark telling wild tales about riding on a horse's back, almost catching two pigeons she was after, helping Old Man McGirt saw wood, and beating two ambulances to the hospital. She would ruin their supper by sitting there eating catsup on cornbread and talking about the man in the ambulance who didn't have a thing wrong with him, not a scratch, till the interns picked him up off the stretcher and his ear stayed on the pillow. Where his ear had been throbbed blood like a fountain. And with that Betty would pop the last of the catsup sandwich in her mouth.

"Where's Betty?" she asked downstairs.

Mrs Merrill was sliding a light bulb into the toe of a sock. "What do you want with her?" A mimosa shaded the windows and she bent low over her basket of darning. She held a needle to the light and poked at it with her pinching-fingers.

"I want to see her about something."

"You're getting mighty mysterious here of late. Secrets secrets secrets, that's all you and Glenn talk about.

"I don't have to tell you everything."

"You don't have to tell me anything," Mrs Merrill glanced over the top of her glasses, commanding her with steady eyes. "Some things I can see for myself."

Debby wished now she and Glenn had never played in the snow, even if Glenn did love her, as he had told her a hundred times since then, better than any living person, including George Washington. That was their big Secret, and it was the one Mrs Merrill was always trying to discover with her questioning and hoot-owl staring.

"I can see for myself too," Debby said, and wondered what they were talking about.

"I thought you did," Mrs Merrill said grimly. "I sometimes think you get by with a great deal you're actually accountable for."

I can make as little sense as she does, Debby thought; then speaking aloud: "I reckon we all do."

"When you say things like that . . . if I only knew . . . then I'd know how to deal with you. Seems that all my life I've had to fight with weak people. Uncle Lee was weak, even when he was mean-drunk. And I don't seem to be able to fight them. I give in. I feel sorry and I give in. But I can't live all my life letting people take advantage of me, take what they want from me, even my children, simply because I'm stronger. Debby, do you think I'm mean to you? I try to divide the work fairly. I never have time to sit and watch the cars passing the way you do. Oh, I don't begrudge you that. Lord knows you need some pleasures. But . . . is it the pay? I've tried to explain to you about money, about the hard times we're having. Is it that?" Her voice was dull, pleading.

"Is what that?"

There was a long silence. Finally Mrs Merrill asked in a strange voice: "Glenn, the way he treats me. He won't even let me be good to him."

Debby remained silent. She didn't like for Mrs Merrill to mention Glenn. He belongs to me, Debby thought and she ground her teeth in defiance.

"You're spoiling him. Spoiling him rotten. Then when I finally have to correct him, it makes him more and more distant. Don't deny it. I've seen both of you sticking out your tongues when you thought my back was turned. You remember, Debby, when Julia and Betty first moved upstairs we went through the same thing, only not so bad, nothing like this. And we didn't enjoy our work together then."

It dawned on Debby: "You want me to leave."

"Debby! I told you when you were sick we'd never talk

about that again. You have a home as long as I live. You won't ever leave us as long as we have a roof over our heads and a bite to go in our mouths. I've had to tell you that a thousand times. *As long as I live, you have a home.*"

The black whirlpool inside her ceased, and again she could think. "What do you mean then?"

"I mean simply this: I think I deserve a little more respect around here than I've been getting. I don't ask anybody to love me, but I do expect a decent answer when I ask a question."

"What do you want to know?" Debby asked in what she hoped was a respectful, obliging tone.

"Merely to be polite, merely to make conversation because I thought you looked lonesome, I asked what you wanted with Betty. It doesn't make any difference though."

"I'm not lonesome," Debby said. Everybody knew who the lonesome one was, who kept her head in a sewing basket all the time. Mrs Merrill bit the thread, slid the light bulb out, and folded the socks into a ball. Methodically she picked up another sock, inserted the light bulb, threaded the needle. She keeps busy, Debby thought casually without purpose or direction.

"Do you know?"

"What?" Mrs Merrill asked as though the subject had never been mentioned.

"Where Betty is."

"She was in the tree-house after dinner. She won't be satisfied till she breaks her arm."

"Did she say anything about my nickel?"

"Not that I remember."

"It's gone."

Mrs Merrill's hands dropped to the basket. "What nickel?"

Debby told her.

"You're certain you put it there this morning?"

"Yes."

"Has Betty been in your room since then?"

"Not that I know of."

"You didn't agree to go in the candy business again?"

"We haven't mentioned that in I don't know when."

"Let's go look."

They searched the bureau, the mantel, the window sills. "Get out your money."

Debby opened her trunk and showed her the green powder box with the four dusty coins.

"I'm sure I gave you six yesterday," Mrs Merrill said, "and you've spent only one? Are you sure?"

"We spent one yesterday and this is all I've got left."

Mrs Merrill became rigid as they went back downstairs, through the house.

"It was my nickel and we were going to get twin popsicles." Every other day they bought popsicles: banana, chocolate, orange—and vanilla that didn't taste as wonderful as it smelled. Mrs Merrill had agreed that it would be fair for Glenn to have one of the popsicles if he walked three blocks to the store. But if he had any money, then he should pay the two cents, Debby the three. Sometimes they cut a bite off of each—down to the stick—for Mrs Merrill to eat with a spoon from a saucer, but that ruined the popsicles. Usually they ran upstairs and made them last as long as they could, until only the taste of wood was left. "I was going to get us some ice cream on sticks."

"Betty! Betteee! Betteee Merrill!"

Betty came out of the Grove with a long six-shooter rubber gun under her arm.

"What you want?" She brushed the bangs out of her eyes.

"Come here."

Betty leaned the gun against the fence, came solemnly forward, not wavering a bit in glance or step. "What's wrong?"

"Have you seen Debby's nickel?"

"No ma'm. I've just got one nickel and I wouldn't take anything for it." It was the polished one she flipped into the air and caught, over and over, while she asked Debby why there wasn't anybody in the neighborhood her age to play with. She reached into her watch pocket to make sure it was still there.

"Look at me Betty. Are you certain?"

"I don't tell lies." That was true. She was mean; she fought; she broke things; she beat little boys up and cursed their interfering mothers; but she never tried to avoid her punishment. And Julia had gone on an all-day swimming party out to Granny Lake.

"Have you seen Glenn?"

"Oh!" Betty's face brightened. "I bet Glenn's the one! I saw him down on Wardlaw Street. He had a paper sack and was running this way. Now I remember."

"What did he have in the sack?"

"Something for him and Debby I spose. I don't speak to him. He's so stuckup."

Mrs Merrill sat down on the back step, apparently relieved. "Debby, think again: did you send him to the store?"

"No."

"Think now, did you?"

"Not that I remember. I had just got out of the tub."

"How about this morning? Did you mention it to him then? You sometimes forget things you know." Mrs Merrill was all the time accusing her of forgetting things; yet she couldn't remember ever having forgotten anything.

"Maybe so. But I know I didn't."

"We'll wait then." So the three of them sat on the steps

in the hot sun waiting for Glenn to return. Presently Mrs Merrill marched over to a peach tree and twisted off a thick switch. With one quick move she stripped the leaves off. "Go find him."

That was the signal Betty had been waiting for so patiently. She ran across the hot back yard, grabbed up her gun and disappeared through the Grove gate. "Bushel of wheat, bushel of rye, all not ready holler 'I.' Coming." Then she let out a savage cry that chilled Debby even on this afternoon. Mrs Merrill walked about, talking low, then louder and louder, snapping her wrist, making the switch cut through the air whistling. "With Britt, everyone saying or thinking if they didn't say it 'You mothered him too much.' Maybe I did. Maybe I did try too hard to make something of him. He couldn't be all that I wanted him to be. But at least he was honest. 'Give them more freedom' that's what Doctor Bronston stood in my own living room saying, 'Give them more freedom. They're going to grow up in spite of everything.' But I mean they're going to grow up honest if nothing else. I've given Glenn his way. Three years now, correcting him only when it was absolutely necessary. Knowing it was wrong to let a child have his way. But I was determined not to ruin him. Now look what happens. He knows better. He's not that young. Seven years old. Stealing." She whacked a leaf in two with the switch. "Spoiled. Spoiled rotten." The switch sang through the air. "When he comes, send him in to me."

Debby sat alone on the back steps. Spike settled down in the shade by her, panting, showing the whites of his eyes, his tongue dripping. "Move away. I don't want an old hot slobbering bulldog breathing on me." Spike waddled down the steps. He fell under the jasmine and licked his face. There was no reason to be mean to poor Spike, she knew but she knew also that she would die if she could not lose some of her anger. She wished the sky would fall in on Mrs Merrill's head, or that big old limb, or the plastering. How, how, how could she ever explain to Glenn what had happened? She wouldn't be able to look at him again. She'd wear a veil. She didn't have one but she'd get one. In the meantime she'd wear a towel over her face with little buttonhole eyes and maybe a place where she could stick out her tongue at Mrs Merrill.

Handsel Tubbs came through the gate. He was holding his hands up. Betty was behind him. She poked him in the small of the back with the rubber gun. "Mama," she called. Mrs Merrill came to the back door.

"Here's one of them."

"Where's Glenn?"

"I haven't found him."

"Quit poking me." With Mrs Merrill in sight Handsel acquired courage.

"Quit poking him."

"But he ate half of the popsicle."

"Glenn gave it to me."

"Yeah but you asked him for it."

"He didn't have to give it to me."

"You're bigger than he is."

"He didn't have to give it to me."

"Shut your big trap. Can't you see my mother kindly wants to say a word."

"Turn him loose, Betty."

"Mama! Here I go out on a hot day rounding up thieves for you and you say turn'm loose."

"Do as I say."

"Beat it then. Thief. Bully! Thief!" She chased him from the yard. "Don't you ever set foot in here. And if I catch you picking on my brother . . ." A rock came sailing over the fence. Betty dodged. "Coward!"

"Tomboy!"

"Squat face."

"Betty."

"Thief! Coward!"

"One more word and I'm going to use this switch on you." Mrs Merrill started down the steps.

Betty flung herself on the grass in the shade of the barn, flat on her back, looking at the sky. "Whew," she said, "it's hot work, chasing thieves. If there's anything I hate it's thieves. When I get to be Alderman of Ward Three, I'm . . ."

Glenn was coming through the Grove. He was taking baby steps. He stopped in the gate and said something so little and low not even an ant could have heard it.

"March yourself right on in here young man." Mrs Merrill bit the words out.

Glenn remained stupefied in the gate. He watched Betty roll over on her stomach in the grass. "You're in for it," she said. He moved past her, turning his head to watch. "Burglar."

"Glenn. I'm waiting."

In dreams sometimes Debby had moved as he was moving now. The brightness of the sun flattened the yard and the buildings into a steaming desert where space could not be measured. It might have been an hour it took him to cross the glaring backyard where he and his shadow were the only moving beings in sight. Mrs Merrill waited, switch in hand.

"Where is Debby's ice cream?"

He looked at the ground. He raised his bare foot and scratched a mosquito bite on his ankle.

"Answer me!"

"I," he paused. He turned around and watched Betty. She was sitting cross-legged in the grass. She pointed a forefinger at him and whittled at it with the other forefinger. "Make Betty stop."

"Where is Betty's popsicle?"

"*Betty's* popsicle!" He wouldn't look at the switch which was almost touching his knee.

"Debby's. You know what I'm talking about." She grabbed him by the elbow. Debby stood up to go. She couldn't watch.

"Wait a minute," Mrs Merrill said.

"Did you take Debby's nickel?"

"Yes ma'm." He twisted his big toe into the dirt.

"Without her consent."

He smiled weakly at Debby. "I was going to surprise her."

"Where are the popsicles?"

"They were melting bad and Handsel Tubbs." He took a deep shivering breath. "I gave him one and I was going to bring the other one to her . . ." he pointed at Debby. If he hadn't pointed at her, reached out his hand like that, she could have stood it. She turned and ran into the house and up to her room.

Before she reached the stairs she heard the whipping. "Mama! Mama! . . . Do you know it's wrong to steal . . . Mama, oh . . . do you . . . yes, yes, yes . . ." she could hear the switch when it hit his pants. "Mama . . . don't, don't, don't . . . are you ever going . . . again . . . quit that hollering." The sounds were muffled. She had dragged him into the house. "No! No!" Debby's dinner was in her throat. In the bathroom she leaned over and vomited sour. Downstairs the sounds stopped for a moment. She hurried to her room. Glenn was pounding through the house, Mrs Merrill's steps behind him. He stomped up the steps. He was screaming with all his strength: "I hate you! I hate you! I hate you!"

From her room Debby could see him standing red faced on the landing, spitting out his hatred, bending forward, shaking his head furiously. "You're ugly. You're mean to me and I hate you. You don't love me and I don't love you."

From below Mrs Merrill's voice: "You're not going to be a thief though."

"What?" he hollered through his sobbing.

"And you're going to respect me, even if it's only because I'm your mother."

"You're *not* my mother." He leaned over and screamed. "Debby's my mama."

"You're going to *obey me*. I can't make you love me, but you're going to do as I say."

He found a bleeding whelp on his leg. He squalled at sight of his own blood. "Look what you did!" He spit down the stairs. "You old whore bitch! You old whore bitch!"

Mrs Merrill rushed the stairs. "Uh oh," Debby said.

"Debby! Debby. Help! Help me!" He was screaming for life. "Debby. Save me!"

Glenn was running toward her across the hall. Mrs Merrill was on the landing.

Debby shut the door.

"Debby, Debby!" He screamed. He twisted the doorknob. He pounded on the door. Debby sank to the rug and pressed her shoulder to the door. "I'm no match for her," she whispered.

"Debby!" It was a last wild plea. Then Mrs. Merrill had him. "Debby," he sobbed as he was being dragged back downstairs, but she did not have strength to open the door—or to move. Her heart was cramped in her. She covered her ears against the whipping.

Three times the room turned black before she heard him creeping up the stairs. He was sobbing and crying softly to himself, whimpering almost like a baby. He went into Britt's room and shut the door. He was fingering the rising pink whelps when she peeped in. "Look at what Mama," he couldn't finish the sentence. He lay back on the bed and cried at the ceiling. The tears ran down into his ears. Debby knelt and fanned him. His legs were striped with whelps and one across the back of his knee was bleeding.

"Debby'll go get some good cool medicine to bathe them with."

In the back sitting room Mrs Merrill was lying face down on the couch sobbing into the pillow. Her body was soft and crumpled. "How," Debby wondered, "did we get tangled up like this?"

While she was silently bathing Glenn's legs with ice water to which she had added a spoonful of vanilla, Betty tiptoed into the darkened room. She laid a chocolate-covered ice-cream popsicle on the pillow beside Glenn. "Here," she said. She drew back her hand. Then without looking at him, she tiptoed to the door. She didn't even ask him for one bite and it had cost her a whole nickel, the one she flipped all day like a big shot.

Chapter 21

THE night of the whipping Glenn would not leave Britt's room; no one asked him to. Debby carried his supper to him and went later to fetch the tray. She had thought though that he would naturally come back to their room at bedtime but he slept in Britt's bed that night. Debby wanted to ask was it because she had shut the door against him, but she was afraid he would say "Yes." Yet in the year that followed she could not understand how such a stormy vow of love could afterward have meant so little. She had thought all that sad evening that Mrs Merrill would know her place now and would leave them alone.

The fault was Glenn's. After school each day he ate lunch and was out of sight until suppertime. No one knew exactly where he played but sometimes when Mrs Merrill was not around, he mentioned the swings in the park across from the hospital. He never offered though to take Debby to see the swings and the shoot-t-shoot. Sometimes she imagined she had merely dreamed the whipping-day because since then everyone seemed to be doing the exact opposite of what he had screamed. Mrs Merrill who had required only obedience —at the top of her voice—not love, now paid no heed to

Glenn's actions except occasionally to call him in for a surprise: a cake pan or chocolate pot to be scraped. Sometimes, rarely, usually on rainy days, or when he was too tired to sit up while waiting for his bath, he would come lie on the rag rug in Debby's room, with one eye shut and trace the slanted ceiling with his finger. Seemingly half-asleep he would tell Debby that he really wasn't a Merrill, that he had been adopted by these people. His mother and father were young and kind and were searching everywhere for him. Therefore he played all day out on the streets and in the park where they could find him.

His voice would become hoarse when he talked about his real parents and he would ask Debby how she had come to lose her own children: Allan and what was the baby's name? "*Glenn*; was that the baby's name: *Glenn*?"

One afternoon in spring she came out on the porch where Mrs Merrill was sewing. Playing with two marbles on the front step Glenn did not even glance at her. "Mama," he was asking, "how old was I when Debby came to live with us?"

"You weren't born then." Mrs Merrill glanced at him over the top of her glasses. "No. I believe you were three days old. Why?"

"I don't know. I was just thinking."

"Thinking what?" Lately Mrs Merrill tried to find out everything that went on in his mind.

"How can you tell if people look alike?"

"What do you mean?"

"When you say two people look alike." He pocketed the marbles and sat tensely with his hands between his knees. "What do you mean?"

"You mean there's something about one person that reminds you of another person. They don't necessarily have to be twins. It doesn't mean they're exactly alike."

"Like they have the same color hair?"

"Maybe."

"Julia's got blonde hair."

"Yes." Mrs Merrill had stopped sewing and was waiting.

Glenn pressed his hands between his knees. "You think Julia looks like anybody?"

"She takes her coloring after Mr Merrill's people."

"Who do I take my coloring after?" He stared at the floor.

"It's hard to say yet. When you were little you had light hair, but it's getting darker. We thought for a while you and Julia would be our blondes."

"You think I look like Julia?"

"Not especially."

He waited a long time. He breathed deeply, almost a sigh, and asked: "You think I look like Debby?"

"No." Mrs Merrill was emphatic in tone. "What are you getting at?"

"Well, you and Debby look alike."

Debby laughed after Mrs Merrill began.

"Now Glenn! You know we don't! We dress alike and we fix our hair alike, but that's all."

He studied each of them solemnly. "You look alike to me. Debby looks like your mama maybe."

"We're the same age. Debby has gray hair but her face is much younger than mine."

"I'm not talking about your age."

"Then how could she be my mother? We're both fifty-one."

"I don't know." He was still frowning. "What makes you kin to a person?"

"Being born into the same family."

"Is everybody that lives in the same house in the same family?"

"Glenn, you know not."

"Is Debby in our family?"

"No, but she practically is. We couldn't get along without her."

He stared at Debby for a long time, silently. "Who do I look like?"

"Some of your features you take after me, some after your father," Mrs Merrill answered.

"And I don't look like Debby?"

"No."

He started in the house. "I'm going to look in the mirror," he said.

That night he made Mr Merrill, Mrs Merrill, and Debby stand in front of the mirror with him. He couldn't hear enough about where he got his features from: Mrs Merrill's eyes and forehead, Mr Merrill's big ears, straight nose, and cupped chin. He couldn't believe at first that Debby did not resemble any of them, particularly not him.

Going to bed that night he raced past her up the steps. "You just live here with us," he said, spanking her as he passed. "You're no kin to us."

During the summer and in the beginning of autumn he could not remind her often enough that she merely lived in the same house with them, that her last name was Hall, and that they were not a drop of kin. One Saturday he and Handsel Tubbs were in the Grove when she went out to kill a hen for Sunday. They watched her grab the chicken out of the coop and wring its neck. While she held the head in her hand, the chicken flopping about over the ground, Handsel whispered—a thing she could not hear—to Glenn. He pushed

Handsel away and stared at Debby in the same way that new women had sometimes done at Stonebrook.

After that he stared at her and asked her a thousand question: "Do you know what six times seven is?" "Where is Mexico?" "What is the capital of Alabama?" "Name the five Great Lakes; the five continents; the largest island." "Who did Pocahontus marry?" "What year was Daniel Boone born?" She wouldn't talk to him when he asked questions. One night at the table he stared at her as though she were an animal and she couldn't swallow another bite. She had had to leave a plateful of food and go sit by the fire until time to wash dishes. Since then she had grown more used to his staring but still it made her uncomfortable. "I'm not an animal," she would tell him. But still he stared.

"Why do you stare at her?" Mrs Merrill asked, Julia asked, and even Mr Merrill. Glenn would not answer. When they were alone upstairs he still talked to her but he talked so silly now. "Debby, this is a window."

"I know it's a window."

"You don't know how to spell it though."

"I don't need to know how to spell it."

"W-i-n-d-o-w, window."

"Anybody knows it's a window."

"Let me hear you spell it."

"I'm busy. Leave me alone."

Then he would begin staring at her again, in that puzzled, curious way. One day, when the leaves were falling and an oak leaf had flattened itself against the screen, Debby noticed, sidewise, that Glenn's chin was trembling as he stared and that his eyes were large with tears. She was sure of herself or she would not have dared it: she went over and hugged him to her. He was tall now, and he pressed his face against her chest. "What's wrong, Glenn?" she asked. He ran out of the room.

The leaves finished falling and on Glenn's birthday—he was eight—Mrs Merrill decided the Grove should be raked. Furthermore, it had to be raked that very day. She promised Glenn that if it was finished by three o'clock he could go to the show with the quarter Debby had given him to buy a present with. He had refused the money until Mrs. Merrill said he could have it. While he was at the show Mrs Merrill made a circle of bricks in the Grove and placed a pile of leaves in the circle and a stack of kindling and wood beside it. Then she went to the store herself and came back with a whole mess of wieners, a box of marshmallows, a bag of Irish potatoes, and two packages of hot-dog rolls.

"You starting supper already?" Debby asked, watching her wash and peel and slice the potatoes.

"These are for Glenn," she said. "I'm going to let him cook out tonight for his birthday."

When he finally came home—Debby had waited on the porch until almost dark to tell him—he didn't, as she had expected, ask her to cook out with him. He ran out the back door and into the Grove, then back through the yard hollering that he was going to ask Handsel Tubbs and Will Moon and maybe Homer. Betty was furious that she was not included but Mrs. Merrill said if Glenn didn't want girls at his campfire he didn't have to have them and that furthermore Betty was entirely too old to be playing with boys. Betty did, however, talk Glenn into giving her two hot dogs to cook over the gas jet, a roll and three marshmallows. Debby stopped stirring the soup when she heard the cellophane crackling as he opened the marshmallows. She watched him reluctantly handing Betty three. Frowning at Debby he said, "I haven't got enough to give everybody some."

"I don't want any of your old marshmallows," she said. At moments like these she didn't want anything except maybe never to see him again. Yet the minute he was out of sight she was anxious for his return. During supper he came in—it seemed like a dozen times—for salt and pepper, the tin picnic plates, cups for the milk, for the four eggs which Mrs Merrill had decided at the last minute to boil, for Mr Merrill's pocketknife. He was almost glassy-eyed with joy and excitement. Each time he went out there was a terrible silence in the kitchen while Betty and Debby glanced at each other, then down at the soup which had fat meat in it.

After supper Betty and Debby stood on the back porch and watched the flames flickering between the cracks in the wooden fence and the sparks flying up through the bare branches of the pecan trees. A blanket of white smoke was leveled for a moment over the Grove. The loud shouts pierced the night air, which was still and touched with cold. With a slight shiver Betty leaned forward and clasped herself around the waist, her arms folded over her stomach. "I've got a cramp," she said. She straightened and walked slowly across the porch, down the back hall to the bathroom. A sudden burst of flames lighted the barn; another armful of leaves had been added. Gradually the barn dimmed, withdrew into darkness. White faced and scared, Betty stood in the hall door: "Where is Mama?"

"Counting out the laundry," Debby answered without hesitation. She seemed always to have a complete knowledge of Mrs Merrill's whereabouts. And Mrs Merrill could tell at almost any second where Debby was and if she were working almost exactly what she was doing. Betty went into the bedroom and Debby heard her crying. Through the wall Debby could hear Mrs Merrill stacking sheets in the closet, not saying a word. Then she cleared her throat for a speech. Debby tiptoed over to the door and listened to Mrs Merrill: ". . . we were talking about last summer when you played so hard you came in dizzy and with a headache. Growing up isn't . . ."

Another one of those talks, Debby thought. Won't they ever get used to the idea of growing up. She had got grown without ever realizing it; but here such a fuss was made about such a simple thing: Britt, Julia, now Betty. The next thing you knew they'd be trying to say Glenn was growing up. Allan had simply disappeared when he was eight and come back, full size, twelve years later. And the baby, what was his name? Not Glenn. I've only been telling him my baby's name was Glenn. Sometimes when she was almost asleep she came near to thinking of his name but then it slipped from her tongue as she sat up awake, and the only name she could remember would be "Glenn." Mrs Merrill knew the name of Debby's baby, but she always shamed Debby for forgetting it. She wondered now if Mrs Merrill still remembered. A flurry of sparks shot skyward. "They're going to set the Grove afire."

"Grover! That's his name. How'd I think of it? Not Glenn! Not, Glenn." She wanted to rush in and say to Mrs Merrill, "I know my baby's name," but Betty was in there crying. She couldn't wait to tell Glenn. Easing the door open, and shut behind her, she tiptoed down the steps. "Grover. Grover Cleveland Hall!" She was delighted with herself for having untangled the puzzle alone. At the gate she stood and watched the four boys who were seated squat-fashion in a circle about the fire. They had finished eating. Apparently, for no one was talking, they had finished their story-telling and were dreaming. Spike too was gazing into the fire, his fat jowls on his outstretched paws. Lazily watching a gray floating ash rise and move on the breeze, Glenn's eyes finally focused on Debby as though he were not sure that she were real, and really standing there. He didn't move, didn't ask her to come into the Grove. "There's Mrs Hall," Handsel said.

"Don't pay any attention to her," Glenn said, and he stared at her coldly.

"Glenn," she motioned for him, "I've got something to tell you."

He uncrossed his legs, stood up, and with hands thrust deep in his pockets, walked over to her. "What?"

"I remember my baby's name."

"Is that all?"

He didn't understand. "It's not Glenn," she said.

For a second he quit frowning. His face relaxed completely, more than it had ever done, even in his sleep or when he laughed. The little tired goblin she sometimes saw in him had hobbled away and left a little boy. Sighing was a habit of his, but he sighed now as though for the first time he was breathing for himself.

"Grover. My baby's name is Grover."

The troubled expression came back, the goblin returned, puzzled, angry, and for a second she suspected, jealous. But then he hollered. "I don't care what his name is. I hate him. I hate you. Go on back in the house." With his hands on her shoulders he pushed her. Staggering backward she was crazy with fury. She grabbed his wrists and shoved him to the ground. "I hate you too," she hissed. She kicked his hips. "I hate you." He rolled over and half-crawling, half-running reached the campfire.

"Crazy!" he screamed. "Crazy. You haven't got good sense! You haven't got good sense! Everybody knows you're dumb."

She was running back to the house, her hands over her ears. "Grandma said not ever let anybody talk to me that way." A rock sailed through the air and hit her sharply between the shoulders. She touched the pain with her hands and felt it with her whole body when she breathed.

"Idiot! You old idiot!" The voice screamed from the Grove.

The screen door would not latch and that was why she began crying. The strange part was that she could not stop. With her apron clasped over her mouth by a smothering hand she tiptoed through the dining room and up the stairs. Even then she couldn't stop crying, nor later when she heard him coming up the stairs. She covered her mouth and hid her head under the covers. If that's what he thinks and that's why he stares, he can just get him a new Debby. The idea almost killed her and if he hadn't at that moment been standing in the door, saying her name, she would have screamed. She didn't answer. She would never speak to him again, for hadn't he thrown a rock at her and hadn't he said things to her that nobody on earth was ever supposed to say?

Chapter 22

NOW that the children were too old to play with her, all of the long days were much alike. Occasionally a fury built up in her against the slowness, the sameness of time. She wished for morning to hurry, for noon, for evening and night, spring, summer and fall. She never wished for winter because she was not as warm natured as she had once been. On the coldest nights her feet and back did not get good warm before dawn. Then too, Mrs Merrill would not let her scrub the kitchen floor or wax the hardwood ones in cold weather. Nothing was so gracious for passing time as being down on your hands and knees, resting your back, and slowly polishing every inch of the floor. At Stonebrook she had learned to tease time past in this way. But Mrs Merrill did not understand: "You certainly cannot scrub the front porch, with these big lazy children around doing nothing." "I'll pay a boy to wax the floors." Often now that Roosevelt and Mr Merrill were making money getting ready for war Mrs Merrill had outsiders in to help with the housework and window washing. "Go rest awhile," she would say. "We're getting old and we've got to learn to save ourselves a bit."

It was during these long rest hours that Debby became so hopelessly confused. Lying on her bed, glancing down the length of her body at her feet, she would see the close resemblance in her clothes to Mrs Merrill's. She would doze off, perhaps for a second, wake up and have the empty feeling that she had disappeared completely, that here, lying in the bed was Mrs Merrill.

Then she would have to go peep in the mirror to see that she was herself. Back in bed she would again become full of doubts. She would imagine that her face was the other woman's: dark wet eyes, wrinkled lids, a pained mouth, a chin that could tremble, sad, aging. Lying there she would touch her own thin nose, her small ears, her heavy eyelids, trace her thin lips, her square hairline, feel the wrinkled neck and again convince herself that she had become Mrs Merrill. This time she would stand in front of the mirror and test her features. She closed her eyes; together; one at a time. She raised her eyebrows, furrowed her forehead. She wrinkled her nose, dilated the large nostrils. She smiled and mock yawned, frowned, and really yawned. Finally as an undeniable proof of her own reality, she wiggled her ears. She would point at the mirror-image and say aloud: "You're Deborah Hall." The voice that echoed back was the quiet, confiding, enveloping whisper of Mrs Merrill: "You're Deborah Hall."

"I'm Deborah Hall!" Frantically she would wave her hands.

"I'm Deborah Hall!" The whisper would say.

Lately, the house, everything about the house, seemed endowed with some part of Mrs Merrill's personality. Always there had been certain articles which were unmistakably a part of her: her sewing basket, comb and brush, the doughboard and one-armed rolling pin, the wine colored dining room rug, the silver pitcher, and all the ferns. Even strangers frequently fingered the fern fronds and said, "Mrs Merrill is a wonder." But now everything had become her very personal possession and reminded Debby constantly of her. She could look at the grandfather's clock, the upstairs bathtub which Mrs Merrill had never even bathed in, or fresh gravel in the drive and feel Mrs Merrill's presence stronger than her own.

The odd part was that she could not remember when all of this had come about. She remembered her first spring here, immediately after her fainting spell, Mrs Merrill had said: "You're run-down. You mustn't load your plate with starches. You need meat, green vegetables, and fruit. Eat what I eat. Watch me and take some, if only a bite of everything you see on my plate."

Since that first spring, too, when Rebecca had fixed her hair like Mrs Merrill's, in play at first, Debby had not worn it differently. And she would not have a dress unless Mrs Merrill had one cut almost like it from the same material. Mrs Merrill though had a habit of not bathing and dressing until Debby was already downstairs in fresh clothes, and so they seldom dressed alike on the same day.

Even before that spring, though, she remembered that when she wanted to touch Glenn, or lift him from his cradle, she could hear Mrs Merrill, who might have been asleep at the time, say, "No." Later when Mrs Merrill would jiggle Glenn in her lap and he would almost jump out of her arms, Debby would feel the muscles jerk in her arms until the baby was again sitting peacefully. And when Mrs Merrill was nursing Glenn, Debby remembered how she often stared at them, hunched over, and felt her own breasts draw.

As long as she was working, it did not bother her to be so very much like another person, for Mrs Merrill was a hard worker and ate a great many things that Debby liked. It was also a comfort to Debby to know that Mr Merrill sometimes became lost when thinking about his wife. He would drive in, walk spiritedly into the house, tossing his new dove-gray hat on a chair, and say: "Where is she?" He walked through the house searching for her and if she were not in, he hurried back out and drove off in the new car. "I can't stand this house when you're not in it," he would explain with no embarrassment at having come home for supper twice in the same day.

Debby would watch the new car back swervingly out the drive and wonder what it would be like to be out of calling-distance of Mrs Merrill, out of the house and out of the yard. One warm day when she had had a particularly trying morning remembering what her own face looked like, she asked Mrs Merrill to take her visiting.

"Where do you want to go, Debby?"

"Let's go calling." She had to get out of this house.

"Who do you want to see?"

"Let's go calling on the neighbors."

"I don't owe any of them visits."

"Do you want to go to walk?"

"I want to lie down if I can possibly finish this patching. I feel a headache coming on."

Debby wandered through the house, and, seeing her reflections in the polished furniture, she again lost herself. She stopped in front of the sideboard and gazed at her features in the mirror. Perhaps it was the curtain-filtered light, or the angle at which the mirror hung, but the face gazing out was Mrs Merrill's. Debby turned and ran out the front door. Glenn was coming up the steps. It was after three o'clock: Junior High was out. "Where're you going, fatso?" he asked.

"Visiting." She started down the steps. Mrs Jackson was

not on her porch. "Watch me across the street." She called from the walk.

"Hurry," Glenn stood on the porch till she reached the opposite curb.

She had never been visiting alone before although Mrs Merrill had often pleaded with her to get out from underfoot. She stood at the door for a long time, but no one answered. Then she saw the bell and rang it. Mrs Abernathy, wiping her hands on an apron, came through the living room and opened the glass front door.

"I've come visiting," Debby said. She glanced nervously over her shoulder at the Merrills' house.

"Mrs Hall! I'm so glad. Come in."

"No. I can't come in."

"Why you certainly can!"

"No. I can't come in."

Mrs Abernathy held the screen door open. "I'd like to know why not!"

"I can just stay a minute."

"Then wait a second while I turn off the oven. Have a seat."

Debby sat on the striped glider she had often studied from across the street. She shook it to see if it squeaked like an old well-chain. It did.

"Your swing squeaks good," she said when Mrs Abernathy came out and sat in the wicker chair.

"Everything here is out of order," Mrs Abernathy explained as though it were a joke. "Everything's old and wearing completely out."

"How is Mr Abernathy's kidneys," Debby asked.

Mrs Abernathy threw her head back and laughed at the ceiling. "You're thinking about Mr Jacobs. He's the one with kidney stones."

"I knew somebody on this side of the street had them," Debby said.

"He suffers terribly." Mrs Abernathy shook her head sadly.

"I bet that's why he drinks so much," Debby nodded sympathetically.

Mrs Abernathy, a loose-necked woman, laughed at the ceiling again. "You're talking about *Mr Abernathy* now!"

It was too confusing. Debby shut up and tried to see who was sitting on the Merrill porch. From here it looked as though Mrs Merrill was sitting on the bench, where she never sat, with her feet on the rungs of another chair. She was eating an apple and was reading. From this distance Debby could not see her features or remember them. "I've got to go now," she said anxiously.

"You haven't been here any time, Mrs Hall."

"I told you I could just stay a minute," Debby flatly reminded her.

"Oh," Mrs Abernathy said. "But I hope you don't think you bothered me. I know people are bound to talk."

"People talk a lot," Debby agreed, wondering how she had ever dared to go visiting alone. She returned home and went into the house without speaking to Glenn who had his nose in a book. Mrs Merrill was lying with a damp cloth across her forehead in the shade-drawn room. Debby was so glad to see her that she could have hugged her properly, but, because it was Mrs Merrill, she didn't dare.

For a month or longer after that Debby was not troubled by Mrs Merrill's ghosts. Then slowly everything in the house began reminding her unduly of that woman. She went visiting again, and for several days she thought about her visit. Then one morning the following week Glenn came into the kitchen and said, while washing his hands: "Mama, I think I'll take Britt's old job after school next year." He turned around and saw that only he and Debby were in the room. She wanted to answer him, but suddenly he was furious. "Where is Mama?" he asked.

"She's upstairs seeing about my sheets," Debby answered. Then she listened while Glenn went through the dining room and up the steps. She sat down and tried to understand how she, Deborah Hall, could be here in the kitchen at the same time Mrs Merrill was upstairs. That night she was afraid to go to sleep. "Who are you when you are asleep," she asked herself the old questions. "And how do you know who you'll be when you wake up in the morning?"

The next morning was Saturday and she was herself. Quite by accident that afternoon she made an important discovery. At the barn when she reached into the coop after the chicken, it flew out past her head and ran squawking across the Grove. "Chicken's out! Chicken's out!" She screamed and the high, excited voice was unquestionably her own. "Here! Chick chick chick chick chicken!" It was a grand feeling to be in command of her own voice again. "Glenn! come help me catch chicken!" Holding up her long skirts she ran in big steps to the back door. She was surprised at her speed.

"Shut the gate, shorty," Glenn yelled from the upstairs window.

She locked herself in the Grove and, still calling, chased the terrified squawking hen in and out among the pecan trees. She was panting and her heart was pounding by the time Glenn arrived and caught the hen. Sitting on a box in the Grove with the bucket of steaming water by her she felt very much like herself. Occasionally she stopped picking the chicken long enough to feel her pounding heart with her feathered fingers. She could not imagine Mrs Merrill screaming, pulling up her skirts and running like merry hell. She laughed and shook her head. "Yea Lord," she said, "if Mrs Merrill wouldn't be a sight trying to catch a hen!" So each Saturday that summer she managed to let a chicken out.

During the following winter whenever she stayed near Mrs Merrill too long at a time or when everything in the house reminded her too constantly of that woman, Debby had only to think about running through the Grove chasing a chicken. She would scroot and eye Mrs Merrill for a spell, trying to see her pulling up her skirts and galloping. Every time she would laugh and then her fears would be gone. Mrs Merrill, however, was sometimes annoyed. "Debby, if you don't quit staring at me and laughing I'm going to be bound to shoot you!"

"You're not going to shoot me either!" She liked for Mrs Merrill to threaten and scold her for that was further proof of their separateness.

Then, after the long winter and a cold, late spring, a sad thing happened. It was the twenty-third day of May. She knew because at breakfast Betty had said, "Only ten more days until graduation." She would be through High School. "And only twelve more days until Julia comes home," Glenn said. "You say it's May the twenty-third?" Debby asked. She seldom knew the exact day of the month and when she learned the number of the day, she remembered it and called every day by that number. Thus for the past four weeks she had been calling every day April the eighteenth. Monday, April the eighteenth was followed by Tuesday, April the eighteenth. But now here it was Saturday, May the twenty-third.

After lunch Mrs Merrill said exactly what Debby had been rehearsing all morning for her to say. "Debby, let's have a big fryer tomorrow." The chicken coop was full of long-legged frying-size chickens. She had not chased a chicken since fall. She wondered if her legs had become too old and stiff.

That afternoon twisting the wooden knob she opened the door and shooed out a Rhode Island red pullet. "Chicken's out! Chicken's out!" she screamed. She shut the gate behind her and ran to the backdoor. "Glenn! Glenn! Come help me catch the chickens. Glenn!"

Mrs Merrill raised the kitchen window. "What is it?"

"Chicken's out," she pointed to the Grove. "Where's Glenn?"

"He's gone to work."

"Oh," Debby said. She had completely forgot about Glenn's Saturday job."

"I'll come help you," Mrs Merrill said.

"No. No," Debby pleaded anxiously. "You stay in the house. I can manage alone." She went back to the Grove and began chasing the chicken in and out under the trees, waving her arms, flapping her apron. The cool breeze in her face and the warm black earth under her feet were refreshing to her as she ran and hollered. "Shoo chick shoo!" She could not at that moment have been more certain that she was Deborah Hall.

"Debby," the quiet voice said from the gate. Had she imagined again that her voice was sounding like Mrs Merrill's? She stopped dead still. "Debby, that's no way to catch a chicken." Mrs Merrill came into the Grove and shut the gate. "You go that way," Mrs Merrill said calmly, walking steadily toward the chicken. Debby walked in the same dignified manner toward the pullet which was gliding along, head sliding backward and forward—actually singing!—along the fence to the corner by the barn. In the corner it stuck its head into a small crack and tried to slip through. Mrs Merrill leaned over with outspread hands and picked it up. Suddenly everything seemed hopeless to Debby.

Chapter 23

TIME, which was the growing of children, had stopped now that Glenn was already taller than Debby. Each day seemed endless to her despite the frequent, excited news broadcasts Mrs Merrill dialed for constantly. But Mrs Merrill, listening, staring into the rug, appeared not to notice when days ended and nights began. At bedtime, when Debby could stay awake no longer and had nodded until her neck ached, she left Mrs Merrill sitting by the radio which talked and talked about war and soap. Britton was in the Army and soap was hard to get. What else was there to know?

Even on the days, often now, when Mrs Merrill's head was ready to split wide open like an overripe watermelon, she would not allow the radio to be turned off. The War, she said, had to end before Britton was sent overseas; but apparently Hitler and Toe Joe did not hear. First the War, then the Depression, now the War again—there was no end to things that could happen on the face of this earth. The War was more fun to listen to and to look at than the Depression had been. Debby studied it on all the shining magazine covers where boys dressed like Britt grinned painfully at her from red skies. "W-a-r, war." Sometimes she could make out the word printed slantwise across a page. It was an easy, short word and she was never really in doubt when she pointed to it proudly and asked, wisely, "That says 'war' doesn't it?" Then she would casually add, "I wasn't sure. My eyes are getting weak."

Mrs Merrill of course was not the only one who had gone hog-wild thinking about the fighting. Glenn was hoping every day, out loud, that it would last at least four more years so that he would be eighteen and old enough to join the marines or submarines. He would box madly about the kitchen at an enemy which he alone could see, until, exhausted he would fall back in a chair. He never told Debby his plans now, but when other boys were in the kitchen with him, dirtying glasses, getting crumbs all over the floor, she would stand in the pantry and hear their secrets. They argued about the Air Corps, the Marines, the Navy. Then when the argument reached the shouting point a silence came over them, broken occasionally by a fist slapped into a flat hand and the outrageous whisper: "We're old enough to go." They had no respect for the seventeen and eighteen-year-old juniors and seniors who were dreading the draft. That was why, when Glenn first began asking, "How old do I look, Debby?" she always said, "Twelve or thirteen." Lately though she had learned that the correct answer was "Seventeen." It was one of the few questions Glenn asked her any more; one of the few words he liked to hear her utter. Usually when she spoke to him, if he answered at all, it was to say: "Dry up. You wouldn't understand."

Mrs Merrill said Glenn talked about the War just to annoy her, and it was true that he did grin and glance sideways at his mother before bringing up the subject. Usually it would be when they were all at the table. He gazed at his plate and said quite calmly, "Wonder when Britt's going overseas." A silence followed in which Mr Merrill glanced quickly at his wife and Betty glared at Glenn and said in a silent grimace, "Shut up." Glenn, though, would continue: "Bet you ten to one, Dad, that he volunteers for overseas duty just as soon as he can. Soon as they start sending big shipments toward Europe." For some reason they all seemed to be at Glenn's mercy; no one dared tell him to be quiet. It was not because they were afraid of him, but because they were afraid not to let him speak what might well be the truth. "Then I'll be next. Maybe Britt and I can get in the same outfit." He would stare at Mrs Merrill's bowed head as though trying to see into the very center of her brain where perhaps there was a tiny gold scale in which she tried to balance her love for Glenn with her love for Britton. "Would you like that, Mama? Would you like for Britt and me to get in the same outfit?"

During the early warm days of that spring, the first spring of the War, Glenn was busy tearing down the barn to make room for the house which was to be built in Merrill's Grove. He worked from school-out until dark, and sometimes after dark, throwing soggy, moss-covered shingles off of the old roof. At supper he was usually too tired and hungry to talk. Debby, however, watched him constantly with the hope that he would say something—not necessarily to her—to anyone. She had no gateway to his thoughts now.

One hot Saturday he worked all day. That night at supper he was so tired that he pushed his plate away from himself after the first bite. He propped his elbows on the table and leaned his face into his rough, nail-scratched hands.

"What's wrong?" Mr Merrill asked.

"It's hot up on that barn."

"Why didn't you start taking some of the sideboards off then?"

Apparently Glenn didn't hear. He was watching his mother, waiting for her to speak. He drank a noticeably small sip of milk and set the glass heavily on the table. Debby wanted to say, "Why don't you drink your milk?" but he was watching his mother, not her. His eyes narrowed slightly, as though the soft kitchen light were too much after the hot spring sun. His mouth turned down in a grin. "Where's Britt now?"

Mrs Merrill looked up from her plate, which might, from the expression on her face, have been a battlefield. "What?"

"Is Britt still in Colorado?"

"Yes," she said flatly.

"How long is he going to be there?"

"He doesn't say. He wanted to know when Julia gets home from school. I don't know if he's expecting a furlough or not."

"Probably an overseas furlough. Handsel Tubbs' brother got one. They always let them go home before sending them overseas."

Mrs Merrill started to ask a dozen questions but seemed completely paralyzed by the slow grin that curled Glenn's lips downward.

"He's been in almost a year," she finally spoke, half-defiantly, half-meekly.

"Sure. He ought to be about ready. Wonder if I can get in that outfit." Glenn held with both hands to the glass of milk. "Would you like for me to be in the same outfit with Britt, Mama?" He had not asked the question for over a month now, but still he sounded as though he were a parrot who knew only that sentence. Debby had a feeling that if she should shake him in the night he would sit up shouting: "Would you like that, Mama?"

"Why do you keep asking?"

"I don't know. It just seems like it'd be convenient for you."

"How, *convenient*? In what way?"

"Well, you wouldn't have to write to me. I could just read Britt's letters."

"Why certainly I'd write to you if you were away from home, in the Army."

"I mean, if I was in Britt's outfit, you wouldn't have to write so many letters."

"It doesn't make any difference whose outfit you were in, I'd still write to you."

Glenn frowned as though he had never thought of such a thing. He forced a yawn and dried his eyes. He looked at Debby and the slow grin came back. "Would you write to me?"

He was poking fun at her again; else, why else would he be talking to her at all? She spoke carefully, "You probably wouldn't care to know what I would have to say." She could not understand the silence that followed or why Glenn once more for the first day since the wiener roast, looked at her kindly. But suddenly he laughed. "I still want to get in Britt's outfit. I can see us now overseas . . ." He described a battlefield. ". . . and then that night I'd begin a letter home 'Dear Mama, Britt was killed today.' " He gave a short hard laugh. Apparently no one heard for they finished supper in the deadest sort of silence.

Spring ended and in June Britt landed—like a great bird—on an island in the Pacific. Julia returned almost immediately to college and Betty went in training to be a nurse, and eventually an ambulance driver. Glenn got up early every morning and waited for the postman. Street noises, the rumbling Army trucks, the overhead droning bombers, and distant blaring radios bothered and distracted Mrs Merrill so much that even on the hottest days the windows and doors were never opened. Mrs Merrill's room was the darkest, the quietest, the coolest in the house.

At first the coolness of that room was as refreshing as water after the heat of the back yard, but then as the leaves put out, grew large, reached out for the window, flattened themselves like hands against the panes, shut out the light, muted outside noises, the chill was no longer refreshing. The air was damp, clammy; and smelled of mold. Mrs Merrill drew the curtains in her room after lunch and lay there on the sofa with the radio playing news at her head across which was folded a cold wet towel. Debby sat in the large rocker, her toe tips barely touching the floor on each forward motion, and thought what a fine room this would be for dead people to live in. Corpses would like the stale cold air, the bodyless radio voices; and they would without doubt be happy with Mrs Merrill who could remain motionless for hours.

"Her head hurts," Debby would explain Mrs Merrill's quietness to herself so often that her own head would begin throbbing at the temples aching behind the eyes. Then when Mrs Merrill tried unsuccessfully to sit up, sharp pains shot like lightning through Debby's head. Yet when Mrs Merrill had a headache, Debby could not stay out of the room. She wandered about the house, touching the familiar, well-dusted articles, and paused at each mirror to inspect her features to make sure that she was still herself. You couldn't be too certain that you had not become Mrs Merrill, especially since you were the only two people in the house almost all day. Sometimes Debby sought refuge for her own identity in the yard—among Mrs Merrill's flowers, under Mrs Merrill's trees, near Mrs Merrill's greenhouse, where Mrs Merrill's extra flowerpots were kept—but seeing that she could not escape she felt safer being watched by the motionless woman herself, than being followed followed followed by the ghost of her. As a dog who does not understand a leash winds itself in ever smaller circles about a tree, Debby wandered about the yard, on the porches, in the halls, ever nearer the center room, until finally she would be seated again staring unwillingly at the ailing woman.

In the gloomful room they listened one evening to the eternal voices which talked incessantly about battles and suds until Debby thought she would scream. She decided quickly however that the front porch would be a better screaming-place. "War war war," she muttered as she went to the porch. "Why don't they stop talking about it?" The fluttering moths beat softly against the door screen; the hard-shelled beetles dashed against the ceiling and bounced to the floor. Without turning on the outside light she opened the door, waving back the moths that sought the inside light. "War war war." She walked to the edge of the porch. "God could stop it if He weren't so High and Mighty." At that, perhaps through fear of a heavenly reproach or divine explanation she glanced nervously up at the night sky.

It had split wide open? Smack-dab across the center of darkness was a band of sunlight.

"Chicken Little!" Debby whispered aghast. She had always known that Chicken Little was right; that the world would come to an end; that the sky would someday fall in on their heads. Now here it was, already cracking open. Terrified she held to the porch column for support. "Come here," she screamed. "Come here." She could not remember where she was or whom she was calling. She did not hear the nervous rapid footfalls coming toward her. "Help," she whispered, beyond screaming.

"Debby! Debby! What is it?"

"The world, the world!" Debby hollered.

"What?" called Mrs Merrill, crossing the living room.

"The world!"

"What about the world?"

"It's coming to an end!"

Mrs Merrill snapped on the porch light. The sight of the old, familiar and faded porch furniture was for a moment reassuring to Debby. Nothing horrible could happen among familiar surroundings—only in darkness and strange, unknown worlds to other people. Still she could not stop trembling. Mrs Merrill stood near without touching her. "Are you sick, Debby?"

Maybe that was it. Maybe she was so sick and tired of war and war talk that she had simply hoped the world would come to an end. She had dreamed the sky had split and would soon begin to fall in huge pieces about their heads. Cautiously she peeped at the sky. It was still split! "There!" she whispered.

Mrs Merrill shook her gently. "That's only a spotlight, Debby."

"A what?"

"A searchlight, for enemy planes."

Debby did not understand, but the calm sanity in Mrs Merrill's tone whispered away her fear.

A shrill whistle from the street split the silence as the light split the sky. "Get those lights out!"

Quickly Mrs Merrill crossed the porch, turned out the light. "Go see about the upstairs light."

Debby was puzzled. She followed Mrs Merrill who was slipping through the house, turning off the lights, tunneling through the darkness like a mole. Surely she didn't think hiding in the dark would save the world! Debby would have no part in such a to-do. If the sky were going to fall, she wanted to see it. A siren was roaring through the night. Someone had already been killed by a falling hunk.

"It's an air raid," announced Mrs Merrill when she realized she was being followed through the darkness. "A drill. A mock attack. Just for practice. Did you see about the lights upstairs?"

"A practice air raid," Debby mused to herself as she climbed the stairs, feeling with her foot for each unseen step. It seemed to her a shabby trick, practicing that the world was coming to an end, simply to scare a body to death. Why would people want to practice such a thing as that? In room after room she switched on the lights and inspected the bulbs. Leaving the entire upper floor ablaze she came back down the steps in time to hear the sharp whistle, a pounding at the door and the same gruff-rough voice shouting: "Last warning. Get those lights out!" Mrs Merrill rushed up the stairs and again the house was dark. Debby was furious. When Mrs Merrill asked her what she meant by such action she said, "You said see about the lights. If we aren't going to have any down here I thought we at least could have some upstairs." She would not admit to a deliberate meanness, but if the house had not been dark anyone could have seen the anger on the little woman's face, which became more intense until finally she was sticking out her tongue at every remembered object in the room. She listened for Mrs Merrill to lie down on the sofa, and when she heard her sigh and the sofa creak, she stuck out her tongue in that direction. To die in the dark was disgraceful enough, but to sit there and pretend to be dying in the dark, that was—she had heard a preacher say the phrase—that was a sin against the Holy Ghost. She shivered at her conjurations.

She waited to see if they would have a headache. Even though the room was quiet she could not catch the rhythm of Mrs Merrill's breathing. When she was able to match her inhalations with Mrs Merrill's she could know without being told exactly how they were going to feel: headaches, fatigue, drowsiness. Now, with the lights off, she could not see the rising, falling chest, the gentle quiver of the nostrils. There was no way to know if the thin deep crease had pointed down between Mrs Merrill's brows, indicative of a headache, signal for quiet. Debby thought about her own head, but having no clues as to how it should feel, she felt merely that she had lost it. She touched it with both hands but it was as though she were fondling a head of lettuce or cabbage. Finally, when the vision of herself as a headless woman became too vivid, she was pressed into speech: "Do you have a headache?"

"I'm hoping," Mrs Merrill said carefully, "that if I don't move, I won't have. It's the faint beginning of one."

Debby quit rocking. Now she could feel the heaviness behind her own eyes, the unduly hard throbbing in her own temples. Speaking before she was even aware that she had words on her tongue, she said: "I wish I had never started fixing my hair like yours."

"Why?" Mrs Merrill asked, distractedly.

What if she answered: Because I hate you? Since polite people wouldn't say such a thing, she said only, "I'd like to cut it off short."

"Mine or yours?" Mrs Merrill asked.

With a sudden twinge she realized that she wanted Mrs Merrill's hair cut, but that was probably impolite too.

"Mine," she said, and understood then that she meant, "either."

"You do need a change, don't you, Debby?"

Did she mean a change of homes? The old fear, the nightmare of being separated from this house and Glenn caught her for a second unprepared; but then, before she could question Mrs Merrill she heard from her memory the soothing refrain: "Debby, as long as I'm alive you have a home."

"What kind of change?"

"I don't know," Mrs Merrill said. "But all your days seem so much the same. We work and then you wander aimlessly around the house touching articles, glancing at reflections. You search around over the yard until I'm sure you must be sick of everything in it. And then you come sit in this room and I know I can't be much company to you when I'm worried about Britt and trying to find some comfort out of the war news. Maybe as you say, a haircut or a new dress would make a little change for you."

"How about you?"

"I think I've had too much change. I think that's why I stay so tired." Mrs Merrill talked on but Debby wasn't listening.

"A *red* dress maybe?" Had Thomas forgotten?

"I don't think a red dress would be quite appropriate for a woman your age, or with your coloring. How about lavender or a pretty powder blue to bring out your white hair."

"I like red."

"Maybe we can find a piece of material in a nice maroon."

"You think Glenn will join up before the War's over?"

"Join what?"

"The Marines."

"Let's not even think about the War lasting that long. He's just fourteen."

"He's growing up though," Debby told her.

"I know. This is the last year, probably, you can wear his old sweaters. But we don't have to worry too much about clothes now. At least we can thank God for that."

"Do you think maybe I could have a new dress and do something about my hair too?"

"Do you think you'd like it short?"

"Not too short. Just an inch or two off?"

"An inch or two wouldn't make much difference you know. Except maybe it wouldn't be so ragged and thin looking."

Again silence and darkness and the slow pain closed in on her. "Let's do something!" Debby fretted. "I . . ." she began again but did not finish. I'm trapped, she told herself. She could not leave this woman and this house, yet if she stayed here longer she would disappear completely. Each day her voice sounded more like Mrs Merrill's voice; her footsteps more like *her* footsteps. Once that would have been fun, but now there were no children to trick into saying, "Mama." Only Glenn remained and he acted as though he didn't know the word.

"What were you going to say?"

Debby chuckled: "I've got a good mind to have all my hair cut off."

"Mrs Hall!"

"Yes I have," she laughed. "Baldheaded! Like a baby."

The silence was Mrs Merrill's, who broke it after a long while by saying: "I used to think when I'd look at my babies and they were so little and helpless, 'Wonder if they'll ever be able to take care of themselves' and if I got the least bit sick I'd become panicky worrying about what would become of them. I'd say over and over, 'You must stay strong.' Now they're all old enough to take care of themselves—even Britt. But the same old nagging fears pester me sometimes about you. I keep saying to myself: 'What would become of little old Debby if you were to die?' When I have these headaches and open my eyes to see you staring at me, frightened, I wonder how and why we ever became so much in need of each other and how it can ever end."

"You mean you don't want me around?"

"I don't mean that at all. It's that I keep wishing I could be sure you'd always be well taken care of, that you knew how to protect yourself. Let the children or anyone flatter you, say a few sweet words to you, and you'll work yourself to death. If I don't watch you all through the day you go beyond your strength. We're growing old, Debby, and we'll have to learn that some things must be left undone. We can't expect to clean this big house the way we once did. You must learn to rest without my telling you every time I hear you short of breath."

"I rest."

"And your food. You still don't know what to eat and what makes you sick."

"I eat what you eat."

"But I always have to tell you. Show you. Why don't you learn? I may not always be here."

Was Mrs Merrill keeping Secrets? "Where're you going?"

"I'm not going anywhere. We never do know though what's going to happen."

Of course Mrs Merrill knew what was going to happen. If she didn't know she wouldn't have brought up the subject. I'll just stay quiet, Debby thought, until she decides to tell me. It hurt her to think that Mrs Merrill was harboring a Secret.

"You never can, but you have to try in times like these to be ready for any sort of emergency: sickness, death . . ."

"Famine and pesty-ants."

"That's another thing—the insect powder. If I don't watch you constantly you drag the dish rag through it or spill it in the cups on the shelves. I can't even make you believe in poison."

Debby counted on her fingers the things she was supposed to believe in: God and Jesus and George Washington. Thomas and Grover Cleveland (the thumb); and on the other hand: snow, nickels, rest, Ford cars. There was only one finger left—yet she must believe in both Mrs Merrill and poison. Could you give one finger two names? She hesitated—poison or Mrs Merrill? both? either? neither? poison or Mrs Merrill?—the finger remained unnamed. "Well, just don't talk to me about it."

"You see what happens, Debby? I always seem to be fussing at you, when you're the last person in the world I'd want to be mean to." Her voice was kind; she could not, in such a mood, reserve the Secret longer. Debby waited to hear it. Mrs Merrill continued, the words on her breath scarcely a whisper. "The Lord understood I could never have gotten along without you, Debby."

Debby whimpered, inwardly, to herself, silently, and an anger flared through her love-grief. A person didn't have a right to say a thing like that, to tear your heart out when you weren't looking, when you were merely sitting in the dark waiting for the sky to fall in.

Chapter 24

WHEN Debby had nothing else to think about, she could always try to decide what to do with the hair on top of her head. She could imagine cutting it slam off and being as baldheaded as a baldheaded baby or leaving it exactly the way it was, as long as Mrs Merrill's. If she had a red dress, something Mrs Merrill would never wear, she wouldn't need a hair cut to be different, to be herself. She could put on the red dress and be Deborah Hall just as big as you please. Even without a red dress she often went upstairs, shut the door of her room, and pretended, by wearing beads and jewelry, that she was Mrs Hall. If, though, she sat too long before the mirror, she became Mrs Merrill wearing beads and jewelry. The length of time she could remain herself before the glass was growing shorter and shorter. And without being told, remembering certain candles and loaves of bread, pools of wax, crusts and crumbs, she knew what happened to anything that grew shorter and shorter and shorter.

One thing she could be thankful for since the air raid and Mrs Merrill's ensuing week-long headache: the radio could not be played constantly. Dr Bronston who toddled up the walk like an old, old baby had told Mrs Merrill flatly she would have to find a new doctor if she persisted in listening to war news, that he could not hope to do anything for her if she listened and kept her nerves jingled jangled jingled. Furthermore, he said that with her blood pressure raging way yonder out of sight, she was in much more danger than Britt had been in or ever would be. "Damn it," Dr Bronston shook his finger in her sick face, "you can kill yourself worrying if you want to. But don't say I didn't warn you and don't send for me when you're beyond going." Quietly though, in the living room, he said to Mr Merrill and Glenn, "Make her relax. Plead with her to rest and go out. I can't keep her blood pressure down with medicine alone." Still mumbling he toddled down the walk, his head as baby-bald as Debby, watching him, wanted hers to be.

She turned back from the front door in time to see Glenn tiptoing after Mr Merrill to the back bedroom. An instant fear for Mrs Merrill's safety chilled her. She followed quickly to the bedroom.

"A week away from home. I couldn't do that."

"Why not?" Mr Merrill asked. "We haven't had a vacation, not just the two of us, since before Rebecca was born."

Embarrassed, Debby and Glenn glanced at each other, aware of their unwelcome here.

"Maybe up to Lakefalls." He was holding Mrs Merrill's wrist turning her hand over and over in his own, examining each line and vein. Debby and Glenn were confused by this simple caress. Two hands touching should not have revealed the complete intimacy that had existed between two people who had gone together through hot and cold running hell. Troubled, shy, Debby wandered to the window and worried the latch. Glenn followed her, then turned abruptly and sat down.

"You must see about the house in the Grove, and your work. If we don't make money and pay our debts now, we'll never have anything."

"One week . . ." Mr Merrill began in an almost boyish voice that prevented Debby from turning her back to the window.

"Who would look after the house?"

"Debby and Glenn."

"And who would look after them?"

"Good gosh, Mama! I'm fourteen!"

"That's what I know."

"I could stay over at Handsel's."

"And Debby?"

Debby knew that she should say something, but she didn't want to be left alone in this house. What would she do with Mrs Merrill gone? Yet she must say something. "I could go back to Stonebrook." If they said "yes" her heart would flutter slowly down to her stomach and be digested there.

"Poor Debby, still worrying about leaving. Stonebrook is gone. Torn down. There's a War Plant where it used to be."

Debby tried unsuccessfully to imagine the site.

"No. Debby and I'll stay here this summer. We aren't working hard now." Mrs Merrill looked from one to the other, firmly, yet wearily, as though she were talking to very young children. "I've had these little dizzy spells before you know. When Britt gave us so much trouble, I had terrible headaches then, but I always lived through them."

"Britt," Glenn began, and he almost smiled sarcastically. Then he turned red and stopped.

"Britt what?" Mrs Merrill asked.

"You don't have to worry about him," Glenn said, but his words sounded as falsely sure as a commentator's.

Mrs Merrill glanced at him mockingly from the corner of her eye. "I listen to the radio too, you know."

"Not any more you don't," Mr Merrill said. "Not after today."

"I'm not going to be treated like a child."

"If you act like one you're going to be."

"The radio's the only way I have of knowing what's happening. I'll go crazy if I have to wait all night for the morning paper without any news from afternoon to dawn."

"I'll listen, or Glenn'll listen, and if there's anything you need to know we'll tell you."

"And all day long when you and Glenn are away?"

"I'll take the radio tubes with me if necessary."

Anybody with two good eyes could see that Mrs Merrill was lying there quietly because she had a plan in her head that would obtain her all the news she wanted, radio or no radio. If she's planning on using carrier pigeons like Glenn was talking about, I want to see that, Debby thought.

The next two days the house was as quiet as cotton. Mrs Merrill lay down, she sat up, she wandered through the house, she walked briskly through the yards, she watched the workmen on the roof of the Grove house until the ringing hammer-blows gave her a headache. Finally she settled herself on the sofa in the darkened room. "See, it isn't the news. I'm more disturbed without it, knowing what could be happening, how near the Japs are to Britt."

Debby said, "Why don't you begin my red dress?"

"I'm going to, Debby, if it's the last thing I do. You're going to have a red dress," Mrs Merrill said, but twice more that week Debby had to ask when they were going to town for the cloth.

Lately though Mrs Merrill had to be reminded frequently. "Debby, don't let me forget to order the groceries." "Remind me, Debby, to have Mr Merrill leave money for the milkman." "When did we send out the laundry? How long has it been?" "Did I pay the paper boy once this week? He was back today." "What did I do with the ration book? Surely Debby, we haven't used this many coupons." Strangely enough, given a minute to think about these matters, Debby could remember. "You didn't pay the paper boy. You went to the quilt-chest for the money but you didn't have the change." Sometimes Mrs Merrill had only to say "Debby" and the little woman, following her through the house, or her eyes about the room, could produce the answer to an unasked question. At such times she would grin all over herself. It seemed the most natural thing ever to be answering questions instead of asking them.

It seemed natural, too, to follow Mrs Merrill and correct her absent-minded actions and oversights: to turn off the water left running when the phone rang, to take the smoking frying pan off the flame, to defrost the frigidaire, color the oleomargarine, and water the potted plants and turn them toward the sun (though often Mrs Merrill would, not thinking, turn them back again).

One day when the headlines were as tall as match stems, Mrs Merrill rushed into the kitchen and glanced nervously about as though she were expecting a pigeon-friend to be flying through. She shook her head, rubbed her eyes and sat down quickly to keep from falling.

"What have we planned for supper, Debby?"

"We haven't had lunch yet," Debby explained, and her voice had never sounded so much like Mrs Merrill's.

"Oh," Mrs Merrill half-laughed, half-sighed. "Lunch. What time is it?"

"Not twelve yet."

"We've got lunch on, haven't we?"

"Long time ago. Before you went out of here."

"Then don't let it burn. I'm going to lie down a minute."

Debby listened as Mrs Merrill went down the hall. She heard the door click and a booming radio voice which quickly became a whisper. When the hands folded on the clock, Debby tiptoed in and turned off the radio. "Let's eat."

"All right," Mrs Merrill said, but Debby had to call her twice more.

"Come to dinner," Debby finally commanded, and became enormous as she spoke. She even had to duck her head as she went out through the low, seven-foot door. "Come on. Dinner." Neither of them ate worth a picky, but it was a grand feeling to have decided when they should sit down at the table. Debby drank two cups of coffee and poured a second cup for Mrs Merrill who wasn't supposed to have had the first cup. All that day Debby directed their activities.

The next morning, however, Mrs Merrill was up early and had read the paper by the time Debby came down. She folded the paper on the table and spoke firmly, tensely, "Hurry through breakfast, Mrs Hall. We're going to town this afternoon."

The tone, short and businesslike, at first frightened Debby, but then she began thinking of the red dress. She was so excited she could not know exactly what she was doing all morning. Glenn came home to lunch and added to the confusion. "Why don't you go to the show?"

"It's too hot. I want to stay up town only an hour at the longest."

"It's cool in the show. The Dixieland is air conditioned."

"I always feel as though I've been hit on the head when I come out of one of those cold places onto the hot street."

"It'll be shady when you come out. If you go at four."

"Do they have that movie with the horses running?" Debby asked.

"Debby, they change the show two or three times a week."

Glenn was always lying to her. Every time she had ever been to the movie she had seen horses running and later a train puffing into the station. "I'd like to see that again."

"Then if we finish our shopping in time."

At some time after three that afternoon, the cloth for the red dress under her arm, the buttons, thread, tape, and red zipper—whoever dreamed of such a thing—in Mrs Merrill's pocketbook, Debby waited while Mrs Merrill slid a five dollar bill through a cut-out place to a girl in a glass cage. You could see only half the girl, and Debby walked all around the cage to see how such a thing could be possible, and how they could have got the girl into the tiny room which was furnished only with a cash register and an electric fan. "I'd hate to live in a little room like that. People staring in at me." Debby walked around the ticket box again. The girl, watching her, smiled nervously. Debby smiled back and gave a friendly sharp rap on the glass to the poor lonesome, caged-in creature. Mrs Merrill, guiding her into the theater, seemed only interested in hurrying inside out of the heat and glare. She wouldn't pause to study the huge colored picture of boys in suits like Britt's.

The long marble hall was cool and in the center of it was, of all things, a fish pond. Water was spilling off of what appeared to be a round table some crazy-body had set down slam in the middle of the pool. "Oh my!" There were colored lights under the water so the fish could see where they were going and would not go bumping into each other and against the sides and bottom.

"Come on, Debby," Mrs Merrill pleaded, tugging at her

arm. "I feel . . ." She didn't finish the sentence. She handed the tickets to an ill-mannered soldier who tore them up right in her face and made her take the scraps. He's a German, Debby thought and gave him plenty of room as she walked through the door. She didn't take her eyes off him until she was standing in the aisle in sight of the Big People.

From that moment on she saw nothing but the huge gray giants who filled the entire window at the far end of the building. And how they did carry on and talk! Just like real people only bigger and louder and sillier. Today they were outdoors crawling on a beach, wading through water, shooting, throwing firecrackers.

"Glenn knew it was a war picture," Mrs Merrill said bitterly. She hid her face in her hands. "Let's go, Debby, as soon as my head quits swimming." But then she began watching the picture and how one of the giants had his leg cut off. Two large terrified eyes peeped in at the audience and music crashed down from the ceiling. A nurse staggered out of a tent and cried, maybe because she couldn't light her cigarette. Then there was a room with an old man in a uniform talking over a telephone, and then an airplane with a man talking over a telephone. There was the nurse again holding a man's hand, the man with the eyes that had peeped into the theater. For an hour Debby sat on the edge of her seat, amazed at the goings-on. There was more shooting. A plane flew through the clouds. The nurse ran out of the building, stumbled and fell. The boy hobbled out, stumbled, and fell. There were treetops and a striped flag waving. Everyone clapped.

The women around Debby blew their noses. Mrs Merrill's face was set in an expressionless mask, as though she had watched through glass eyes. "Let's go," she said when people had stopped shuffling up the aisle.

"Let's see another one."

"It will be the same thing again."

"You mean just what we've seen. Again. They'll have the same War again."

"Yes, the same War again."

Debby had hoped all through the picture that the big giants would be able to think of something different to do next, something besides fight and kill. She followed Mrs Merrill up the aisle past the people sitting in the dark, past the fish swimming in the colored lights.

Outside the late afternoon sun blinded them. Groping along after Mrs Merrill across the hot sidewalk, Debby suspected she was being led into an oven. "This isn't our car," Debby said as she was pushed still half-blind through a door. Maybe Mrs Merrill was going to bake her into a gingerbread lady, like the witch in Handsome Rachel.

Mrs Merrill gave the driver the address twice and made him repeat it. Then exhausted, with her eyes closed, she lay back in the hot leather seat. Tears were streaking her face and sweat, her neck. Little dewdrops of sweat popped out above her lip and on her forehead. "Debby," she shuddered violently all over, "get me home."

Chapter 25

DEBBY lay on the bed and stared at the ceiling. Who would have guessed that her life here in this house would end so suddenly and completely. Her eyelids were sandy but she would not let them close because when she did she saw again Mrs Merrill lying on the seat of the taxi; the driver carrying her in his arms up the walk, into the house, into the bedroom; the doctors sadly shaking their heads to the questioning Merrills and saying that she could not live a week after such a stroke. For two days now Debby had wandered over the house, unable to eat, to talk, to answer questions; unable to stop breathing. She could not stay away from the door of the room where Mrs Merrill was lying unconscious. But always there was a nurse there, day and night, who pushed her away with finger to lip and never a word.

The Merrills still talked to her vaguely as they wandered in their separate dazes about the hush-filled house. Julia was home. Betty was home. Glenn was home. Mr Merrill was home all day. Britt sent red crosses. And Rebecca could not come back because she was out west having a baby and a divorce. When the children wandered into Debby's room she watched their soft lips—which she had memorized a thousand times—moving but their words were as far off and meaningless as the cawing of a distant crow on a snow-filled evening. There was no need for any talk; all of them knew that with the end of Mrs Merrill was the end of the world. Fear tingled Debby's entire body. She went with swimmy-head to the bathroom to see if she could be sick just one more time.

She held to the water tank and gazed down at her face in the toilet. The fine web of wrinkles about her mouth and eyes wiggled in the water. Her wrinkled neck hung smooth from the weight of its own flesh. She opened her mouth twice and breathed deeply. Her stomach was empty. She dropped a square of tissue which she had torn to clean her lips with should she be sick. It floated unevenly, side to side, down into the bowl and blanked out her face. She flushed the toilet and watched while the square blank face whirled faster and faster and disappeared in a splashing roar.

She let cold water run over her fingertips and pressed them against her glassy, hot, heavy-lidded eyes. A cold chill frosted the triangle between her shoulder blades. Thoughts passed through her head so fast yet so dimly she could not grasp them as she wandered back and fell across the bed. For two nights she had not been able to sleep, yet if she relaxed the least bit all outside noises crept in and became part of a strange dream-world where she and Mrs Merrill were going about the housework together, on tiptoes, quietly because the baby was asleep in his cradle. She could not bear to awake from this dream again to discover that Mrs Merrill was not working but was lying unconscious. Debby pushed herself up, got unsteadily to her feet, and straightened her wrinkled Sunday dress. Mrs Merrill had told her to wear the dress to town and now there was no one to say "Wear this wear that." Still since there was no work and there were so many whispering strangers, each with food or flowers to be thanked for, each day was like Sunday.

Holding to the stair rail, Debby went downstairs. At the door of the living room she stood and studied the ghost family. What would become of them all? Mr Merrill had never been able to stay in the house when his wife was out visiting. Julia, sitting with folded hands at the silent piano, would fade completely away like ground fog in a warm wind. Rebecca, her phonograph records warped and dusty, was already gone and not coming back. "Betty, will Betty take me to live with her in nurse-training?" She studied Betty who was frowning in a fitful nap on the sofa. "Or Glenn?" She watched where he sat behind a magazine, pretending to read, yet peeping over the top when the nurse, far off through the house, opened a door. He hid his grief in anger so that no one dared speak directly to him. She tried to see through the magazine-shield which he held between himself and the world. Would Glenn come back to her and take her to live with him? "Glenn," she spoke quietly. He turned blind eyes on her.

Pain cramped her stomach and she went to the dining room. Not a bite had been cooked in the kitchen because it was too near the sick room. In the center of the table was a ham Mr Merrill had sent up from a restaurant and around it on fancy lettuce-bed dishes were pounds of potato salad which the neighbors had brought in. Roses and potato salad—if you liked either of them you could live forever in this house. Debby had never liked potato salad and now the sight of roses, which Mrs Merrill knew better than anyone how to grow . . . "Pea turkey," Debby whispered, angry and frightened, "she'd better not die and leave me here."

She filled a glass with water from the sweating silver

pitcher. She sipped water as she walked around the table. The sight of Mrs Merrill's empty plate was a warning to her to eat carefully. "Eat what I eat. Eat what I eat. Now Debby," the voice whispered as she reached out her hand, "you know pickles don't agree with you. Eat what I eat. Take the crackers, leave the salad alone." "You know what ham does to you." She put down the knife and walked to the sideboard where there was a coconut cake. "You don't know what's in that cake. No telling what. Eat what I eat." Hunger pangs were gnawing like lizards in her stomach yet she could not eat. Twice the day before and the day before that she had asked Julia: "What are they giving her to eat?" And Julia answered: "Nothing. She can't eat. She's not even conscious."

"But," Debby said, "she can't live without eating." No one had been paying any attention whatsoever to Debby though. She waited to see if the nurses slipped food into the room, but when she saw that they only carried bowls of cracked ice, she decided that she would just wait and eat when Mrs Merrill did. Each time she cracked ice for the nurses she saved a glassful and drank the water from it as it melted. She stood now and sipped the water as she glanced with nausea at the greasy potato salad. She ate two soda crackers and went again to the door of Mrs Merrill's room.

I'm by myself, she said to herself. Alone. There's not a person on God's big fat green earth who wants me. "All they want out of you is work work work, and when you've worked your fingers to the bones for them and are old, you'll see that they care about you exactly what they can get out of you." That was Mrs Merrill whispering. "But as long as I'm alive Debby, you have a home. I hope to God though you'll die first so I'll know you were always well treated!" Debby sat down heavily on the cassock by the door and thought so hard that Mrs Merrill was sure to hear her thoughts. Don't leave me. Don't leave me. Don't leave me. She buried her face in her apron and allowed a few of the tears that had been boiling in her head to roll scorchingly down her face. Damn you damn you damn you, she muttered at Mrs Merrill.

Betty opened the door and backed out of the room. Hadn't she left Betty asleep in the front room? Cat naps, that was all Betty would allow herself. "Debby, I've told you a dozen times you mustn't sit here." She pulled Debby to her feet and led her out into the back yard. "If she were to hear you crying like that, it would only make her worse."

"I can't help it," Debby sobbed. "I . . . I go all empty and weak inside and my stomach hurts."

"Well cry somewhere else, not outside that door." Betty tried to act like the other two nurses. She gave sharp orders and joined with them in keeping everyone out of the room. She slept on a pallet in the back hall at night so that when the sheets needed changing she would be there to move her mother. "If anyone picks her up, or moves her, besides me," she said when the other two nurses were together, "there's going to be hell. Considerable hell." And even though her back was now so sore she could hardly walk, she still insisted on sleeping on the hard pallet outside the door and being called when the linen was to be changed.

Betty left Debby standing in the middle of the glaring back yard. Debby fetched a porch chair from the sideyard and placed it next to the house, under the sick-room window, behind the shrubbery where she could see every move without being seen and hear every noise in the room above without herself being heard. She shut her eyes against the glare and tried to remember all that had happened. A stroke. You stroke dogs, cats, Spike, animals, people you love. Who would strike a body so hard it lay shuddering without a moan in the backseat of a taxi? Trying to recall the scene to herself she saw Mrs Merrill open her pocketbook for cabfare and pull out, not money, but an ice mallet with which she hit herself over the head: "Bong." "Lightning comes in strokes." The word made sense now and for the first time Debby knew that the doctors were right. But again her stomach cramped for the doctors had said Mrs Merrill could not live a week. Mrs Merrill walked toward her smiling, bent low and whispered, "I'm dying." Debby shook her head and mumbled fretfully, "No. no." She opened her eyes and there again was the glaring backyard and above her the nurse near the open window saying, "Call the doctor. Quick, she can't stand another convulsion." Ice water poured through Debby's stomach for it was not a dream, never a dream. There would be no waking up. Awake or asleep Mrs Merrill was sick unto death of living.

A blue jay called out and with a sharp slap slap slap flew out of the mimosa. Truly then it was not a dream. Before her the bright bare back yard stretched under the hot afternoon sun; behind her the darkened room gave out the sound of whispers, feet-running drumming, and moans and whimpers as Mrs Merrill was shaken by another convulsion. Debby dug her fingernails into the calloused heels of her hands, holding tightly onto nothing, and dared not breathe while waiting for her heart to beat again. Quietness came gradually to the room above—a long pause in which Mrs Merrill's life and soul might escape slap slap slap out the window—and finally the reassuring voice of the nurse saying, "See if you can get a doctor here."

It is a dream. I'll wake up. We'll all wake up and then when I come down the steps one of these mornings soon, there *she'll be*, sitting with a newspaper and she'll say,

"Well, Debby, we have another beautiful day today. We may even get to work with the flowers if we finish early." The back yard glazed in her sight, turned dark as though under a cloud, darker than dusk, blacker than midnight. The taste of ice water and soda crackers rose in her throat. She tried to swallow the sick taste, but her throat burned sourly. Quickly she knelt beside the chair. Pressing her forehead against the mossy bricks she vomited sourly onto the soft earth beneath the window where Mrs Merrill lay, perhaps dying.

That's not polite, Debby thought, her throat raw and burning. She scooped up a handful of dirt and sprinkled it over the mess. Quietly beneath her breath she laughed to herself. I feel like an old sick cat. And then her laughter gradually, without notice, turned to sobs. Still kneeling she rubbed her cheek against the mossy bricks and wished that God would, this very moment, change her into an old cat who could live just anywhere, alone.

Chapter 26

NOW the quiet of night had come to the house, but no one slept. Mrs Merrill had become a stranger and all beneath the roof were waiting, politely, hopefully, for her to leave. The family had listened to the doctor say at eleven o'clock that tonight would be the night and to his few mumbled words that death would be the easy way—not taking into account that Mrs Merrill had always avoided ease. When the doctor departed, a silence settled on the family. They said solemn farewells before wandering off dazedly, each to his own room, there to eat out his own heart. Debby left sitting alone in the dining room before the long bare table dug her fist into her cramping belly. She bent forward and pressed her cold, sweating forehead against the table. She knew that she needed food, would have to eat. Then it occurred to her that since Mrs Merrill had not eaten in three days either, her stomach must be cramping too.

She unlaced her shoes, slipped them off, and padded stocking-footed down the hall. Betty in a bewildering outburst of tears had given up all hope and with it her nightly watch. The back hall pallet was empty. Through a crack in the door Debby could see the night nurse hovering over the bed. Now was the time. She hurried into the kitchen, into the pantry, and as quietly as a robber, began taking down everything she needed: the muffin tins, lard to grease them, the mixing bowls, soda, cornmeal, and from the frigidaire, eggs and milk. This done, she settled herself to baking what was to be and must be the best cornbread ever made. Because she had to be so quiet and because she cooked with the oven door open for fear of burning this special bread, the night was half gone before she finished. But no one, not even the night nurse, had heard her.

She chose a fat-topped golden brown muffin and placed it—exactly so—on a saucer with a square of butter. Over it she spread a linen, company napkin. She turned off the kitchen light and stood, saucer in hand, in the dark door, scarcely daring to breath even when the pains in her stomach demanded screaming. Five, ten, fifteen, twenty minutes. A half an hour—and then with no warning whatsoever the nurse whisked out of the bedroom and into the bathroom where she pushed the door almost shut before turning on the light. In short baby steps Debby ran down the hall and into the bedroom. She dared not glance at Mrs Merrill or even at the bed. She placed the cornbread, saucer, napkin and all on the table.

"Here," she said. Then she was gone.

Back in the kitchen she closed the door, switched on the light, and crouching over, began devouring the cornbread, feeding herself greedily with both hands. She ate four muffins without stopping. Then, standing straight, for the pain had become less demanding, she took time to butter one. She made a sandwich of the next one, spreading peanut butter and mayonnaise on it. After that she ate a muffin soggy with catsup. When she turned the bottle up over another muffin, the catsup floomphed out, splattering the muffin, plate and table with thick clotted blood. Debby vomited.

When she opened her eyes on the reeling room she saw the nurse standing in the door. When she opened her eyes again she was lying in the back hall on Betty's pallet. The nurse's hand was cool against her wet forehead. "You must have a high fever." Again she was sick. When she opened her eyes again Betty was beside her with a pan of water. "Debby, why didn't you tell us you were sick?" Betty was as far away as the moon. There was no need to talk to her, to answer her silly question. But to herself she said, "I can't hurt this way. I've got to . . ." She was turning wrong side out again.

The nurse and Betty were whispering:

"Seven muffins!"

"Wouldn't account for a fever of 103."

"Or that breath."

"Or the constant cramping."

Between the blackness and the weak sick spells Betty sponged her forehead with cold cloths. "Debby, I hadn't thought about you. Who's been looking after you?" Betty kissed her on the forehead but that didn't help any. Debby began moaning to the pain.

"Shhh, Debby."

"I can't help it. It hurts."

Early dawn, gray and cold with the first chill of autumn, was in the hall. Betty disappeared and reappeared with Glenn.

"I'm sick," she whimpered to Glenn.

"I know you are Debby," he whispered. "We'll get the doctor in an hour. Soon as he's had a little more sleep."

"We're going to move you up to your own bed," Betty explained.

Glenn lifted her as easily as she herself could have lifted

a baby—as easily as she could once have lifted Glenn. And in her delirium it was she who carried Glenn up the stairs, up up up, and deposited him gently on the bed. She moaned and thrashed the sheets.

Her slanted ceiling glared in the noon sun. Dr Bronston stood at the foot of her bed. Betty and Julia were here too, in her room again, waiting for bedtime stories. "Do you feel that?" She could see that the doctor was squeezing her toes through the sheet a mile and a half away. Tears rolled down her cheeks and pretty as you please into her ears. How could she tell bedtime stories, or even listen to them, if he was going to squeeze her toes. She didn't know any bedtime stories anyway.

"Debby, answer him. Can you feel your toes?"

They were numb. But that was because she'd had a stroke in the taxicab. She pulled at the corkscrew. Her navel had turned into a corkscrew and was boring a hole slam-damn through her belly. It twisted again and she screamed.

"Debby," Julia knelt beside the bed and tried to dry the tears which were wetting the pillow.

Why doesn't she leave me alone? Debby wondered. "I don't know any stories. I never did know any. Debby was the one who listened to the stories. I just kept your socks patched." She looked at the doctor. "Go get Debby. I want to see Debby. You haven't let me see Debby since I been sick."

"Debby," a voice on the other side—Glenn of all people—whispered. "You're Debby. You're Deborah Hall." Wasn't that just like Glenn? Didn't even know his own mother and her with a belly ache.

"Where's Debby? Glenn, you ought to love Debby and take care of her."

"We're going to take care of you, baby. Here's Doctor Bronston. He won't let anything happen to you."

"You don't understand. It's not me I'm worried about. It's little Debby."

Glenn could hardly speak: "We're going to take you to the hospital. We can't have you and Mama both here sick. So we're going to take you to the hospital. I'll go with you in the ambulance and you won't be afraid, will you? You remember those pretty long blue ambulances that used to fly by here. Remember how you used to run to the front door hollering 'Fire' when you'd hear one? You won't be afraid to ride in one if I'm with you?"

It was Glenn talking to her. He was talking to her again; he had come back. What would Mrs Merrill say to that? Debby turned her head and memorized his face, the trembling chin which tried to work away the tears, the nose with a bad pimple on the very tip of it and a tear drop on the tip of the pimple. She didn't have to listen because he was talking to her again, not to Mrs Merrill, not to Julia, or Betty, but directly, openly to her, Deborah Hall.

Two soda jerkers lifted her onto a stretcher and she let them because it was only a dream. "Bump bump bump," their feet sounded on the stairs. It was not a dream! Her trunk had sounded thus at Stonebrook. They had tricked her. They were taking her away. And Mrs Merrill didn't know it!

"Help me! Help me!" she screamed to Mrs Merrill who would save her: "Help!"

"Shhh, Debby," Glenn held the side of the stretcher going down the walk to the ambulance. As they slid her in—like a loaf of bread into an oven—she tried to see everything about the Merrill house and yard, so that no matter how far they carried her, no matter how many corners and curves they turned, no matter, she could find her way back here, back home.

Chapter 27

LATE afternoon sunlight slanted through the white blinds which could be let up and down like shades on the window. A cool breeze was blowing and in it came playground sounds from the park across the street. Some children were playing hide-n-go-seek: "*Bushel of wheat, bushel of rye, all not ready, holler* I*!*"

"I know where I am now."

"You're in the hospital. Remember we came yesterday in the ambulance and I had to hold you down all the way. Remember." Glenn smoothed back the broken hair that a breeze lifted about her forehead.

"*All ten feet around my base are caught.*"

"We're across from the park. You and me. When you was a little boy oh" a fire burned in her stomach ". . . we, we went one Sunday afternoon. They let us out of the car and we swang in the swings."

"I don't remember that."

Now how could a body ever forget anything like that? She didn't care. It didn't make any difference now. A-tall. He had come back to her. All night she had only to open her eyes and he was there for her to look at: sound asleep with his hair amess and his mouth open. And through the night Julia and Betty came and went and whispered with the nurse. Sleep, wake, sleep, Glenn didn't leave her here, way far away from home. Once in the night her eyes were clear. A doctor had his hand on Glenn's shoulder and was saying: "You've got to buck up, son. We've done everything we can until she gets stronger pulse, higher blood count. If she doesn't, there's nothing more anyone can do for her except to make her as comfortable as possible." What more could a person want? She wished she knew as much as doctors. "I wish I had some water.

"And them sticking needles in me and me sick. I want some water, get me some water, Glenn, I'd give you some water if you was sick. Water. Make them give me some water. I know they've got some water here." Debby was whimpering. Her always deep-set eyes had sunken farther into her head, leaving hollow sockets. Glenn dipped a new pad of cotton into the white enamel pan and dabbed her blue lips and the parched yellow skin of her forehead. When she fainted, which was often now, she turned white. All morning the doctors and internes had appeared frequently in her room for talking parties and guessing games. A nerve had gone dead, they finally agreed, a nerve that controlled the blood supply to her abdomen had through injury, shock, or possibly extreme, prolonged, fear, gone dead. And now, little by little, her intestines were dying.

"Does gangrene grow like moss. I don't want a green belly. Make them give me some more medicine. My belly hurts. Water. I water drink a water. Some more medicine. Glenn! Nurse. Nurse! God oh God! Make them give me something. My belly hurts."

"Shhh. Don't talk Debby. Please. The doctor said for you to save your strength." Glenn placed his finger on her arm where the needle, feeding something from the hanging bottle, was like a splinter under her skin. He held her wrist so that she could not move her arm and break the needle loose. Another nurse would be coming soon, sticking more needles. "Water."

Glenn mopped her lips with wet cotton. "Debby, don't ask me any more. I can't give you any water. When the night nurse comes on duty I'll make her give you some."

"I want some now." Footsteps sounded far down the hall. She opened her eyes in time to see Mr Merrill enter the room. "Water." Maybe he had a jug of water on him. Mr Merrill disappeared in the muddy lake which filled the room. Presently he appeared at the park-side window, through which came the singsong chant, the voices of the children counting out, a summer twilight evening song, and another voice to which Debby listened:

As I draw this magic circle
Someone will sign it
With a d-o-t, DOT. . . .

Drowned out by the shouts of those who would hide those who would seek.

Mr Merrill finally spoke: "Good news, boy. We can breathe easy now. I came by to tell you."

Glenn didn't take his eyes from Debby's face.

"She's regained consciousness. She's out of the worst danger."

Glenn laid his palm flat on Debby's forehead.

"Did you hear me? I said your mother's out of danger."

For a long minute, Glenn was motionless. His voice was hoarse from unvoiced sobbing: "Did you tell her about Debby?"

"I had to. She asked about her."

"Did she ask for me?" Glenn spoke each word slowly as though it grated in his throat.

He stood up.

"Water." Debby moved her fingertips to touch his hand. He sat down and again applied the moist cotton to her parched lips.

"Did she ask for me?" Glenn repeated.

"She's still very weak," Mr Merrill said. "She didn't ask for or about anyone except Debby. She wanted to know if Debby had got home all right."

"You mean to our house?"

"I suppose that's what she meant."

"What did you tell her?"

"I thought it better to tell her the truth."

"You told her there wasn't much chance."

"No. Only that she was in the hospital. Very sick."

"What did she say?"

"She can't talk much. It's hard to hear and make out what she's trying to say."

"I'll bet she knows how sick Debby is."

"Probably. I had a feeling she knew when she first asked." Mr Merrill turned and looked out the window toward the park where a child was shouting:

"*. . . one flew east one flew west and one flew over the cuckoo's nest and out you go you old dirty dish rag you!*"

"Your mother said a strange thing when I told her Debby was in the hospital. I was afraid the news might upset her but she just said, '*I hope she dies.*' Then she turned over and went off into a sound sleep. I think she's worried a great deal about what was going to become of Debby. Maybe that was it, I don't know. She's sleeping now though like a baby. Doctor Bronston says that's very encouraging." Mr Merrill walked over to the bed and stared down at Debby, his face floating against the dark ceiling. "Is she conscious?"

"I don't think so. All she mumbles is 'water.' "

"*. . . and out you go you old dirty . . .*"

"Dish rag," Debby's eyes glazed. A milk-fog came between her and Mr Merrill. "I been tricked out. She's tricked me out of her house." Gradually, dimly Mr Merrill's face floated into view, then Glenn's. She mumbled to Glenn, and he bent to hear her words: "You weren't worth saving."

Then Mr Merrill's face floated nearer nearer until his lips touched her forehead. It was too late for that. She didn't want to go on living now. She twisted her head.

"Poor Debby. Still scared of me after all these years. Maybe it was a good thing that you remained frightened of me. She would have made you miserable if we hadn't continued as strangers. There was enough strain over the children. Now seems like she's winning."

Debby's fingers circled Glenn's wrist.

"I wanted you to know, Glenn." Mr Merrill walked to the door.

"Tell her . . ." Glenn was crying now. "Tell her I didn't know it was a war picture."

"I'll tell her," Mr Merrill said.

Glenn buried his face on the side of the bed. He cried softly for a long time, then angrily he said: "Debby, it wasn't you I wanted to die! I didn't really want anybody to die."

Her fingers remained circling his wrist with all her strength. Bargain or no bargain she had him now.

"Debby," he sniffed and dried his eyes with the back of his free hand, "you don't have to hold me so tight. I won't leave you." The sobs broke out again. "And don't you leave me."

The room was gray in the early dusk. Beyond the window,

lamp posts were drifting against the dark, tossing trees. Through the twilight the playground singsong rose higher and higher:

"Bushel of wheat! bushel of clover!"

Debby loosed her fingers from Glenn's wrist for a second. It was true: he would not leave her. She moved her hand to her aching navel. It was gone!

"Bushel of wheat! bushel of clover!"
All not ready, can't hide over.

"Glenn Glenn!" she screamed. She sat up in bed, her eyes wild and searching. "It's gone! Hide me. Hide me!"

"Debby!" He pressed with his hands against her shoulders and with his head against her breast. Her heart was trying to free itself in jolting tremors.

"Don't! Let me go, Glenn. Let me go. I know a hiding place. Let me go. I got to hide."

She shut her eyes, lay back, and ran, past the north field, past Stonebrook, through the yard, through Merrill's Grove, to the boxwood graveyard at Katie Powell schoolhouse. There was snow on the ground, cool and wet against her parched lips as she sank down down down into the grave. It was, she knew, a perfect hiding place; for after all, who would think to look in the grave for a little lady whose navel was on the wrong side?

Voices of the South

Doris Betts, *The Astronomer and Other Stories*

Sheila Bosworth, *Almost Innocent*

Erskine Caldwell, *Poor Fool*

Fred Chappell, *The Gaudy Place*

Fred Chappell, *It Is Time, Lord*

Ellen Douglas, *A Family's Affairs*

Ellen Douglas, *A Lifetime Burning*

Ellen Douglas, *The Rock Cried Out*

George Garrett, *An Evening Performance*

George Garrett, *Do, Lord, Remember Me*

Shirley Ann Grau, *The House on Coliseum Street*

Shirley Ann Grau, *The Keepers of the House*

Barry Hannah, *The Tennis Handsome*

William Humphrey, *Home from the Hill*

William Humphrey, *The Ordways*

Mac Hyman, *No Time For Sergeants*

Nancy Lemann, *Lives of the Saints*

Madison Jones, *A Cry of Absence*

Willie Morris, *The Last of the Southern Girls*

Louis D. Rubin, Jr., *The Golden Weather*

Evelyn Scott, *The Wave*

Lee Smith, *The Last Day the Dogbushes Bloomed*

Elizabeth Spencer, *The Salt Line*

Elizabeth Spencer, *The Voice at the Back Door*

Max Steele, *Debby*

Allen Tate, *The Fathers*

Peter Taylor, *The Widows of Thornton*

Robert Penn Warren, *Band of Angels*

Robert Penn Warren, *Brother to Dragons*

Joan Williams, *The Morning and the Evening*